I X I
COMICS

PRESENTS

SPECULAR

L.K. BROOKS-SIMPSON

Titles available in the IXI COMICS series (in reading order):

SEQUENCE 1

SPECULAR

First Published in Great Britain in 2018

SPECULAR
ISBN Print edition 978-1-912791-01-9

To every person who dreamed with me and helped bring this project to life − thank you!

To my cousin Shaun - rest in perfect paradise.

CHAPTER 1

I See Me In You

"Natalie, this can't go on, it just can't!"

"I know, but the most important thing is that he was not hurt."

"He hurt someone else though, badly!"

"I just don't understand. Something's wrong, these incidents are not like Tre at all."

"No kidding."

"It's like he forgets all discipline, all the lessons we taught him."

"We need to do something now."

"So, what do you suggest, Cecil, should we just beat him senseless because that is surely going to do the trick?"

"I never said—"

"This is our Tre; no one said raising a child was going to be easy. He is nine years of age; of course, he is going to make mistakes."

"The mistake was letting him go out and play with the other kids down the road, if we kept him in none of this would have happened."

"We can't protect him from the city forever."

"He can protect himself pretty damn well judging by the state of the other kid's face."

"It was your godforsaken idea to have him out there anyway, Cecil."

"Initially."

"Initially. Do you hear yourself?"

"Well yeah, he should have other friends than Miss Hill's daughter."

"What's wrong with her daughter?"

"Nothing is wrong with her daughter, it's her. She's a weirdo."

"She has been nothing but lovely to our family."

"I don't consider a free psychology consultation as, 'being lovely'."

"Mum, Dad... Am I in trouble?"

The two parents found their exchange discontinued when their son spoke for the first time. The neck of the young boy craned upwards, everything about his demeanour spelt naivety: he rubbed his small palms together, he held his lips inward and his eyebrows pulled closer in fear of reprimand. Despite all of this, his attire spelt a different story entirely. Dried blood could be seen from his right fist all the way to the rips in his beige jumper. The mother fixed her eyes on her husband in such a manner as to prompt him to address their son's question. The boy's father knelt until he was at eye level with the young boy, and as were the symmetric of genetics; it was as if he was looking into the face of his past self. Both were umber brown in skin tone, had defined cheekbones, closed, unreadable expressions and coned eyes with the strength of a cyclone inside. The pair's most prominent features were their clear skin, long eyelashes and low haircuts that held afro waves so strong they could bring a tide of eyes along.

"Yes, Tre. I know I told you to always defend yourself, but you did a terrible thing today." The man cuffed the back of the boy's neck and looked deep into his junior's eyes as he continued, "there is a whole world out there, full of possibility, full of opportunity. You need to ask yourself if you want to be the kind of person who helps people or hurts people. Who do you want to be? Both ways you can have the world at your feet, but there's always a difference." His voice was susurrating by the time his words ended. The boy's head knelt now.

"Now go to your room and really think about what you have done, and I mean it." After those words, the young boy named Tre found himself scaling the staircase with nothing more to say.

"Take off that jumper and wash the blood from your hands!" his mother called after him. Once he had left the landing, she still had her large eyes tagged on her husband.

"What?" Cecil exclaimed.

"We don't even know what happened, Cecil. He didn't say anything for the entire journey. If you ask me, he is trying to cover up for those shady block boys," Natalie seated her arms in one another.

"It's clear what happened. They were playing and Tre and the other boy got into it," he shrugged back.

"That boy's damn nose was broken! Does that seem like something Tre is capable of? I tell you those block boys are no good," she flared in her quietest voice, all the while glancing at the staircase. Her husband made a point to close the distance between them.

"Those 'block boys' were just like you and I once, dear. Everyone has to grow and everyone has to learn, even Tre. It is not too late for any of them."

Once he had heard enough Tre proceeded to his room. Their family house was moderately sized, as was the typical house in their district neighbourhood of Hive Borough, in Indiana U.S.A. He removed his stained jumper and washed his hands, and with fleecy socks on foot, slowly slid across the Merbau Komodo Molti patterned flooring. The different colours of the wooden flooring paled in comparison to the shades of his emotions. After washing the blood from his hands in the bathroom unit, he continued to his room. The boy held a pained expression from the corridor all the way to the entrance of the attic that also doubled as his room. He pulled down the steel ladder extension and swiftly climbed his way to his personal space. The triangular room held a dark blue umbrella lamp, a small sofa, a computer console, a line of posters in the shape of the mercury retrograde model, a flat screen television, a junior's telescope, a *Sega Dreamcast*, elementary physics cue cards, multiple bean bags; the colours: yellow, green and red, comic books and a wide double bed. In short, it was a young boys' dream room and Tre would have continued happily had he not been consumed by the need to blow fumes. Once the trapdoor was shut, Tre began heaving, his figure creased over and his hands reached toward the nearest bean bag. He would have ripped it apart if he had the strength. He would have spread his arms and sprouted right then, if wings were a thing. The blood washed from his hands was a reminder that as far as he could remember, he had never had a true handle on his life. Just like it so often did, his head began to ring and he found himself stumbling to the long, lone mirror at the far side of the room. He could no longer tune the other voice in his head out and in a bizarre sequence of events, he began speaking to himself.

"*That was unfair, to send us to our room,*" a strange, ghastly voice came in his head.

"No, it wasn't!" Tre retorted back immediately, "you did something very bad today, very bad."

"*Oh please, Brother. The boy cheated, he deserved what was coming to him.*"

"Hurting people is not nice and you made Mum so upset. She was crying in the car!" He pointed out to his reflection in the mirror. Only the blue light from the umbrella lamp shun, so his reflection in the mirror was cast in a sinister light; his face would contort malevolently every time the strange voice came to mind.

"*Well she wasn't there to see what happened; besides, it was your idea to bet with money. Now imagine they found out we were betting too?*" it threatened.

"NO please! They have enough to worry about already." Tre placed two palms on the mirror in plead.

"*Good, then you better start saying 'we'. We hurt that boy. We punched his cheating face in until his nose broke. We took his blood, then the money he owed. We both disappointed our parents and I don't know about you, Brother, but I'd rather stand up for myself and get in trouble than be weak and get praised. I wouldn't be able to sleep at night.*"

"Well I don't think I'll be able to sleep tonight after this, it doesn't feel right."

"*You are so soft sometimes.*"

"Mum says I'm a responsible boy. Well she said – she probably thinks differently now."

"*What if we didn't have parents though, what would you do then?*"

"Don't say stuff like that. It's not funny."

"*You care too much about what our parents think of us. Don't you know that sometimes parents don't know best?*"

"Leave me alone; just get out of my head!"

"*Get out?*"

"You're not real, you are just bad thoughts!"

"*How could you say that, brother how could you?*"

"You're ruining my life, making my parents sad!"

"*Take that back now! "*

"I hate you! I hate you!"

"*All I have is you...*"

A forceful flush came and Tre was able to drown out the voice in his head just in time to hear footsteps underneath him.

"Tre, you have a visitor!" came a voice that certainly belonged to his mother. Afterward, the trapdoor rose upward, helped by a short, thin arm that certainly did not. A bright eyed, young girl with a blooming afro climbed onto the landing, looking extremely pleased with herself to have made it so far up. With one hand massaging his brow, Tre waved at the girl. It was Caprice Hill, his best friend.

"Tre-Tre!" yelped the small girl before throwing him into an adorable hug, Tre's tepid reply was lost in her large, brown, mane of hair.

"Sweetie, why are you holding your head like that?" The concerned crown of his mother came into view.

"My head hurts that's all," Tre said over his friend's shoulder.

"I think you are dehydrated again, all that running around. You need to drink water, hold on I'll get you some."

"It's okay, Misses Moon; I brought some water with me," Caprice informed her as she pulled out a small bottle of water from her lacquered backpack.

"Aw, Caprice you are such a sweetheart. If you two need anything, just call." With a closed smile and the close of the trapdoor, the two friends were left alone. As soon as she reckoned Tre's mother was out of earshot, Caprice released a few flossy sniggers.

"What is funny?" Tre mumbled, still browsing his forehead region with a hand.

"Your last name is funny. Moon... hehe," she teased.

"Yours is not any better. Hill. What kinda name is – AGH!" The sharp headache resurfaced and the voice in his head poised to make a resurgence, "*Don't block me out! Don't you dare block me out!*"

"Here." Caprice unscrewed the bottle of water, lifted Tre's head upward with a soft hand before pouring some into his mouth. When she was content with how much he had consumed she assumed a motherly stance.

"Make sure to drink the rest. It'll help." Tre watched her for a few moments. Her pecan coloured afro reminded him of an intricate bird nest: ringlets and curls of all sizes were layered on top of one another. Her eyebrows were fair but full and her lips were full but fairly spread. Her skin was butterscotch in complexion; a result of mixed parentage. Her features were from both sides of the tree; however it was her hazel, green eyes that kept Tre's rooted. Caprice's eyes were like a mesmeric woodland, should nature be confined to the anterior border of the iris. The Rayleigh scattering in her eyes were like groves of birch, beech and buckthorn; beautiful charters of chartreuse. The melanin scattered across the eye was like soil across the marshlands; full of life, full of potential. Caprice was all of these things. Just looking at her sparked something inside the young boy, however, his preliminary notions of attraction only allowed him to view her in the narrow ways only a nine-year-old could. Caprice Hill was pretty, but not in the same way his mother was pretty. Moreover, he liked to spend time with her, but not in the same way he liked to spend time with the block boys. She was a tender soul who was hard on the people she cared about. Still, her soft touch was hardly enough to ease his burden.

"Who is that?" Caprice pointed at the largest of all the posters on his wall. It showed a triumphant man, in a fantastic transparent suit of some kind; it was also Tre's most recently acquired poster and by far his favourite, as this was the man he looked up to most.

"That is Aaron Heron." Tre admired the poster for the countless time. Caprice, however, did not seem impressed.

"Who is he? It's not as 'sciencey' as the rest of the posters."

She had a point, alongside the ambitious spectacles of space and chemistry captured on the other posters, the portrait of the man pictured in the city of Signot's Hive district, hardly compared. Tre's infatuation did not falter.

"You know, Mr Heron built that suit himself. He's going to change the world one day. I want to work for him when I'm older."

"Golly. That's amazing that you know what you want to do already. A lot people in our city don't survive to even be that age."

"I guess. You've just got to ignore the bad things and focus on yourself. That's what Mum always told me."

"Sure. Drink up, Tre." Caprice lifted the base of the drink he was holding.

"It's not going to work by the way. I'm not dehydrated," Tre admitted.

"I know. There's a painkiller in there. It will help with the headache," Caprice assured him; she kneeled and pulled herself closer to her friend.

"So, what is causing it then?"

"Don't laugh."

"I won't."

"Promise?"

"I promise!"

"I haven't told anyone this, but I can hear voices inside my head and when I try and make it stop, it hurts. It hurts so much." For the first time, Caprice saw her friend's strong eyes crumble into vulnerability. Despite his disclosure, Tre kept the true nature of his condition close to his chest; she would never know how this voice was also responsible for his perceived decadence. How he was not in full control of himself. How he did not like to sleep at night, for the fear that he would give control to it. If one was to look close enough they could see bags under Tre's dark eyes, thankfully, his dark complexion blended them out somewhat.

"Like an imaginary friend?" Caprice tried to rationalise.

"Sort of, except I can't control what it says. It talks to me, tells me to do stuff – You don't believe me do you?" Tre cut his confession short when he saw Caprice's expression stuck somewhere between disbelief and disturbed.

"I do actually. My mum is a psychologist and sometimes she talks about people who see things that are not there." She squinted ever so slightly to imagine such an affliction, but her slight shake of the head signalled this was beyond her.

"Your mum helps crazy people, does that mean I'm crazy?" said Tre slowly.

"No Tre-Tre. You're special, that's all." She placed her small hands on either side of his face and waited until his smile reached both sides. He could not help but feel better about things when Caprice was around; she was not like the average girl. She brought him balance; a challenge that could not be undersized given he was blighted with a damaged psyche. Despite her brightness and her gift for foresight, even Tre knew that it was highly unlikely that a vicodin or the test of time would stop the battle he was fighting inside.

"Crazy?"

"You hate me do you?"

"No one is truly there for you but me!"

"I'm the one who knows who you truly are. Who we truly are."

"I'll show you, Brother."

"You've always had to learn the hard way."

That very same night when Tre closed his eyes, he let his guard slip. It was the young Tre Moon who fell asleep, but it was a shadow of himself that rose from the bed two hours later. The scene was more chilling than *Phantom of the Opera*, as the phantom operated the body of the small boy. Its expression was one of humiliation, its walk, its demeanour and its blinks were indistinct. It clenched its fist so tight that nails began to sink into the creases on his skin. He began by disabling every fire alarm in the house. Next, his breathing began increasing when he grabbed a bottle of whiskey from the Moon household's liquor cabinet. With no regard whatsoever, the boy began flailing the liquor across the landscape of the house: sofas, carpets, electronics, tables, cushions, food, drapes and most notably, routes of escape. Once he had emptied the last contents of the bottle, the wicked spirit decided to double it over with another bottle of spirit. Spurred by vindication now, he grabbed a third bottle solely to cover the entirety of Tre's attic. Sensing his act culminating now, the boy watered at the mouth as he clawed at the chest of drawers for the final tool for his plan. A packet of matchsticks.

With one possessed swipe, a single match was lit. He held it to his face. With silver light eyes that did not belong to himself, he inspected the point of fire, almost as if there was some tranquillity to be found inside it. Almost as if he liked the singing sensation he felt when he held it close to his nose. Almost as if he was infatuated with it. If he needed, nothing was too hard to let go. So, the lit matchstick fell. In one bombastic instance made of combustion, gushing sounds and an unforgiving grin, the rivers of alcohol set alight. After a second the entire corridor was sectioned. After a minute the culprit was missing. After five, the living quarters were swallowed alive. After ten, the fire was hungry again. Twenty minutes passed and black fumes began to mask the house, cast a black fog within the bathroom, which made escape impossible for even a master of parkour. On the thirty-third minute after the fire began, the first human sounds could be heard. The horrible wheezes and coughs of Natalie and Cecil Moon as their respiratory systems tried to get rid of the poisonous carbon monoxide fumes. Helpless yells of panic and confusion. Shrieks of pure pain as they tried to battle the heartless flames and rescue their precious child from the blaze. The whimpers when they realised it was no use. Their final screams of the name, Tre.

The home was unrecognisable by the time authorities, neighbours and Fire Control responded. The Cherry Street residents gathered in the streets in horror. The Moon's home began to crumble under the pressure and questions of how it started began to spread, faster than the fire itself. The answer was not hard to find. Standing directly at the front lawn was a small boy, five-foot-four with a packet of matchsticks in hand. Like he always did, Tre returned from his awfully hot slumber, but when he realised what he awoke to, he was truly living a nightmare. He shuddered and looked erratically at the blaze. To the neutral observer, this seemed a strange change in behaviour, but in the eyes of the truth, this was a boy watching his life falling apart in front of his very eyes.

"NOOOOO!" screamed Tre, he dashed toward the fire thoughtlessly. The box of matchsticks dropped to the floor; however, the nearest fireman was ready to take action at the drop of the hat. The young Tre was only able to put one hand into the flame before the man scooped him to safety. His right hand was seared but on the back of his confusing, selfish act, this was nothing. Even in the face of the fire, his tears would never leave.

CHAPTER 2

<u>The Mysterious Case Of Tre Moon</u>
<u>2008</u>

Word of the murder of Natalie and Cecil Moon quickly went around the city of Signot, Indiana. Word started in the Hive Borough, where the Moon residence was situated, and continued to the outer reaches of the huge city. Inevitably, word of the incident also reached local news, then the legal system. With no lawyer, witness or irrefutable evidence to defend him, in June of the year 2003, Tre Moon was convicted of murder on two counts and given a mandatory life sentence. He was to serve his sentence in Signot's Juvenile Detention Centre until he was eighteen years of age. When he became of age he was to be transferred to Hallows Island; an isolated, maximum security prison for America's worst offenders. At the age of nine Tre had everything taken away from him. His mother. His father. His best friend. His home. His hopes. His freedom. His innocence. Throughout all his loss, one thing did remain however, the voice inside of his head. The voice provided him with constant company during the first year of his sentence, a feature that he reckoned, ironically, kept him from falling further into insanity. Besides, he knew for a fact that no one else inside the detention facility had an ominous counsel or a savage alias to handle the rough aspects of Juvenile Hall. And it got very rough. During the first five years of his sentence, Tre became very familiar with the offenders' lifestyle. On any day he was liable to see: fistfights followed by revenge in the form of knives formed of whatever abrasive material one could find. Gym practice and betting championships with all types of tactics and juvenile algorithms employed to get the advantage. Religious sessions and prep talks were held in improvised lecture halls. Readings and plea deals, which led to weaklings, robbed of their free meals. Tre Moon was not like the offenders around him and so he tried to keep to himself, however he found it increasingly hard to do this. His reputation as a cold murderer preceded him and ego grown individuals began to pick fights with him to establish the pecking order. The aphorism '*you are a product of your environment*' proved to be true time after time. The pecking order changed, Tre picked up weights and developed popping pectorals to handle whatever problem came his way, or in the case of his phantom, to compensate for the inmates that short-changed them back in the day. Tre was not always alone though. In the third year of his sentence a boy one year older than him came into the detention centre. The boy's name was Chevron and allegedly was a part of the Block Boys Tre once new, who were now a full-fledged gang. He immediately gravitated toward Tre, giving the young boy some further reputability inside the detention centre. Though Block Boy Chevron's sentence was a feeble year compared to Tre's lifetime sentence, even when he left, word of Tre's associations remained. He was not proud of it, but he took advantage of the respect nonetheless. With this new freedom, Tre was able to reform back to his former ways somewhat. He took intensive studying sessions in his free time and though he always knew he had a fascination for science, he discovered that he had a pension for physics in particular. His academic progress became hard to ignore and so he was given his age range exams to take, only to pass them all. This was a notable and uplifting achievement for the young teenager who was conditioned to believe his life would play out in the darkness from the fading light of his former life. Neither qualification, nor any outstanding certificate in physics would be able to change the scars on his hand. The scars were a reminder that he narrowly escaped the fate he deserved. Tre, like every other inmate was nonethewiser, led to believe his horizon contained nothing more than further institutionalisation.

Five years and one hundred and thirty-three days into his juvenile sentence, a miracle struck. He had a visitor and it was not an aspiring reporter trying their luck. A rather tall, ebony skinned woman came into the visitation room. She was dressed in a white professor's coat and had eyes of hazel green. Compared to the hard-boiled guards that were constantly on duty, the woman looked more than out of place. There was something of an urgent air when she spoke, but it turned out that her words were exactly what Tre thought he would never hear, but exactly what he needed to.

"Tre, you might not remember me, but my name is Edith Hill. I am Caprice's mother and I was also a friend of your mother. I am a psychologist and if you don't mind I would like to have a few words with you because I think I can help you get out of this place. Forever."

The woman named Edith Hill led Tre into a room in the detention centre he had never been before, despite this fact, it was still like every other room in the facility. Grey, low lit and held four walls that seemed to inch closer by the second.

"Please have a seat." Professor Hill invited him to sit opposite her at a marked table in the centre of the room. Tre cut uncomfortable eyes toward the floor. Given there was a prison guard at the door, as well as visible markings of conflict scratched into the table's surface, ('F*** Indie Police' and 'HELP' were the largest) he thought it was shaping more to be an interrogation than a discussion. Edith Hill caught on to this quickly.

"Excuse me," she turned to the guard blocking the door, "I am carrying out a psychiatric exam, and I will need complete confidentiality."

"Okay," replied the guard plainly. He did not move an inch however.

"Well?" she said in a higher pitch.

"Ma'am. You probably don't know what this inmate is capable of but for your safety its best I stay in the room," he said. Her neck seized up.

"Get-out-now," Professor Hill whispered. After a few seconds of quiet dissension, the guard left the room, courtesy of her scalding stare. Once they were left alone, Edith took a moment to search Tre's face. She found a sensitive, scarred soul that had been hardened by predicament. She saw potential that had been dampened by penitentiary. She saw something else in him that she could not put her finger on and she also saw that Tre's strong features would not break to reveal any more. He returned the searching look and all he saw was Caprice in her eyes.

"You should not be in here," she said finally. Tre's glum expression did not move in the slightest. All he could think of was how under qualified she was to make such a statement; he doubted that she could even begin to scratch the surface of what happened on the night of his arrest. Of what was still happening inside him to that very day. He was forced to think of that tragic night five years ago, for the past thousand nights; nights that did not allow him to rest easy under the feasibility that he would ever be declared innocent. He was both innocent and guilty. Both responsible and regretful. It was the unequivocal truth and whether or not he chose to vocalise his strife, the law would remain inequitable in the court of the inconceivable. Tre tried to balance each side of his situation and consequently Edith Hill was bothered by his levelled demeanour.

"Don't you care about getting out?" She put a hand into her large, curly afro.

"You can't help me," Tre said shortly.

"I can help you and whether you think I can or not, I will," she responded in an authoritative tone.

"No one can help me," Tre maintained.

"No one needs to, as long as we have each other." The voice rung in his head. It seemed Edith Hill was through with debate as she drew for some writing materials from her lap. She inhaled deeply and straightened out her paper before proceeding.

"Tre, I have been involved in some low-key research for the past couple of years and some of the findings are incredible. The implications for someone like you are too important to overlook. I am going to ask you some questions, is that okay with you?"

"You're wasting your time," Tre mumbled.

"Just because you have given up on yourself doesn't mean everyone has." Professor Hill readied her papers.

"This woman is annoying."

"Okay, first question. How would you describe yourself?" she continued.

"Really?"

"I'm quiet; I pretty much keep to myself. It's easier that way. Especially in here," Tre answered.

"Uh huh," she jotted down some notes, "what kinds of things are you interested in?"

"Not being patronised, that's what."

"I used to like reading comic books and playing games, but they don't have those things in here. So, I guess you could say I've forgotten about that stuff."

"What do you like doing in here then?"

"Having the respect and power. No one ever comes near us when we are at the gym anymore."

"In here, the only thing I like is learning about physics. It's hard to understand some of the theory without trying it out though; they would never trust us with the lab equipment."

"Okay," she said. "I heard that you were friends with some gang members back at home, is this true?"

"We weren't friends; the only friend I had was Caprice."

"I hope you didn't mean that. I'm your friend too."

"Are you okay, Tre, you seem to be a little distracted?"

"I'm fine." The longer the exam went on, the harder he found it to keep concentration. Every question brought on the onset of his inside voice's opinion, whether warranted or not.

"Speaking of your mother, how was your relationship with your parents?"

The answer was simple, but the propensity of emotions this brought about put some trouble in his deliverance.

"I-I..." So many words tried their way out, including those of the voice inside his head.

"Who does she think she is? Why is she bringing it up? I didn't want to do it but you made me angry! I miss them just as much as you, but I had to teach you a lesson."

"Tre?" Professor Hill said again.

"I loved them. So much." He managed to find his own voice.

"Then why did you kill them? Why did you kill the people you love?" She leaned in sincerely; her eyes skated to every inch of Tre's face. She saw his solid expression weather under the pressure of his dualistic infrastructure.

"I-I..."

"Why did you kill them, Tre? Tell me, tell me the truth—"

"Listen lady!" Tre blasted, however, his voice was now completely different, *"I have had enough your questions. Are you trying to make me look bad? Are you trying to turn my*

brother against me? I've already apologised." Where Tre's will broke, his counterparts did not. It was now in control. Professor Edith Hill dropped her notes completely.

"Who are you?" Her eyes were now so wide that her hazel retinas looked like an island amongst a sea of white.

"*I'm me,*" it shrugged lazily.

"What is your name?" She held out a hand toward the upper corner of the room. If the occupier of Tre's body was paying any attention it would have realised she was sending instructions to the hidden camera placed there.

"*I've never really given that any thought. Tre has never let me introduce myself to anybody...This is the best question you have asked all day!*"

"So, you are not Tre Moon?"

"*Tre is my brother.*"

"Did you kill Natalie and Cecil Moon five years ago?" she asked slowly, now gripping the sides of the table.

"*I'm not a bad person,*" it replied indignantly.

"Did you kill Natalie and Cecil Moon?!"

"*I don't like the way you are talking to me. You can talk to Tre; I don't want to see you again.*" In a moment that was like a hypnotic kick, Tre snapped back into control and once he realised what had happened, broke into heaves. He tried to frown through the tears as if they would somehow reverse what Professor Hill had just witnessed, and he bit hard into his lip as if to drown in his own blood. Edith unseated herself and kneeled beside him.

"It's okay Tre," she began. "You do not have to say anything else. I am going to get you out of this place and introduce you to some people who can help you, okay? You are not a bad person; you are just suffering from an illness okay, hunny? Everything is going to be okay; you'll be out of here soon." She spoke her most soothing words to the young teenager in an attempt to undo all of the wrongful pain, labels and trauma he had been through. She could not begin to imagine how torn he must have become, dealing with a piece of himself trying to tear itself from him. With a past so tainted in darkness, the most she could do was give him the light of hope going forward. The story of the Moon's murder of 2003, just like Tre's battle inside of himself, was deeper than the surface.

It took a month for Edith's Hill retrial request to be processed and when it finally did, it took place in Indiana's Supreme Court in front of Head Judge, Nincy Valentine. In other words, the decision on that day was to decide Tre Moon's future. Due to the nature of the retrial, it took place with relatively few people including, Professor Edith Hill herself, Tre Moon, Judge Valentine and another impartial body. Edith Hill was to present evidence that Tre Moon was not responsible for the murder committed the day of his parent's murder. She showed the video footage capturing Tre's anomalous behaviour during the psychiatric exam; she also proved that there were indeed two separate entities inside of him by studying his brainwaves during another session which involved an MRI scan. She told the judge that Tre Moon was suffering from a rare psychological condition called Dissociative Identity Disorder and that he exhibited all of the signs of the condition such as loss of time, sense of self and inability to recall actions when the other identity had taken control of the body. Due to the lack of research in pathophysiology and comorbid disorders, there was a grey area in the law where the members of the retrial could not cast definitive judgement. Therefore, a bout of reasoning took place; Tre's first sign of retribution. Judge Valentine's argument was weighted heavily toward logic: if two identities could reside within the body, should it not be that both parties share the responsibilities of one's action. Edith Hill argument was that of a humanitarian: one person's actions should not be held accountable for another person's future. She personally vouched for him as a functioning individual; she brought up behaviour reports from his previous school as well as during his time in the detention centre. She told the judge that Dissociative Personality Disorder is a serious condition and that they should not treat it lightly. At that point Judge Valentine budged some, but he was far from won. The judge voiced that he did not feel that just letting Tre free would be a service to the people, given he is still, technically, a risk factor. In response, Edith Hill informed him that her research over the past two years addressed symptomology and treatment for such psychological disorders. She proposed that Tre be subject to regular psychiatric tests and to be put on suitable doses of anxiety reducing drugs, as he is most vulnerable to give up control when he is nervous or distraught. She continued by telling him that even if they try and do not succeed in suppressing his Dissociative Disorder, it is quintessential to the principles of what they stand for as professionals, to try at least. After some time of deliberation, Judge Valentine agreed to Edith Hill's stipulations. He told her that she was a good person for going so far for a child everyone else had given up on. Edith Hill made good on her promise to Tre and so by the grace of a hard-working lady's miracle and in the face of a nameless future, Tre was freed from Signot's Juvenile Detention Centre on the 3rd October 2008. It was a one in a millennia occasion. The missing number in the equation. The mysterious case of Tre Moon - 2008.

CHAPTER 3

<u>Signot</u>

The city of Signot was the largest of Indiana's three central cities (including Heavens Conquest and Babil City) and was predicated on the new age equation. If you took the views of nature money could not buy and added the multiple high-rises money could, you had yourself something quite beautiful. Signot's national park was at the heart of the city's artful creation and with a circular plan of urbanicity to surround the island of nature, Signot resembled a signet. It had a ring to it. The city's other main attractions included Heracles Sports Ground, located in the Hive Borough and The Liami Sphere located in the Claxon Borough. The final attraction was Signot's annual carnival: the Belly which was found at the coastal borough of Hetashi. Heracles Ground was the biggest of them all, boasting a four mile complex for every professional sports club the city had. The Liami Sphere was a high security arts and sciences centre. It was patterned like Saturn. The looping designs that covered its transparent body added with its grandiose incline and conspiratory timeline made it one of the top five visited places in the country; therefore, the grandest of events from both worlds took place there. Lastly, the Belly Carnival was the least prestigious of the three but was destined to hold its place in the far reaches of the city due to popular demand. It was the go-to place for the teenagers because it optimised the youth culture. Its gothic, fun-fair theme made it stand out even amongst the many corporate lanterns in the business ends of the city. Signot city had all the aspects of a successful one: attractions, modern design and natural views, but, it was also a true sign of the times. A city once destined for retribution now had to settle for the creeping symptoms of destitution. Economic depression resulted in an economy unfit to fight the few swelling corporations. Containing crooked CEO's who dodged city tax as if it was the plague itself. The protocols to deter such activities were in place, but the people of Signot lived to learn that money could make even the most obvious crimes outlast litigation. The corporations were not going anywhere, anytime soon. At the neck of the high collar crimes were illegal street activity. With so much missed opportunity, Signot was a breeding ground for misdemeanour, hit and miss political campaigns, miscellaneous pop-up stores and hit and runs. The city was running amongst the highest for inner city crime rates in the entire country, but this statistic stood shy next to the numbers behind the scenes. Millions of kilograms of drugs were being imported and exported into and out of Signot each year, signed and sealed by the Bulgarian Conglomerate. The drug business remained largely intact because of poorly exercised measures against it. The Indiana Police force was not as prolific as they needed it to be. The council did not have the capital to combat the growing areas of crime. The populace was too preoccupied in their personal lives to push for policies against a power that was not directly troubling them. After all, the more drugs that moved, the less lives were lost. That was just how things were. That was just how the city of Signot let things be; scared into acceptance, scarred into dependence. The Bolivian Conglomerate had such a stranglehold on the city that they operated mostly through smaller factions and bases in the various boroughs. They hardly moved a finger, so when something did demand their attention, they struck with force. With eyes and ears in the backstreets to the outer city and everywhere between, there were not many places their influence did not reach. Though the fate of the city belonged to the highest bidder, the price of crisis paved way for the highest of hopes. Hopes that would one day take flight and find a way to fight the plights of the city and strictly, these wishes came true at night. The five o'clock news would report biweekly occurrences of assurance: a corporate head resigning. A drug bust seeing trial. All small signs that the people should hold their heads high. Not to look below or behind, but to look out for a hero in the sky.

"Your move, Moon." Even with all the cards stacked against him during his early years, Tre Moon once again found himself awaiting judgement. It was not by the jury however, this time it was at the weekly poker club at the University of Claxton, of which he was a regular. On a daily basis, Tre could not escape the thought of how the tables had turned for him. While he was facing a life sentence in the detention centre, he would count his days away. Now, he had poker chips on the counter, the countenance of the law and more blessings than he could count. A fresh start and a government funded university grant. A place in his university's science research team and most importantly, freedom.

"Pass," said Tre, keeping his line of cards curved toward himself. If life had taught him anything it was that gaining nothing was a considerably better deal than losing something. This very principle served his conservative playing style in the arena of poker. Two of the students exhaled impatiently. Like the jury at his original trial, the fellow competitors at the table wanted him to fail and though it was not in the blockbuster, block boy ways of his past days; he was still, ironically, playing with odds. Stacking them, betting them and beating them. As the course of the game circled in its conventional clockwise cadence, there was no short of competitive counter play, therefore all cards were kept clutched to the chest and coughs and cold looks were commonplace as the players all tried to coordinate their composures.

"Pass," announced Tre once again when his turn came.

"To win you have to play," taunted a boy a few places from him.

"To win you have to play smart," replied Tre with an unbothered air. The boy peered at him some, then, with the exact intention Tre meant, the boy glanced unsurely at his own cards in play. Tre Moon's ace in the hole was his still demeanour, his expression remained largely unchanged and in the face of tense poker game, this trait was as precious as a diamond. His immersion in the game was lost when he spied the figure of Caprice Hill waiting outside the poker club room.

"I've got to go guys— I'm sorry, I forgot I had to do something!" Tre's concentration dropped as fast as his cards when he leaped from his chair, sending many chips flying. His opponents could not help but spy his winning hand. Despite his full suit, king and queen cards that would have put him on par for victory, his greatest setback proved to be his heart. The backlash of the club members came next.

"Really, Tre?"

"Again?"

"Look at that hand, he must be crazy?"

"This is the fifth time you have bailed out of a game halfway; you're banned for the rest of the term!" cried the convenor.

"Sorry!" winced Tre. Before he exited the room he straightened his trench coat downward and gave himself a bad breath test in the form of a light, discreet cough. When he had met his own standards of satisfaction, he strode out of the room and feigned surprise.

"Caprice? What are you doing here so early?!"

"Tre-Tre!" Caprice spun around on the spot. Her turn proved to be quite a struggle as she had to swing no less than a dozen shopping bags with her. "I thought poker club finished at seven pm? You're twenty minutes early?" she returned with equal surprise, stuffing all of the bags out of his line of view, although he could identify most of them by colour. He resolved to not address her strange behaviour.

"I found myself drifting off during the game, was gonna head back to the apartment early to sleep. How comes you're here early?" He smiled down at her. Since the age of nine, eight years had put seven inches of height between them. Tre's six-foot frame sat high above her five-foot-four figure, however, since his release from juvenile prison three years ago, the pair could not break free from the single thing that had kept them close for so many years, their friendship. From behind her, Caprice revealed a small bag and from it she withdrew a small telescope. It was extremely well crafted and had the words 'Heron Institute' branded into its base. Tre's mouth widened as she presented it to him and as she often did, captioned her actions with sentimental and, admittedly, bloated words.

"Okay, so as I was shopping this afternoon I wondered into a miscellaneous store and, at first I was going to walk straight out because half of the stuff in there were either strange or most likely illegal. But something caught my eye. When I went over to the geeky, science section I saw it. I know I should really be saving for my camera, but I had to buy this for you. It is not as powerful as the one your parents got for your sixth birthday, but I thought it would be nice if you could at least have a piece of your past back."

In a moment of indefinable gratitude, Tre locked his best friend into a hug. If he had not been so preoccupied in appearing cool to her, he could have shed a tear. Seventeen years of age had changed Caprice Hill some; a few of the strands in her afro had undergone the fashionable change to the colour alabaster, moreover, she had strangled her free flowing hair into hairbands so much as to resemble an ugly top knot trend that had captivated most of young, female America. She had developed a long neck like her mother, a slimming figure and a particularly callipygous lower half. Her face could not escape the freshness of old and for that reason she looked younger than she was. Finally, her hazel eyes sat behind a set of thick glasses, like gems in a jewellery shop window.

"Looks to me that you could have done some saving." When he finally let her go, he eyed the numerous other shopping bags she held. Caprice gave an offended tut.

"Before you give me anymore stick I'd like to let you know that the microscope your very generous and thoughtful friend just bought for you, cost twice as much as everything else in these bags. Heron Institute equipment is not cheap!" Another trait Caprice had developed over the years was making third person references when trying to make a point. It was overused, but appropriately amusing all the same.

"Twice the price? That is even worse, that did not help your case whatsoever,"

"Also, two of the bags are food," she continued strongly, "someone had to do food shopping cos we both know you would not get around to it."

"How did this become about me?" Tre laughed.

"University is stressful and shopping relaxes me okay? The new camera can wait until after my photography major I guess. C'mon let's get back to the apartment it's getting late." The pair made their way from the site of the main campus, through the meadows of the national park and into the lower district of Signot's Claxon Borough. Throughout the journey and though they were engaged in conversation throughout, Tre's attentions were secretly on his desire to get the camera for her. He had no doubt that it would take some time, given its price tag, but, he knew it was something he could do. Less because of the fact he could exercise more restraint than her when it came to matters concerning the material, but more because the smile on her face when he would gift it to her would be priceless. Tre received a break of his scholarship every month for being part of the state of Indiana's Science Youth Research team, so to wait a few months was not going to be hard, especially for an individual who was forced to serve years. After some ten minutes of walking, the pair reached a particularly ruddy stretch of estates and the state of the area surrounding the complexes was telling. The roads were as neglected as the surface of the flats, the inhabitants refused recycling and this could be seen in the items of rubbish planted under the sheet of autumn leaves. The flats themselves had chipped paint, stained windows and dated designs.

"You got your keys? Nope." Caprice answered her own question upon seeing Tre's unsure reaction.

"They must be with Left, I share mine with him cos the fool keeps losing his," Tre explained as they stepped inside their flat. It had fewer rooms than Caprice had shopping bags in just one hand, the ceilings where more crouched than Tre's stature as he had to duck under the doorways and the passage was narrower than the look Caprice gave him next.

"All of that doesn't even matter right now anyway. I'm stuck."

"On what?" Tre placed his telescope down.

"My photography project, I have no idea what to do it on..."

"I thought you decided you were doing it on the Belly Carnival? That's what you said right?"

"I changed my mind."

"Why?"

"It's too predictable plus I think that damn Alisha is going to do it too. Argh – she is so annoying I—"

"Straying off topic a lil'..."

"I'm just saying, also have you seen my contact lenses?"

"You left them in the kitchen cos you were rushing out this morning, yeah right beside the sandwich toaster." Tre directed her at a lean. When she had located her contacts case, she threw her large glasses off her face, making a more hurried attempt to thank him.

"Tre-Tre, what would I do without you?" She gave him a peck on the cheek which resulted in the tall, seventeen-year-old to swell up.

"More than you could ever know," Tre managed to say normally. He did consider Caprice as one of the most fluttering individuals he knew, but he also knew she was capable and brilliant, especially as a friend. If he was to ask himself that very same question it would be a very different story. Tre did not express his affection for her as openly or often as he wanted, but he knew that without Caprice his life had little meaning.

"A compliment? That gift must have really buttered you up?" She was now flashing mascara over her eyes in the nearby mirror. With a kick of courage, Tre decided to take a stand on a proposal he had been thinking about for a few years to say the least.

"So, Left is out of the house. Maybe it would be a good time to hang out together like the old times maybe?" Due to the loudness of his nerves, these words came out as an extended mumble.

"What?" came the unfocused reply of Caprice, she was in the process of cosmetic carpeting; layering her lips with a matte pink lipstick.

"Err, you going back out or something?"

"Not even, I'm just – oh that's him right now. Can you get the door Tre-Tre?" Caprice jumped a little as her phone vibrated on her makeshift dressing table. Tre's expression dropped as much as his hopes did. As he put his hand to the door he could not escape how primed and pretty Caprice looked. Before he unlocked the door, he pruned over the insignificance of his pet name and when Caprice's guest came pushing in smelling of propane, pride and potent smoke, he could not help the plethora of pejoratives that came to mind. It was Caprice's unofficial boyfriend, Lancis Green.

"What'up big soldier," Lancis threw Tre a rugged salute sign.

"Soldier," Tre acknowledged him with a slight raise of the head. Lancis Green was nearer Caprice's complexion than Tre's, had a hairless baby face and donned a navy tracksuit with its hood upwards. Under it, you could see a haircut that had been measured to the millimetre. If the boy's haircut was to be described as fresh, Tre's, in comparison, was a frantic fresco of waves. The smoothness translated in the manner he addressed Caprice also; he swept toward her, swept her into one arm, all while Tre's eyes swept to the corner of the room.

"Did you miss me?" Caprice squeezed him tightly.

"You did," Lancis replied before lancing his tongue in the direction of her mouth.

"Really?" Tre muttered under his breath, trying not to hear the slippery, tongue twisting noises that followed. Five seconds too long passed and Tre had enough.

"Alright guys, I'm going be in my room."

"No worries, Soldier, we were just going ourselves," Lancis announced and in a few playful moments Caprice and himself were shut behind the door to her private room. Tre shook his head and picked up the microscope Caprice gifted him. At the opposite end of the flat was his own room. If having his preposition thrown in his face was not enough, what he saw upon entering his room was enough to make him palm his face. He had to face the most daunting prospect yet; a night with his final flatmate; Left Davies. Left had a thick but lean figure. He had greasy, blonde hair and a peppered beard across the sides of his face. Their shared room was cramped, holding only a bunk bed, a stationary work desk, two shelves and a PlayStation corner, which Left had set up during their absence.

"'Sup?" slurred Left in a tone so blasé, Tre would not have believed there were multiple half full soda bottles and packets of spilt crisps on the floor, unless he was standing there, right then. Though it proved impossible in the past, Tre tried to 'un-see' what he had just witnessed for the sake of diplomacy.

"Left... Left!" Tre repeated as he tried to win his roommates' attention from the games console, which proved as effective as trying to keep an elastic band stretched.

"Which left, the next one?" Left asked urgently. Tre was utterly confused until he realised that Left was playing a racing game. Between the mess and the misunderstanding, Tre became too short to reason with either. This led him to switching off the entire console from the main plug.

"Bro," Left gasped in disbelief, "there are three things you do not do in this world. You don't walk in front of the TV during a game, you don't jeopardise another man's gaming session and you do not, and I mean do not, ignore someone when they say greet you hello. That one hurt the most. Admittedly."

"Can you please clean up this damn room?" Tre brushed a few of the chips together with his left foot.

"Rough day at the office, hunny?" Left said in his highest pitch.

"We aint' friends. Just clean up the room." He placed his Heron Institute microscope on the higher of the two shelves. Next to it was science books, medical manuals and a single photo of a younger version of himself with his parents. It was a candid picture taken almost twelve years ago by Edith Hill and, once again, gifted by Caprice. The lower shelf was filled with game cases, movie cases and lost assignments. If the shelves were not indication enough of two types of personalities inhabiting one place, then the room itself was. Tre's side was relatively empty, but also clean. Left's side was crammed with posters (gaming and vixen alike), electronic equipment and the fair share of careless mess.

"Okay I will. Don't worry man; I know how it feels to sit by while the girl of your dreams gets further and further from you." The lazy Left did not abandon his wheeled chair as he cleared his mess; he merely skated over to the appropriate sections.

"Did I miss something?" Tre responded. He thought of ignoring the comment but a part of him could not resist the act of recompense.

"C'mon bro. Even the blind could see you are in love with Caprice."

"Don't talk about things you don't understand. She's my friend."

"You follow her around like a puppy."

"We study a lot and we live in the same place. Look, I don't know if you've noticed but we do a lot of things together."

"Not enough things, clearly."

"Your greasy ass always has something slick to say huh?"

"You just need to tell her how you feel man."

"I can't believe we are even having this conversation right now. I could be studying."

"Guess who aint studying right now? Caprice. She might be focused on something else though."

"Wow. Where did they get you from bruh? You're hella' annoying."

"You're lucky they transferred me from New York man, otherwise you'd have no one to carry the rent with you. You'd both be ass out behind payments. Probably having to sleep outside, cuddling together for warmth. Which sizes up better compared to this friendzone situation you got going on here."

"They all up in other people's business in New York too?"

"Just tell her how you feel. Anyways I prefer Indiana way more than NY," Left changed subject.

"And I'm sure you're going to tell me why," Tre predicted, throwing himself on the underside of the bunk bed."

"You bet I am. It's usually courteous to ask before going on somebody's living space. But anyway, Indiana has vigilantes. Hero Vigilantes. People fighting the battles we can't." Left had the odd habit of handling multiple thoughts in consecutive sentences; therefore, one had to remain attentive to catch the words of relevance. This was ironic given that if Left had to do the same, his fickle attention span could hardly contend.

"Hero, vigilantes? What does that even mean? Seriously, the stuff you come out with is ridiculous sometimes."

"I'm guessing you do not watch the news?" With one sweeping assumption, Left caught Tre's ignorance in a net.

"Err—"For a person so flimsy with their living space, Left was quite sharp with the assertions.

"I thought so. You need to read up every once in a while. It's real. Your neighbour city, Heavens Conquest, has a super vigilante, by the name of N.O.M.A. - a real life hero! He has like a suit and everything. They say that the reason the Bolivian drug empires weakest point of trade is in Heavens Conquest, is because N.O.M.A. protects it." Tre had never seen Lefts back as straight as when he explained these facts to him.

"If it's true why isn't it in headlines and stuff?"

"The media control what they put on there man c'mon, everybody knows that. If they show what N.O.M.A. has been doing, it will give people hope. Stay woke."

"Sounds like a conspiracy." Tre shrugged.

"It is. He has been to Signot too."

"What does N.O.M.A. stand for?"

"There are a lot of theories, but No-Man-Army is the most popular. North-Of-My-Asshole is the funniest." The two boys held eye contact for only a second before they both could keep their straight face for no longer. Left's eyes crinkled into blue dots and his face blotched red as he laughed up his recent words. Tre cracked a smile, but reality sobered him almost instantly.

"Interesting thought, but I've seen too much bad stuff happen to believe there is a hero watching over us."

"Can't save everyone. That's why if you can, you should. Same applies to love bro." Left's words of wisdom could barely hit home as a rap on started on their door. The rap was too rapid to be Caprice, so his next guess was right on the mark.

"Yo Soldier, come for clearance for one minute," Lancis Green ushered Tre.

The Signot lingo was like chasing a mole in a hole; hard to follow unless you knew where to go. This kept the strangers of the youth culture astray even in public situations, whether it was the streets or the subway. It provided the young generation with their own claim to individuality in a city which biggest factors where the predictable benefactors of the corporate and drug empires. 'Clearance' was a breed of the newest lingo the city's street culture had adopted, and accordingly, it was made by the gang initiated, to address the drug affiliated. In short, Clearance was the term used to initiate a drug deal and was the exact same reason Tre Moon and Lancis Green were making their way to an obscured side street.

"It's getting cold man," Lancis tried to start conversation when they found a suitable spot, but Tre had little patience for small talk.

"Not today. You got the thing?" Tre found himself rubbing his hands anxiously.

"Yeah I got that for your impatient ass," Lancis laughed his broad, white grin, "but I have got a question to ask you before this."

"I need the drugs, make it quick." Tre clamped his hands together to stop them from shivering. It was only slightly chilly outside.

"So, as you should know, I get around town getting this money and I hear things. I hear that you served time a few years ago. From what I hear you're heartless. Why you wasting your time at this uni broke, living in this cheap ass flat? Why don't you get in on this lil' thing we got going on? We make real money. We playing by our own rules and there's always room on the team for someone like you."

"Who said I was heartless?"

"Some of the bangers in my gang, some of them did time with you in Juvy. They said you had the worst charges in there. Listen in this lil' thing of ours they call me 'The Chef', cos I make sure everyone around me is eating good. Getting what they're supposed to get. This city aint what it used to be and it's looking like it aint getting better anytime soon. Money and fear run Signot and we have all of that. We got powerful friends. As long as that's the case we have nothing to worry about, we'll be able to live in glory. I've known you for a few months now and I can't lie, you are one of the most laidback people I've ever seen. But I also know that people don't change, no matter how much they try to deny. So, what do you say? Are you going to eat with the wolves?" The Chef held out a hand, one which held a magnificent pinkie finger ring that was surely a small indication of the nice things the drug business had brought him and his friends.

"I'm good, bruh. Drugs ruin people's lives." Tre did not consider his decision for one moment. In fact, the speed of his reply prompted an affronted look from the aspiring drug lord.

"What?"

"I said I'm good. I don't want to ruin someone's life."

"You ruined your parents already didn't you?" Chef slashed. Tre was intrinsically destined to be bound by the horrors of his past and if it was not for the barriers of security and reassurance Edith Hill had brought to his life since rescuing him from a life sentence, perhaps he would have faltered under the latest test. But alongside his improved fortitude, he now knew that Lancis Green a.k.a The Chef was a person that would go to any lengths to get what he wanted, and to further lengths when he did not. No reaction came from Tre's statuesque face.

"Have you got my thing?" Tre withdrew a twenty dollar bill.

"The price doubled, as of now," Lancis whispered with hostility. He stared Tre straight in the eye as he withdrew another twenty and handed it to him without so much as a qualm. The endlessness to Tre's patience seemed to only shorten his; consequently, two more acts of disrespect came.

"Take your damn drugs," Lancis threw the packet at Tre's chest with force, "a broke, addict who doesn't know when someone is trying to hook him up. Caprice needs to pick her friends more wisely," he sneered before blinking his sports car into start-up. When Lancis left the road of their flat, the sky darkened just a bit more, but for Tre it was a bright evening. An evening without regret. An evening without consequence. Another evening in control. He looked down at the packet of xanax, and then he picked one out with his finger. Even though Lancis Green had left him, and he was totally alone on the Claxon roads, a voice was still with him. The livid voice inside of his head.

"How could you let him talk to us like that and walk away alive? I'll kill him!"

"I'm in control of my life now. You don't have a say and you never will again." It was a rare moment because Tre gave a victorious grin, one he reserved for moments where things that could have gone bad previously, were now under his control. He put the tablet of xanax on his tongue and as the solvent slipped more and more from solid form, the voice inside his head became less and less audible.

CHAPTER 4

<u>Xanax & Xenium</u>

Tre's addiction to Xanax was a trip with no destination, like a ship with no sail; stuck until the waves of the drug would sweep him away. His trips were hazy and more often than not, accompanied by the weightlessness of life's obligations. The drug gave him a patience that was not of his own natural temperament and put to rest the other occupier of his mind. All the rage, bad thoughts and manipulation were now latent, a reminder of what he did not want to be and a marker of how he wanted to proceed. Caprice Hill was the person he cared most about but she did not know of his secret affair with insobriety. In more ways than one, he wanted to be there for her, but like most things he was used to in life, he could not control how she felt about him. More than anything, he wanted to take the blindfold from her eyes in the form of a confession and let her see the bond they had, but perhaps it was him who did not see things in perspective. After all the clearances to his name, he was still by definition a murderer. He was still an unstable teenager who suffered from Dissociative Identity Disorder. Tre could not imagine what sane person would want to live their life with someone who brought such uncertainty. He could not blame her. After all, taboo was truly a titan to tackle and stigma was a sensitive appropriation to shake. If religion could clear his conscience, he would have attended tabernacles many times a day. Therefore, Tre settled for enigma, he kept a low profile when he could and did not form deep connections with those he did meet. This kept the subject of his past a relatively untouched one and his dark secret of murder was only with the two souls he trusted, Caprice Hill and her mother Edith Hill. He did not know how exactly Lancis Green knew of his past, but he knew that it was unlikely for it to be used against him. Especially since he had no plans to get in his way. As long as he had Lancis Green as his connection to the drug, he could lead a normal life. His first and last reason for drug use was to pacify the demon inside.

Tre awoke the next morning to dry snores below him. Upon checking the alarm clock on his shelf, he saw it was 7 am: in other words; two hours until his lecture and also two hours shy of his flat mate's progressive loudness. With the incentive of not having a conversation with his messy roommate, (who left an area of litter for Tre to prance around) he got ready relatively quickly. To finish his routine, he pulled a dark cap onto his head and pushed a bar of Xanax onto his tongue. When he felt the wilting effects of the drug take over his body, he set off. As Tre made course for the university campus he could not help but think how much he liked the city of Signot. The city was almost always busy, so it was easy to remain just another face in the crowd. The design of the city was both sublime and subaffluent, depending on where you went, but still diverse enough to not pay attention to the next person. Lastly, the citizens of Signot were bred with an innate fear of the things around them, so there was a large tendency to keep your head down. This very fact put incongruity in his belief system; he believed people should be and feel safe but if that was achieved, he was most likely to be picked out as the insane kid who murdered his parents. Not feeling he had a place at either signpost of morality, he was content on walking the uncomfortable line between. Upon arriving to the campus, it took him fifteen minutes to reach his well hidden lecture. This was because Indiana's Science Research Programme (ISRP) was held in the highest reaches of the university building. As if attending their extra curriculum meetings did not require dedication enough, the climb to the meeting room made sure that only the most committed would attend. Tre, who was of average fitness, found that his cap reduced his head to a greenhouse by the time he reached the top. One by one his peers steadily joined him in similarly heaving entrances.

"At least we're early today."

"They need to change the location of these meetings."

"They really do."

After a few minutes, the last student of the fifteen students had arrived. Unlike the rest though, Tre was stationed against the wall by himself. Throughout the year most members had tried to incorporate him into their conversation, but it was quickly concerted that he preferred to be an outsider. While they saw an anti-social, arrogant boy, it would only take one peer into his life to see he was hardened by sorrow, numbed by drugs and had little trust to spare.

"Do you plan to say anything to anyone today?" a rosy voice glided beside him and due to the interminable effects of his insobriety, a person followed sometime after. He turned to his left and he was met with a girl he knew to be named Damia Ascot. The first noticeable thing about her was her attire: presentable and smart. White shirts and flaring work trousers were a feature of her usual outfits. She had a star line of beauty marks from her left eye down to her throat, and had brown, loyal coils for hair. Her forehead was wide, but much wider was the openness she showed when she approached him. Her dark eyes switched between both of his in wait of a reply. None came.

"If you ever need help with anything class related, just know you can come to me. We're all here for each other," she continued with a warm smile.

Tre supposed there was a defect in her understanding, so he spoke only to clarify.

"I can handle everything. Thanks though."

"Damia Ascot," she introduced herself. At this point Tre was uncomfortable, the thought of giving his name and possibly seeing a reaction of terror made him abstain from completing the introduction.

"Damia, of course."

"So, what made you choose to be part of this programme? Apart from the fact that it is one of America's best fast-track programmes into the scientific industry." She spoke in a half modest, half factual way.

"Well, I hope I can work for Heron Institute when I'm older. Aaron Heron was my idol when I was younger," Tre replied.

"Oh. Did you hear that he and his wife have been missing for a few years now?" Damia said gently.

"Yeah, I heard, why wouldn't I have?" Tre could not let her hide behind what she had implied, especially if it meant she knew who he was.

"Nothing-never mind, it's nothing. I'm sure by the time we get to our goals, they will have found him and I'm sure you'll meet him," Damia tried to play off her words but ended up tripping over her own dismissal. Stammering and all.

"Right. I got to make a call, I just remembered. Nice meeting you—" Tre was in the process of backing up until a hand found a way to the back of his collar, stopping him in his steps.

"I don't think so, Mr Moon. The meeting is about to begin." With impeccable timing, the founder of the research programme arrived: Professor Noel Jinx.

The science research meeting room was held in the mansard of the university's structure; therefore, it was a draughty place. Sloping sides, portable radiators and executive lab equipment were a feature of the room; moreover, the research meeting was not complete without Professor Noel Jinx himself, conducting an animated, inspirational speech to those seated. Though he was not an official member of Claxton University, he was Tre's favourite lecturer by far. The fact that he was also a former employee of Heron Institute was a bonus.

"First of all, I would like to congratulate everyone for the work on the colloidal silver project. Hopefully in the next few years we will be able to maximise the medical uses of silver. Truly remarkable." The Professor sighed fondly before continuing, "When people think of the field of science they think of the answers that is has provided. General relativity. Oxygen theory of combustion. Natural selection. We live our life with somewhat concrete beliefs due to what science has discovered, but the truth is we know hardly anything. Every day we discover something new or understand something better. The truth is we can never be too certain about anything because we could always discover something tomorrow, a discovery, that changes everything we thought we knew. That is why I always say, as scientists, we should feed ourselves a healthy dose of scepticism when we conduct our research. I see ourselves like adventurers; we are exploring the world and everything around us in order to understand it more. Is that not what adventurers do? Before me is Indiana's finest minds; the future of scientific research, and no matter your field, it is an extraordinary thing. To want to dedicate your life to uncovering secrets and knowledge that will benefit humanity. Different interests and experiences have brought you to where you are today but no matter who you are, or what you been through, what unites every single person in this room is the desire to be pioneers in the scientific field," Professor Jinx spoke in a forced whisper because he believed what they were doing justified the sincerity of what he was saying. You could see droplets of sweat bloom from the top of his dark, balding head and his thick brows pulled together in such seriousness, that they now formed a bridge. During his speech he periodically preached in front of each student, sending them into impromptu shyness or a fight against the giggles, as his fuzzy moustache seemed to take on a life of its own when he spoke. The professor garnered reactions from everybody except Tre Moon, who seemed unfocused.

"I'm sure you have heard me speak enough this semester already, so today I am going to ask something different of all of you. I want to give each and every one of you the taste of what your future holds for you; making breakthrough research. That is why I am putting you in groups of three. By the end of this academic year, each group will bring me a research project of their choice." It was this unlikely announcement that nudged Tre out of his druggy slur.

"Yes," Professor Jinx noticed Tre sit up some, "I expect this research to be of the highest order. To have a clear thesis, method and research material. Pretty much what you are used to, except I am giving you all the freedom to choose what the project is about. As you may have figured, I expect this project to be done independently of your university studies, but I—"

"Wait! With all due respect, Professor, you must know that we all have social lives, jobs?" a particularly vocal member of the research team interrupted. The name of this student escaped Tre on that occasion, however, he could identify him by his sharp beard and his brash mannerisms which made Tre question, on a number of occasions, how he had a place on Indiana's finite research team, in the first place.

"As a scientist, sometimes you are going to have to make sacrifices Quiqhin. You'll learn that at some point, and better sooner than later," Professor Jinx informed the young man, but before he walked away he added a reminder in the form of renunciation.

"Also, I'm not sure chasing girls around campus constitutes as more important than this research project."

"Sir!" intoned the boy named Quiqhin, sensing that a few avenues may have closed at those words.

"I'm just saying youngster, this is more important than you think. I understand that it might be a stressful project to put together, but that is why I have assigned you to groups. Also, do not underestimate the value of this research project. Your work will be officially credited toward the Scientific Institution of America, meaning that it could be used as reference for future works; you are contributing to the well of knowledge. Hopefully this will motivate you to conduct the best research of your life. In order to give you the widest and best resources possible, I am giving each group a pass to Heron Institute archives and it goes without saying that everyone should be signed up with Signot library." A few nervous coughs came at the end of these words.

"That will be the end of the meeting, I'll leave you to form groups and discuss preliminary ideas. One person from each group should email me the members and research idea, when you have decided, and then from there we can discuss whether it is viable and how to go about it. Remember everyone; I am your fourth member!" Professor Noel Jinx exclaimed, concluding the shortest meeting to date. Without the authority of the professor to keep them at bay, Tre watched Newton's law play out as the students gravitated to the biggest personalities in the room. The exception to this was Quiqhin, as the females in the meeting seemed to zip particularly quickly from his general direction. By the time the other groups had formed, only Quiqhin, Tre and Damia Ascot remained. Tre found himself eating his words from earlier.

"Looks like we're a group," Tre pointed out, as he took a seat beside her.

"So, it seems," Damia confirmed, "Damia Ascot," she introduced herself once again as Quiqhin conceded that it was destined to be his group.

"How comes I never see you around campus, only at meetings?" Quiqhin questioned her immediately. When he spoke from close it was impossible to miss the London accent that had bypassed them several times before.

"Trust you to notice," she remarked, "I don't go this university, I live and study in Heavens Conquest."

"And you travel here every week, just for the meeting?" Quiqhin's mouth was so wide it implied that if her answer was yes, it would be one of the most ridiculous things he had heard in his life.

"Yes." Damia nodded.

"That is one of the most ridiculous things I have heard in my life."

"Travel is long and expensive but being a part of this is important for me. If it was my decision, it would be based in my city, but we just have to deal with things in life," said Damia. "By the way Quiqhin, this is Tre, Tre, Quiqhin." She crossed both hands and inverted them to complete the introduction between the two males. Both took in each other's appearance during her words, and as Tre inspected his slick, styled hair, smart, sharp beard and matured, middle-eastern features, it occurred to him that this was a face he had seen on his campus before.

"Everyone calls me Quick, it's easier," Quiqhin said, still taking in Tre's face for himself. "I know you; you're always with that fit girl? Caprice, right?"

"She's got a man, soldier," Tre said.

"Swear? You know what, I'm not even gonna go there. On the basis that you told me peer to peer, research partner to research partner, man to man, I respect that. Do your thing, bro," Quick testified with a hand to the chest. Tre nodded in receipt of his words but chose not to correct the minor misunderstanding. The concept of Caprice and himself being together was an idea he liked.

"Okay. We need to think of a research topic, so everybody write down their name and number on this piece of paper and I'll make a group chat," Damia brought the matter at hand back to attention, before handing Quick the paper. Once he finished writing he passed it over to Tre, who wrote his details underneath the name, 'Quiqhin Isles.'

"Moon, that's a cool surname." Quick glanced the words on the paper as he passed it back to Damia. His first reaction was to shield the paper, but it was already too late, his name had been seen. The next and only thing to do was to take the words for what they were.

"Thanks," Tre said sincerely.

"Well as soon as we come up with our idea I'll schedule the acceptance meeting with the Professor. I guess I'll see you guys then." They had only been a group for less than ten minutes, but it was becoming increasingly clear that Damia was the more organised of the three, and consequently, most qualified to lead. Quiqhin was the first to his feet and made his exit in something of a hurry.

"I'll have the idea by tonight latest. Check your phones! Tonight!" he called back through the closing door. Apart from Damia and Tre, the only people in the draughty meeting room were one other group, who were discussing something in detail. Damia Ascot grabbed the single bag she had and stood herself.

"I know who you are," she uttered, discomfort was spelt all across her face and this sent Tre's heart into a race. His heart was like a fire alarm, pounding in his chest and rightly so, Damia had the power to rip apart everything he had established.

"I am so, so sorry about what you have been through – what you are going through. I won't tell anybody." Damia left looking troubled but she also left Tre with an unspoken token that was trust.

It was a young, mauve afternoon by the time Tre left Claxon University's campus. The young teenager had one too many thoughts on his mind, but all he could be thankful for was that it was only thoughts of his own. He began upon the long route toward the Signot's national park until the shrill horn of a car made him stop. When he could not recognise any of the vehicles along the private road, he continued, to which the horn sounded again. Tre was not left searching for the origin of the noise for long because he could see Lancis Green waving out of the window of a particularly expensive looking car. He approached reluctantly.

"I ain't seen Caprice today." For the sake of avoiding any more knots in their relationship, Tre got straight to the point.

"I ain't here for Cap, I'm here for you, soldier," Lancis replied smugly, his teeth were laced with gold grillz.

"Yeah?" Tre's fist tightened. His time in Juvenile Detention taught him that most strains of ill feelings could be solved through warfare.

"Chill, man. I've just come to say sorry 'bout the other day." Lancis kept both hands on the steering wheel, in sight. This was enough to egg Tre down.

"Oh,"

"Yeah man, what I did the other day didn't sit right with me. You a good guy Tre, you ain't done nothing but be a loyal customer and be there for Cap. You got one hell of an addiction to them xan's but I shouldn't have treated you like that. I'm just quick to anger. I apologise, soldier. You ain't gotta live life our way, you got your own life." To complete his gesture he pulled out a blue bag filled to the brim with xanax bars, while smiling a glistening, xanthaodontous smile.

"This for you, man, Chef got you." He held out the bag from the tinted windows.

"'Preciate it, soldier." Tre was fast to forgive because he better than anyone knew that it was possible to do and say things that were completely out of character and though Lancis was not facing the affliction he had, if second chances were not a thing, he would not be walking free at that very moment.

"You gonna take it then?" Lancis looked up and down the street cautiously.

"If you want to do me a favour, I would rather you take me somewhere. It's a bit far but probably nowhere you ain't been." Tre's mysterious proposal was nothing short of a gamble, but with guilt and his prior gift considered, he had to give in.

"Aight', get in. This better be important." Lancis shook his head in disbelief.

"There's nothing more important," Tre promised him.

After almost two hours of driving, the two boys had reached a place far from the comforts of the city. Their thin road was surrounded by forest, fields, fences, fen nettle and a mist eerie enough to end Lancis' gesture prematurely.

"Yo," he clamped the brake down in exasperation, "where the hell are we?"

"This is close enough, thanks man." Tre exited the vehicle and with no hesitation, made toward the thick of the forest. Lancis threw confused looks back and forth, he was utterly at a loss.

"Bruh, do you see where we are?! Have you lost your mind?"

"Half of it." Tre acknowledged.

"I can't lie, but I'm not waiting for you." Lancis solidified his dare by revving his engine in declaration.

"I wasn't expecting you to," Tre called back.

After some moments, where he guessed Lancis thought he was trifling, Tre did not hear a sound, but when he had reached deep into the forest, he heard the faint sounds of a car rearing away. The noise pollution caused a chain reaction within the forest; there were flutters from above, maybe eagles, bats or owls, then he heard howls and had to bow his head as raindrops began to pound downward from the upturned leaves. The forest was beyond dark, but Tre continued to make his way from the light of his memory; he was not far from the resident rose bush. He was forced to push his hands into the pocket of his trench coat because the chills of the forest mist seemed to intensify the further he went. Tre had left the bag of xanax under the passenger seat and the very fact that Lancis considered that drugs were an appropriate measure of reconciliation showed him how little he understood him. Then again, no one alive truly understood him. His dependency of xanax was a contradiction as well as a coping mechanism. He took it to quiet the voice in his head and to maintain complete control over it, however, he had progressively taken it to dampen the depressogenic waves that came with every good thing that he had done up to that point in his life. When he was released from Juvenile Detention, he questioned whether he truly deserved freedom. When he was chosen for Indiana's Science Research team, he questioned whether an individual like himself was deserving of such a gift for physics. Every time he would see Caprice, he feared that he could somehow hurt her. Every time he had control of his mind, he questioned how long until the other voice would return. Living life in fear and in doubt was worse than any drug he could put into his body and though Tre would never admit to anyone outright, he had little value for his own life. If he was to die tomorrow, he would see it as karma paying its dues. Self-contemplation had fast tracked his journey because he was at the rose bush. He picked one rose because the rest had wilted beside it. He continued to walk until he reached a clearing in the path. Beyond it laid a small graveyard. Tre climbed down from the stretch of forest, making sure to keep the rose intact as he did so. By the time, he reached the lower ground of the yard, his trainers and the knees of his jeans were patched with soil, but the teenager did not mind as the earth was to be his bed for the night. Usually Tre Moon's face would remain stronger than any of the many gravestones around him, but as he approached a tandem of two close ones, he felt his face crumble under the magnitude of the moment.

"Hi Mum, hi Dad." He smiled with dry lips. Through the crinkling waters in his eyes, he could see the words 'In memory of Cecil Moon' and 'In memory of Natalie Moon' written on each gravestone.

"I only brought this today," he said, placing the red rose across their beds to join the multiple, now wilted flowers from before. "This was kind of a spontaneous trip; otherwise I would have brought more. That rose bush back there is not looking too good, autumn is getting to it, it seems." Tre lowered himself to a seat before the graves.

"Man, do I have some updates for you guys," Tre started in a joyous manner, but he stopped and stared blankly forward. He could hear faint words repeating.

"Tre, I said I'm sorry."

"Tre, I said I'm sorry."

"Tre, I said I'm sorry."

"*Tre, I said* —-" Tre swallowed another bar of xanax and the voice disappeared down the same well in his mind it came from. There was one exception to his principle of forgiveness and that was himself.

"Yeah, so today was something. Prof Jinx has decided to give the research team an extended project today. He put us into groups, which I have mixed feelings about, but apparently our research will be officially credited to the Science Guild of America. He also said we will get a chance to use the Heron Institute archives! Can you believe it, Dad? Heron Institute!" Like a shell meant to endure the hardships of life, Tre Moon revealed the true aspects of his personality. He was sweet and excitable, moreover a truly ripe mind, a trait that he could not hide from his lecturers and the reason for his selection oun the research team.

"Speaking of Heron Institute, you guys will never guess what Caprice brought me. A Heron Institute microscope. She is great. I want to show her how much she means to me more than anything, so I've been thinking to get her this camera she is always shouting about. It is a limited edition range, 87 Titan series – something like that. My scholarship money comes in three weeks so I'm going to buy it then. I can't stop thinking about how happy she is going to be. Seeing her happy makes me happy. She is the only thing that has kept me happy since you guys left." At the trail of his last sentence, Tre's idyllic energy switched to something more sombre. His head swamped downward as he continued.

"Since you guys left me, I've been testing what helps and what doesn't. It is the ninth month without losing any type of control to the voice in my head. I found a way to silence it. I can hardly hear it these days. I wish I knew how I could make it stop before that day..." Tre was able to level the feeling of self-hate that was rising. "Everything would have been different. I could have stopped it. Edith thinks that her counselling sessions are helping but it's the drugs. You wouldn't want to hear this but, sometimes I think that I should be down there instead of you and maybe I should. It would have solved all the problems. Sometimes I think maybe I should join you since it's too late. But I must be here for another reason. Another purpose. Like you said, Dad, there is a whole world of possibility out there. I'll hang in there. I love you and I always will. I hope you haven't forgotten about me." Fresh tears met the soil and for the rest of the night Tre sat with the only company that could bring him true solace. Even a location so desolate, in a yard full of the dead, with another persona inside of his head, it was Tre who felt the most empty inside.

CHAPTER 5

<u>Origins</u>

Three weeks passed and the city of Signot was cast into the deep of winter. With shorter days and longer nights, the city was caught in the tide of the rising crime waves. The term '*crime pays*' seemed to apply less when the only toll criminals would face was missed opportunity, should they decide to hibernate. It was an expensive time of year and not due to the approach of Christmas, but rather that being outside could cost you your life. The seasonal gift for Signot would consist of a growing list of crimes and wishes for better times. The arrival of winter also brought one of the four surges of popularity for the Belly Carnival. Between Easter, Halloween and summer, winter was the third most anticipated. Nonetheless, the Hetashi Borough was swarming with teenagers and young adults as the Belly Carnival was Signot's thematic statement of arrival for every significant time of year. It was also one of the few places in Signot which could make the people forget about the gloom outside its walls. Given the dark days that Signot was currently facing, for an individual who had been living in the dark all of his life, it was as if the world was late to join Tre's realisation.

Tre found himself in his nearest miscellaneous store, scouring every shelf, low and high, in search of his prized item: Caprice's camera. The usually cool teenager worked up a sweat when more and more shelves came up empty of what he was looking for. The miscellaneous store was exactly what is was titled; it held a compilation of the most random and unassorted objects you would ever find in one room and due to the disorganisation, Tre was left rubbing his brows after twenty minutes of browsing.

"Yo," he called over an elderly man who was the owner of the store, "that camera I asked you about last week. Where is it?"

"I've sold like ten cameras since last week, kid."

"Listen," Tre approached the front desk half desperate, half worried. "I need that camera, man, it's important. I told you hold it right, I told you hold it for me?"

"I get new things every day. People offer good money for these things, especially the electronics!"

"I can't believe this. Do you remember what the camera is called, maybe I can get it somewhere... what?" Amidst his panic he could not help but notice that the elderly shop owner was beaming at him. Beside his reaction being inappropriate, Tre reckoned the smile was even too wide to justify the few occasions that he had acquainted with him previously. Something was amiss.

"What?!" Tre repeated with some bother in his voice; the man still held his stare and there was even something sentimental about it now.

"Oh, I just have a feeling that you are buying this gift for a lady friend that's all." Tre wondered whether he had been wearing his heart on his sleeve all these years without noticing. The young boy's silence only served to confirm the shopkeeper's intuition.

"How long have you liked this girl youngin'?" he continued. He now had his chin resting on a fist.

"She is one of the reasons I wake up every morning," Tre replied.

"Oh, love huh?" The shopkeeper walked from his side of the counter in order to stand closer to Tre, "Listen, if you want to show a girl how much you really care about her, buying a gift is the wrong way to go about it. Sure, she will love it but there is always going to be someone who can buy a bigger or more expensive gift. Even if you do get the most expensive thing in the world, people become accustomed and eventually it will not mean as much."

"What else then?" Tre folded his arms. The man's direction of logic made sense to him and so he was on board.

"If you want to win a girl's heart, you have to do something she will always remember. Help her grow," the old man finished with a magical whisper. These wise words were tattooed on Tre from the moment they were spoken. They earned a spot at the top of his concerns, he pondered for hours of how this profound gesture could play out within the bounds of his restrictive university lifestyle. He thought a confession was too fescinnine. To leave her guessing was at his detriment. He needed to be the last person in her life to leave a lasting impression. If love was truly a drug, then for her he would give up everything.

"Harnessing energy in synthetics. That is our project!"

"Err, could you elaborate what exactly this project entails?"

"It's pretty much self-explanatory, Prof, but I'll give you a sneak peek I guess. So, as we all know, certain materials have certain properties that allow them to be conductive, tensile, light, etcetera. What if we could change the properties of these materials, or better yet, what if we could harness multiple properties from different materials, chemically, to make a far more superior material?"

"You do know there is only a finite amount of ways that atoms can form? Do you think your topic for research has enough depth?"

"Like you said, Professor, we could always discover something tomorrow that changes everything that we believe today."

"Right you are, Quiqhin. It is ambitious I cannot take that away from you, but it also sounds expensive. Testing, safety trials. You might want to undertake a project that is more financially realistic."

"Funding will be taken care of by me. Besides, this is a project that could lead to a business prospect I have been planning for a few years, so I see it all as necessary expenses," Quick rolled on confidently. Quiqhin, Tre, Damia and Professor Jinx were all sat in the science meeting room, however, Quick had been at the forefront of the discussion for the entire duration.

"Sounds like it's more of a personal project and not an agreed one?" the Professor said.

"Oh, not at all. We have discussed this prior. It is not just Quiqhin's idea," Damia quickly informed him, though the rush of scarlet to the sides of her face said otherwise.

"We're all with it," Tre budged in to keep them from a second line of questioning. They could see their lies loosely in the reflection of Professor Jinx's shiny head. There was a minute of silence where it seemed their spontaneous team effort would backfire. Quiqhin had to put hands of prayer over his lips to physically stop himself from protesting. Damia's flush of scarlet had now decided to migrate to the other regions of her face, namely her forehead and lips. Tre, like on most occasions, was cool on the exterior, however, his heart was pounding for every ounce of inconvenience that would be caused for having to spend extra time formulating a rehearsed research plan. A drop of sweat almost escaped from the waves in his hair.

"I approve," the Professor finally said, to which the postures of the three students relaxed drastically.

"Thank you, sir, you have our word that it will be both thorough and innovative," said Damia.

"I expect nothing less from Indiana's brightest." Professor Jinx unseated himself, before making his way to the end of the lab. He carefully opened a samples fridge before pulling a tube out. "Before this meeting ends I thought you all would like to know that our colloidal silver project has taken on the right path. The Scientific Guild of America is willing to invest in further research for this finite version of silver." He held the tube to the light and the artic silver liquid was visible. They could see it climb to the sides of the vial like a liquid however it never truly separated from itself; it was as if it was in a state of inertia. A wonderful and strange visual experience. It was as if it was too elegant to conform to the shape of the vial, but too rare to be kept in anything but one.

"That is great news!" Damia said, clashing her hands together in excitement.

"You're welcome for the help," Quick congratulated himself proudly.

"The research you asked the class to gather was rudimentary. Properties – research of silver and similar alloys. If this was for your own independent project, what exactly is your thesis?" Tre asked.

"Well what we had before was colloidal silver, but to enhance its medicative uses, I have altered its state. Not me specifically, but a good friend of mine at Heron Institute. In a process called intact-photopheresis, we were able to intensify the properties of silver. It is in a highly reactive form at the moment – heck it will vaporise if exposed to oxygen. That it is why it in this air tight vial. It is may look like ordinary glass, but it is unbreakable by ordinary means. If we are able to stabilise and harness this 'supersilver' I believe a lot of people could benefit around the world. We could reach a new age in medicine. It has the ability to regenerate cells at incredible speeds." There was no look quite like a scientist looking upon the culmination of his hard work.

"Amazing!" Tre and Damia said in unison.

"Sir-sir-sir," Quick trilled, looking down at his ringing phone, "I think your work is incredible and thank you for letting me be a part of it, but I gotta go somewhere, so I'd appreciate if you'd let us go, if that concludes the meeting?" His knees were bent before a reply even came.

"Sure th—"

"See you in a bit, guys," came Quiqhin's colloquial farewell.

"Quiqhin. I think we should at least plan our next move before we leave, don't you think?" Damia tried to reel their research partner back but he seemed to have stronger loyalties elsewhere.

"Just text it in the group chat init." There was not a step of impartiality in his stride when he rushed out.

"Can you two give me a hand putting this back in the sample fridge?" Professor Jinx asked. Both obliged. Damia pulled the doors of the fridge open, while Tre readied the containment holder. Professor Jinx placed the vial of colloidal supersilver back into the holder before it was locked in the fridge once again.

"You are good kids, with a very bright future. One word of advice though: don't let him (he pointed a hand toward the door) get too controlling over the project. Egos and science are one of the most dangerous combinations you can have." The Professor Jinx left, and he also left Damia and Tre with such hard hitting advice that the proclivity of their partnership had been turned on its head and they were left with something of a problem now. As soon as the professor was out of earshot, Damia spun toward Tre, to confide in him.

"We need to get him on board; otherwise this could all go terribly wrong."

"He's on board, but not with us though," Tre reckoned.

"What is he even trying to find with this research project? It seems slightly farfetched," she said.

"Did you come up with a better one?" Tre was surprised when she drew for an excuse rather than an example. She stopped at the doorway in such suddenness that Tre automatically stopped with her.

"I didn't have time. It's been a crazy few days for me,"

"Why?"

"There have been political protests this past week in Heavens Conquest because of registration for the city to be the new base for Sargent Boston's private military. As you can imagine we don't want our home to be a war ground. When people started protesting, military resistance came. Boston ordered the transport around the city to cease in order to reduce the amount of people joining the march. My train was one of them. So, I could see it all. The soldiers began throwing riot gas into crowds of protesters. There were innocent children at the march. A few people became furious and belligerent because of the soldier's blatant mistreatment of the protesters, and when they did, the soldiers opened fire at the crowd..."

"No?" Tre was lost for words.

"Yes, opened fire at everybody," Damia said, her assured eyes were now faint.

"How many people died?" asked Tre, even though he was not quite sure he wanted to know the answer.

"None." She watched as Tre inched toward her as if his hearing had just failed.

"What do you mean none? How?"

"I saw it with my own eyes," she uttered with certainty.

"Saw what?"

"N.O.M.A. He – it swooped down and somehow blocked all of the gunfire. Within ten seconds it had taken out the row of soldiers, by itself. I learnt three things that day. N.O.M.A. is real. Sergeant Boston is an evil, heartless bastard and that Heavens Conquest is not a city I want to live in anymore." From her eye to her neck, Tre could count a beauty spot on her face for every shake of anger in her voice.

"Sorry to break the news but Signot is not any better," Tre said.

"When a private army is trying to militarise your city and turn it into the latest warzone then maybe you'll understand." The pair began walking again.

"Signot is a warzone, trust me. You're just not around enough to see it," he maintained. Damia did not dispute his latest sentence; she just eyed his regularly worn, black, trench coat, his rucksack, then, his manner during his cool delivery.

"I'll try to watch myself around here then. I'm going to call you this week to talk about our project. I'll see you next week, Tre." When Damia left, so did the pressing issue of the research project. Tre found his focus was back on the single track it was before; admittedly his science life added another dimension to his, one that he now knew he appreciated. It was a welcome distraction.

"A call later this week? Someone has an admirer." Out of nowhere the teasing voice of Caprice came and caused Tre such alarm, that he batted the air as if to defend himself from the suggestive words themselves.

"Caprice, what are you doing here?! The room keepers are going to be here soon to lock the classrooms." Ironically, on this occasion he was not expecting his best friend.

"Sorry its short notice but I seriously need your help." Their years of friendship equated to only a second for him to see her sincerity.

"Tell me what you need," Tre said.

Caprice pushed Tre back into the research meeting room, before leading him to a seat. She was in such a state of jitter that she decided not to sit herself. She pushed the arms of her glasses to her temples before she began relaying her problem.

"It is deadline day tomorrow and everybody has their photography concept except me. I've literally been stressing myself all week, trying to come up with something unique. It is not easy. (Tre raised his eyebrows slightly.) I was ready to give up and just fail the whole module until a couple of hours ago. I want to do my project around one of your scientific studies Tre-Tre. No one else will be doing it and it will give me points in originality since half the class has been doing Signot's most popular attractions," she finished; looking extremely pleased with herself for her last minute save of grace. Her brown and alabaster curls were tied into a frustrated ponytail, you could see bite marks in her bottom lip from worry and her oversized woollen jumper was cuffed over her palm. Her ray of optimism dimmed slightly when Tre did not return a look of accordance.

"Cap, you do realise that the majority of work I do in my physics lectures is theoretical?"

"Meaning?" She sunk her incisors into her bottom lip again.

"There is pretty much nothing visual for you to photograph, except my essay papers. Besides, it is way after the university's lending hours, how are you going to shoot anything with no camera?" Caprice reached into her leather satchel and withdrew a particularly polished looking piece of equipment. Under closer inspection, he recognised it to be the 87 Series Titan, the exact camera she had wanted, and that he planned to buy for her.

"No way? You got it?!"

"Yeah!" she squeaked as she put it around her neck, then into operation. "Lancis brought it for me a few days ago and surprised me with it today! I'm surprised he could even keep his bragging ass quiet for so long."

"I'm so happy for you." Tre forced a grin because this statement was half true. Yes, he wanted the best for Caprice, but to see someone else bring the smile that he could not, made him feel as if the hapless ways of his past had clung on to him somehow.

"I still have nothing to shoot. I'm going to be in so much trouble at the proposal lecture tomorrow." Caprice ran her eyes around the room for inspiration but in the most pivotal moment, it eluded her. There was a moment of three minutes where the pair shared a silence so stirring, at least one of them was bound to whip up an idea. Inspiration struck Tre first and he announced it with electricity.

"I've got something!"

"Yes-Yes-Yes-Yes." Caprice bounced on the spot. Tre disobeyed all lab conduct and dashed toward the samples fridge and removed every tray it contained. Caprice was won when she saw the various eye catching colours of the chemicals. In a session of pure ecstasy lasting fifteen minutes, Tre and Caprice propped the tables with different types of vials and pallets. The rush of spontaneity. The thrill of being caught by classroom keepers and the act of accomplishing something with your best friend. They were all ingredients for the unforgettable moment. Once Caprice had caught these pallets at a pentangular of angles (as well as making Tre feature in a silly photo shoot of his own), the reality of being caught truly kicked in.

"We need to go; they are going to be locking up the rooms anytime now." Caprice was laughing through her sentences as she was still experiencing the after effects of their brief querencia.

"I don't know if you noticed but it's easier to make mess than it is to clean it." Tre pointed this out light heartedly as he packed up. He honestly could not remember the last time he had anywhere near that much fun; there was a new glow of life about his face now.

"How comes that vial has a different cap than the others?" She directed his attention to the lone vial of colloidal supersilver Professor Jinx had shown them earlier.

"This is Professors Jinx's personal project. It's highly reactive so it's in an air tight case," Tre responded, making a note to leave the most delicate of the samples for last.

"What kind of a name is Professor Jinx?" she guffawed.

"What kinda name is "Chef"?" Tre countered quickly. Caprice burrowed the surge of instinctive laughter as soon as she realised she was laughing at her own boyfriend. She then changed the subject so as much as to change the telling look on her best friend's face.

"Thanks Tre-Tre, I'll never forget this. You won't either. I have photographic evidence that you are capable of smiling, it's all here." She tapped on her camera.

"All right, just get outta here before you get in trouble," he said, but when she approached to help with the workload he issued another warning, "seriously! If they see you in here you'll get in trouble, if they catch me I'll just say I noticed a spillage, now go!" To Tre's relief, Caprice was far from stubborn and so she left him with a hug tighter than usual. Satisfaction proved to be a force in itself, because it seemed to accelerate the process of cleaning up. The colloidal supersilver was the last vial he put away and it was because it occupied its own pallet, as well as its own shelf. On his way to storing it, Tre observed the peculiar liquid for some time. Once again he thought it strange how it stuck to the walls of the vial despite having the appearance and consistency of a liquid. It had an ephermal transparency about it; it was clear, but the space behind it was not visible, instead fractions of the entire room were. It was quite unlike anything he had seen within his days and though it was strange, stranger still was that no one had yet come to lock the meeting room. It must have been his lucky day. When Tre slid the container into the last empty slot in the fridge and began to close the door, he noticed that the single vial was now empty. A flux of panic immediately came; he erratically retraced his steps and looked for spillage in the fridge, however, the vial was intact and could not be opened by traditional means.

"This can't be happening?" In disbelief, Tre put a hand to his forehead, but what he saw next made this same disbelief inflate more than he ever thought possible. His concept of realism was shrinking right in front of him. The colloidal supersilver he had just seen in the vial moments ago was now on his fingers and worse yet; it was somehow sinking underneath his nails, beyond the surface of the skin. With a greying, quavering hand before his face, his question of how quickly became how long until. Warmth was quickly draining from his extremities and his migraine returned with a vengeance; a head splitting pain and a splitting scream from its other occupier. With a slam of the sample fridge, Tre dashed from the meeting room as fast as he could. His screams for help were lost in his own throat; the cold seemed to evaporate them altogether. His progress to the entrance of the university became increasingly hard to navigate as the moderate lights of the hallway intensified like supernovas in the ceiling. Every staircase was a step closer to the unknown; every hallway seemed to slow the passage of time and for every door he passed, entered more fear. Blinded, freezing and choking, Tre tumbled into the nearby toilets on his current floor. The culmination of his ailment was equal to battling physical birefringence.

"CAPRICE! CAPRICE!" Tre wheezed twice. Not one reply could be heard. With all of his might, he grabbed the nearby sink and pulled himself up. Between all the painful flares of light in his sight, he could see a horrified, blue skinned reflection of himself staring back at him in the mirror. Just as he had a glimpse through the lens of the surreal, the glaring white light swarmed his sight over just as it appeared.

CHAPTER 6

<u>The Belly Carnival</u>

Edith Hill's counselling room was found in the skies of Signot's Hive Borough, but the prized views were far from the only eye catching aspect of the room. Her office had the right amount of sun rearing through the okna starkmark roof. The sky pod shared the beams generously throughout the space, highlighting its other features. The walls were covered in an overtone of sesame, perfect for one to embark on a session of mental sessility. The bel air lethaire sofa gave the room a dainty flair, additionally, its competitive price was to ensure comfort was all but accommodated for those who visited. The lengthy, shaggy benuta rug could have been sheared from the chest of a yeti, yet its downy touch could not be denied. On each of the three reclining chairs were cushions with dodecahedral patterns that were soothing to the eyes, but widening for the mind. Stacks of therapeutic and positive psychology books lined the shelves and the owner was even able to capture the elements of the planet in detailed and highly sophisticated, artistic renderings of, earth land, volcanoes and natural disasters, which were framed around the four walls. Even deep in the metropolis, Edith Hill found a way to incorporate nature. She had impressive origami animal sculptures hanging from the ceiling; a garden with ardency toward all that ~~was~~ is natural. With all the personality her counselling room had to offer, Edith Hill seemed to tuck hers behind her professional mien with little effort. That was one feature Professor Hill and Tre shared; they were not easily ready to discuss matters concerning themselves. Conversely, if Edith Hill was considered a closed book, then Tre was perhaps one with pages scorched to the point of illegibility.

"How do you feel today, Tre?" Edith Hill started. She was dressed in a white shirt and a long cotton dress, sat upright in a single reclining chair with paper and pens at hand yet again, as if it were an extension of her person. On the other side of the room, Tre was laid across the bel air sofa and despite its comfort; the teenager was in an uneasy position.

"I feel aight," Tre said, while looking at the frame of an erupting volcano.

"Try to close your eyes during these sessions, Tre. The room can be distracting sometimes." she encouraged him kindly. Tre obliged, however as he closed his coned eyes all he could think of was how 'sometimes' was quite an understatement. Upon all of his monthly visits since his release from Juvenile Detention, the growing collection of origami decorations had never failed to pull his interest.

"How have things been this past month?" she asked. Tre could not help but let his eyes flicker to the frame of large waves on the left side of the room. It was funny how the power of his own irresolution could multiply one question into a million more.

"I'm not quite sure. Different." Tre closed his own eyes again, trying to visualise his own thoughts.

"Hmm, elaborate?" The professional in Edith was bound.

"Life is usually straightforward. I've only considered there to be one road for me, live and then die. Recently my eyes have been opened. There are so many roads. So many that I am not sure which one to walk, let alone where it leads. It's pretty overwhelming actually."

"I see." Her comment was accompanied by a familiar jotting sound. "You are saying that you see more possibility in life than you saw before, do you consider this a good thing or a bad thing?"

"I'm not sure yet."

"Why would you not consider more possibility a good thing?" Edith Hill seemed to be asking the question for herself as her pen was positioned crosswise on her notepad.

"Because there is the possibility that something bad could happen." Tre's pessimism featured in yet another session and so Edith had no choice but to note it.

"Would you say you have had a revelation of some sort recently?"

"Yeah I would." Tre remained plane, but his coned eyes levelled on the professor.

"I'm not depressed again by the way, I promise you that."

"How did you—" Edith curved her notepad further toward herself; the latest words on the paper were 'There is a chance the patient is experiencing depression again, may have to increase number of consultations per month.'

"How are things between Caprice and yourself?" Edith chose to dismiss Tre's deduction as a hunch of intuition.

"Are you asking me as my counsellor or as her mother?" He pushed himself upward until he could seat himself on his elbows.

"Both."

"We are good, as always. She's just stressed with her work. She'll get through it though, she always does."

"Keep her safe, Tre. I know you two don't tell me about everything that is going on over at your university, and I expect that. But I trust you more than anything. Since you have lived with us, and though you may disagree, I can tell that the terrible things that have happened to you, have shaped you for the better. It's matured you. Caprice doesn't always know what is best for her, so I couldn't have anyone better to protect her. I know you are more than capable of taking care of yourself. You've made it this far and now you are an intelligent, handsome young man with a lot to offer the world. I know she means a lot to you. Just remember to do the right thing." It was a rare moment for their counselling sessions to have, but Edith Hill put down the professional barrier. A compliment was like a cold touch to Tre, it did not happen often but it reminded him that he was alive, that he was not an empty shell, that other people saw something warm inside him.

"Uh." Tre did not know which part of her words to reply to first, but Edith Hill coughed twice to signal that the session was to resume.

"How have you been handling your disorder? Have you been maintaining control over your actions and ignoring intrusive thoughts?"

"I have not heard the voice in two weeks." Tre was as surprised to speak these words as Professor Hill was to hear them. Since the colloidal supersilver incident, he had been his own man. Even in the absence of his xanax use, the voice was no longer in his head. He was now lonely in every sense of the word.

"Incredible. Have you changed anything in your diet, any drug usage?" He had never seen Edith look so pleased, nor had he seen her shocked by anything in their past meetings. She was always usually in a seat of expectancy, but now she was at the edge of her seat.

"Nothing."

"Well this is incredible, but let us not get ahead of ourselves," Professor Hill started and she seemed to be lowering her own expectations more than anything. "Your separate identity has its own thoughts and life, so it is possible that it is dormant or trying to deceive you in order to undo all of the work we have done."

"Thank you, Edith, for being there for me when no one else was. You gave me another chance." Even these words fell short of the gratitude he truly felt for the woman who could be described as nothing less than his guardian angel. Edith Hill returned his words with the smile that reminded him so much of the girl he cared so much for.

"You deserve everything, Tre. I hope you figure out which road is the right one for you."

"Everyone this is Quiqhin, Quiqhin this is Caprice, Left and Lancis." Tre, Left, Caprice and her boyfriend Lancis Green were gathered outside the entrance of the Belly Carnival. Tre thought he would never be in this position for two reasons. Firstly, due to his apprehension of crowds; he pledged many years ago that he would never attend the popular carnival. The second reason was that he never thought he would merge his only two social groups; his roommates and his science group. If it were not for Damia Ascot's insistence, it would never have happened. Her logic was that an event outside of the lecture halls would bring their research group closer, but the irony lay in the fact that his didactic peer failed to turn up herself. For this reason, Tre was left by himself to play the host to Left and Quiqhin, who were hardly his favourite people. Inversely, he would pick to have their company over the trodden task of a third wheel for Caprice and Lancis, every time.

"Hey Quiqhin, so lovely to meet you," Caprice said. Tre could always count on Caprice to smooth over his rough duties.

"What's good, soldier?" Lancis said shortly. Tre expected nothing less than neutrality from a polarising figure like Lancis Green.

"Always nice to have someone else in the crew. Though Tre has never mentioned you." Left plunged an eager hand forward and Tre plunged a metaphorical palm to his face.

"Ice-Tre here has never mentioned any of you either, he doesn't talk much." Quiqhin matched Left's handshake with a nod.

"Let's go in guys... look they are getting along," Caprice whispered to Tre, while leading the group's progress inside the mouth-like opening.

"Glad someone is at least. Damia was supposed to be here too. The girl you saw me speaking to on the day we did your project," Tre clarified when she pulled a face of confusion when he named his missing peer.

"Oh yeah, I remember. By the way, I never asked, did you get in trouble at the end of our little photography session or nah?" Caprice looked up at her best friend only to see an inscrutable expression on his face.

"Just a bit. Everything is okay now though." The tightening of skin over his cheekbones spelt something else completely. The group of teenagers were caught in the thick of the crowd as they reached the narrow of the mouth. The entrance was literally designed in the image of a mouth; it had pointed foam to resemble fangs and a mossy velvet carpet for a tongue. As they approached the mouth, their surroundings became incalculably dark for most, but for Tre it appeared in the same way as say, a poorly lit room. For this very reason, all of the subsequent jump scares that followed made Tre seem like an unimpressed, frequent visitor. He could see the bafflement in the method actors, wearing luminous costumes as he watched them crawl from hidden doors inside the mouth. He also noticed they had some type of night vision goggles to see inside the dark.

"OH MY GOD!" came the infrequent screams of Caprice, alongside the feeling of her small hands grabbing a handful of his trench coat. By the time they made it to the belly of the beast, so to speak, the sight of what awaited them made Tre's stomach turn. The turbulent, twisting tracks of the rollercoasters were impossible to miss, but what was easier to miss was the wailing, dragon-like coaster bursting in and out of sight at such speeds that he had to take time to consider if he was wanted to proceed. The loudest noise in the whole carnival park was the screams from the occupants of the Tower Drop, when they were sent into a brief, one hundred foot free fall. He by no means had an irrational fear of heights but similarly, he did not think it irrational to not want to be thrown from them. As the cart of falling teenagers shuddered into gradual descent, Tre shuddered in apprehension.

"I can't wait to get on that thing," Left said in awe.

"Maybe we should give the risky activities a rest for now. My heart still has not recovered from the jump scares," Caprice said. Her wonky spectacles were a testament to this.

"Why don't we do one activity everyone wants to do?" Tre suggested, leaning a single finger on the upturned side of Caprice's glasses.

"I think everyone should go and the do the events they want, cos I gotta go in a couple of hours," Quiqhin explained in his usual pressed way. Damia was due to be disappointed but for an individual who was wary to let expectations take flight at all, Tre foresaw this.

"That's cool bruh, but the larger our group the quicker we'll get through queues," Lancis added.

"True," agreed Left. Quiqhin made one painful look toward his expensive looking timepiece before conceding to the majority vote.

The Belly Carnival contained farcical but enjoyable events. It had the regular arsenal of mini games such as: hook a duck, table puck, the laughable (but arguably regretful) foam wrestling and test your strength. But more impressive than the spread of ambitious rides, or depth of festive activities, was the light displays of the carnival itself. The electronic lights that lined the carnival stands and headers were mesmerising. They danced different patterns with such precision that even the wiresmith themself could admire it. Against his wishes and against his better judgement, Tre faced all of the carnival's trials and lived to tell the story. As they approached their last event, (the tame Ferris wheel that Caprice claimed they absolutely must try), he reckoned that height was at the discretion of one's perception. In other words, he had seen his vertigo to its last days and his life was growing stranger with every passing one. Before boarding the Ferris wheel, they were prompted to put their cell phones in collection boxes before entering the section. Tre noticed Left trap his phone between the large waist of his pants.

"Looks like me and you are up." Left pointed out Caprice and Lancis holding hands two places in front of them. Tre would have had to hold his jealousy behind the surface on any other occasion had he not heard Quiqhin flirting with a girl directly ahead. His exaggerated British accent and pseudo-Casanova approach could have made for its very own show. Eventually Left and Tre were directed onto the seats lowest and only when he was locked in with nowhere else to go, did he realise the depth of the mire he would have to endure for the next ten minutes.

"Seeing them hold hands must have made you wheely mad." Left found himself so unbearably funny that he could not even finish his sentence with a straight face. On the contrary, Tre found him unbearable. He made a half turn away from his annoying roommate, praying that the hands of time could somehow rotate faster.

BANG! BANG!

In a sudden turn of events, everybody suspended in the air threw their necks as far forward as possible. The unmistakeable sound of gunshots could be heard below.

"There's a group of muggers holding everyone getting off the Ferris wheel hostage," Tre said this with such certainty that Left lashed out in alarm.

"How could you know that, we can't even see what's going on down there?!" Tre's roommate had a point as from the apex of the wheel; the contraption blocked the view under them.

"When we get down there just do what they say, they are tying us up," Tre instructed.

"Are you crazy, let's call the cops while we still have the chance?" Left pulled out his phone, however, Tre lowered his arm.

"If the police come they might hurt someone. I'm going to need you to trust me when I say this."

"Say what?"

"Let me handle this."

In a moment more unlikely than the Ferris wheel segment of the carnival park being closed off by thugs, Left put a blind leap of faith in his roommate and refrained from calling the authorities. Tre and Left were the last people to be taken from the wheel and bound with rope. The muggers were all wearing black masks and there were five in total. Two of the masked muggers were guarding the two entrances to the area and the remaining three were placing the hostages on their knees, in a single file. In the line were teenagers, adults and even small children.

"Now this is going to be as painless as you let it be. This is what's going to happen; if anyone shouts for help, someone is going to die. When my friends here go into your pockets and bags for your items, do not resist otherwise you are losing a limb." Each of the three muggers brandished their machete knives. After, the menacing coordinator continued,

"You speak when we ask you a question and if you talk out of turn I'm going to assume you don't need your tongue. Also try and keep the tears to a minimum, we're not here for blood, just your nice things." The leader smiled while he closed Caprice's whimpering jaw with the edge of his blade. Tre clenched his.

"If you know what is good for you then you'll get away while you can," Lancis snarled.

"One of the Bolivians send outs I'm guessing? I could kill you right now." The vocal mugger pulled out a pistol from his coat and put it to Lancis' jaw.

"You know if you kill me, it'll get a lot worse for you." Lancis smiled at the gun.

"You're right!" exclaimed the masked man, then he viciously pistol whipped the young man. The whole crowd broke into cries of panic as the Lancis' unconscious body slumped to the floor. Caprice's mouth was wide in terror, however, her eyes were wider having learnt of Lancis' drug ties.

"That doesn't mean I won't kill anybody else, boys start searching them." The gun wielding robber swept the gun across the crowd, causing everybody to thrust their head aside in fright. There was one exception and that was Tre. While everybody was deep in prayer or pure terror, his hands were one inch deep into the thick of rope. His hands were emitting a white hot glow and a few seconds later the rope was completely severed.

"Oh, this one has a lot of things." The muggers were halfway across the line and had accumulated all items of value, from designer winter jackets to cell phones, however, when they raided Quiqhin's pockets they were positively riveted.

"This is a nice watch kid." One of the robbers flaunted Quiqhin's expensive timepiece on his own wrist. "You must have bank. Whose name should I use when I go shopping with your credit card tonight?" Quiqhin held a silent frown.

"You can also lose your tongue for not speaking." The sharp edge of the knife was pointed once again. It seemed Quiqhin was about to speak, but the only thing that came the mugger's way was a hurling ball of phlegm.

"YOU'RE GOING TO DIE FOR THAT!" cried the disgusted mugger. He pulled his machete hand backward, but little did they know, Tre had already sprang into action. The fact that all three robbers were focused on Quiqhin, and with the screams from the females masking any other noise, Tre was able to approach undetected. Tre pulled the gun from the hand of the leader, before tackling the aggravated robber mid-swing. The resulting action left, Quiqhin unharmed however the machete had found a considerable way into Tre's left arm.

BANG! BANG!

Everyone, robber and hostage alike stopped to assess the situation as everything had happened so quickly. After a few moments Tre rose with the gun pointed at the frozen robbers.

"Drop your weapons or I will shoot," Tre ordered. With a clash of metal, the muggers surrendered immediately. No one could believe their eyes. Not only was the machete still in Tre's left arm, not only was his sleeve soaked in blood, but there was not an inch of fear, nor pain on his face and this perhaps put more fear in the criminal's hearts than any pistol could. The only cries of pain that could be heard was from their partner who currently had two bullets in his leg. The two muggers who were guarding the doors came running over having heard gunfire, but when they realised what happened, they also folded.

With the entrance to the Ferris wheel unguarded, the other visitors of the park discovered the rescued hostage situation and called for the help of the authorities. When the Indiana police Department arrived and put the grounded criminals into handcuffs, Tre could finally breathe easy. In truth, his breathing had become increasingly heavy from blood loss. The ordeal after the authorities had arrived was honestly more overwhelming for him. Authorities howled that he needed medical attention, the survivors thanked him endlessly and the crowds of gasping spectators pointed to his gashed arm. Not to mention, Tre knew first-hand that Caprice handled stressful situations badly.

"Tre, you need to get help now!" The whole experience left Caprice more erratic than usual.

"I'll be fine, get me Quiqhin please, just please." Tre could feel his vision narrowing, he would soon be unconscious.

"No, you won't!" There was now rainfall in the forest that was her hazel eyes.

"Just—" Tre emphasised. He tried to look as well as he could and at the same time, he was trying to kneel his head in fear of being recognised by someone in the crowd. Caprice grabbed Quiqhin from the crowd of police officers who were now contacting the ambulance. When Quiqhin approached Tre, he was wearing an expression the equivalent of 'have you lost your mind?'

"Mate, I don't know why you are calling me, you need a medic. Saving everybody is not going to save yourself!" Like every other hostage, even Quiqhin looked beside himself. His usually neat, flair of hair was now flailing in front of his face and his mouth was so thin, it was lost in his beard.

"I'm not going to die, but I can't go to a hospital. Can you help me?" Tre's body lapsed in strength for a split second and he bundled forward into Quiqhin. The British native secured Tre mid-fall however.

"I got you – I got you mate." Quiqhin hoisted his good arm over his neck. "What do you mean you can't go to a hospital?"

"I'll explain later, but right now I need to get out of here. Do you know someone who can help me?" Tre muttered over his shoulder. He could feel his eyes rolling backwards. Quiqhin wasted no more time and began pulling Tre from the crowd.

"Where are you taking him, the ambulance is coming?" a police officer cautioned when he noticed Quiqhin leading him away.

"My father is Isaac Isles. My friend is registered with our private healthcare service. I can get him to help faster," Quiqhin declared.

CHAPTER 7

The Quarters of Isles

The Isles family quarters bore great similitude to the great Estonian city halls. Every wall was a treasury, every hall, the opposite of penury and every clerestory a clear view of the family's wealth. The art hanging from the walls were one of one, the sculptures were double the price and one was free to assume the value of the other expensive looking features. There was not one component of an affluent home missing, from dressing room to kitchen, cooks and assistants were known to live and drop ship at the drop of a whistle, just to probe the ego of the so called richest man in the district. Quiqhin's father, Isaac Isles – founder of the Isle's oil industries. Living lavish was a diminishing facet in a city of such depravity, so Tre could not believe his eyes when he finally came to. He awoke at a jumpstart.

"Is it just us here?!" Tre said, and shockingly enough to Quiqhin, his first concern was not his own wellbeing. Tre's neck played an axis for his head and his sockets an axis for his eyes, as he took in the luxurious surroundings.

"Yes, like you asked," Quiqhin told him. The collar of his smart, black shirt was rough and it seemed to have been unbuttoned in incidental fashion as there were now a few missing. Tre's return to health seemed to pick holes in his understanding, so much so, that he was now pulling at his beard in confusion.

"Where are we?" Tre was a little beside himself.

"We are at my father's beach chateau,"

"Chateau? You famous or something?"

"I'm not... yet. My dad is the owner of an oil industry, big in Europe but hasn't reached here yet."

"Are you serious? Your dad owns an oil business?!"

"That is beside the point. You need to tell me exactly what is going on. You are supposed to be, you know, dying!" Quiqhin leaned over Tre's medical bed and lifted his left arm. A tight bandage had been squeezed over the place where his wound should be. "At the carnival you were going to die from blood loss. I mean, you passed out and everything. When I got you here, the wound was... closing up. How is that possible?" As Tre opened his mouth, he found that the obscurity of his answer was due to be much greater than his propensity to explain, and this was because he, himself, was in the nascence of this new chapter.

"You wouldn't believe me if I told you."

"Well you have no choice now. You agreed to tell me everything if I brought you to safety. You didn't even take Caprice's help." Quick folded his hairy forearms into one another.

"Is she okay?! Her, Left–"

"Yeah everyone was fine. That Lancis guy got taken to the hospital too. Now cough up." Quick pinned every potential topic of procrastination and Tre blew an anxious breath upward. Despite an establishment of such wealth, Quiqhin's reaction was sure to be priceless.

"Do not, and I mean do not tell anybody about this. Especially Professor Jinx. Got it?" Tre's stern expression creaked into something close to seriousness, Quick, however, was well on board.

"Yeah man, what's going on?!"

"It happened the day of our research proposal meeting. After you left early, Professor Jinx and Damia followed."

"Who's Damia?" Quick interrupted.

"Are you serious – our damn research partner!"

"Oh, the chick with the weird line of birth marks?"

"Do you live in a bubble, man?" Following his question, Tre looked around at the lavish setting he was currently in. Clearly Quiqhin did.

"I know a lot of females; I get names confused. Anyways, continue your story." Tre did not let himself fall into the figurative pitfall trap that was fantasising about Quick's female affairs, instead, he ploughed on.

"Right, I was the last to leave, but before I left, I bumped into Caprice..." Tre paused in order to choose on which note to reveal the extraordinary events that followed, however, Quick exhibited more symptoms of a bad listener.

"So, you took her into the room right?" An audacious smirk began to travel across the line of his mouth.

"Yeah but—"

"I misjudged you." Quick sent a laddish nod his way.

"Are you going to keep talking? How do you even get to know girls if you talk so damn much?" Tre said, putting a finger to the top of his nose, where he felt a frown begin to sink.

"Who said I get to know them?" Quick quipped, however, he let silence follow when Tre gave him a strong look.

"She wanted something to shoot for her photography project and I thought it would be a good idea to use the class samples. I went into the sample fridge, let her take pictures of all of the chemicals. At this point the room keepers were coming so I told her to leave while I cleaned up. I put all of them back and I'm not sure exactly how it happened but the colloidal supersilver escaped its case and came into contact with me. It was like I was absorbing it. I ran for help as fast as I could but I couldn't breathe. The coldest feeling I have ever felt began to creep over my body and I passed out. My face was blue, blue from silver poisoning. The next day I remember waking up in my flat. I thought it was just a weird dream until these weird things started happening." Tre recalled the murky and confusing original story with every detail he could summon and thankfully he was not met with ridicule or over-concern, but with pure fascination. Quiqhin was leant, had full eye contact and widened eyes, so it was safe to say Tre had his undivided attention.

"Weird things like what?" Quick peered at him with a curious angle on his face. Without a word, Tre Moon's entire body fluttered out of sight for nano-second increments, giving the impression that he was being rapidly pulled out of their dimension. Quick toppled backwards in alarm.

"What the f*%$!"

Tre ceased the fragmented effect when his point was proven. Though his body looked to be rapidly disappearing from sight, it was unaffected.

"How did you do that?" Quiqhin's cool, confidence seemed to have gone missing also.

"Also, the ropes that the muggers held us with. I was able to burn through them with my hands. That's how I was able to break free". Tre displayed his palms to Quick, afterward they began to glow white with heat. As Tre negated the heat coming from his hands, both teenagers watched before their very eyes as the scalds and burns that the heat caused began to instantly reform into healthy, unsinged skin. Quiqhin could not get a handle on what he had seen; it was as if the hands of time wound backwards, as if the implications of physical laws were inactive. Before Quiqhin could cook up any further quotes, a light began beaming from his chest pocket. When he took his phone out and looked at the screen, an eyebrow perked upward. He then showed Tre; the screen read 'Incoming video call from Girl with the weird birth marks'.

"Yo, you actually saved her as that?"

"Let me tell her to call back—"

"No, answer! She might be able to help." Tre sat up some more.

"Are you sure you want her to know about this man?"

"Yes." Tre confirmed. He could think of no better person to keep in his circle of confidentiality. She was already keeping one secret for him and from the science meetings she had shown that she was as knowledgeable as they came. Quick slid across the screen and a live video feed began. The screen was not the largest, but the boys could make out that she was in a moving crowd, with multiple people holding indiscernible signs and banners.

"Oh my gosh, is that Tre? Where are you guys, it looks like you're in a palace." Damia was having trouble looking into her own screen and even though this was the case, her comparison was not far off.

"Yeah he's alright though, maybe more than alright." Quick held out the phone with an outstretched arm, to give Damia the best view of the both of them.

"I heard about what happened at the carnival, I had to check if you were okay? I'm so glad nothing serious happened." Unlike their side of the feed, hers was jolting all over the place due to the constant movement around her.

"Dian-Damia, listen." Quick's near mistake of her name gave Tre little hope that they could one day be a thorough team. "Tre had an incident that involved the colloidal supersilver and now he's got – *abilities.*" Quick finished at a hush.

"Insecurities?" Damia misheard over the rising chants of 'Free Heavens Conquest!' from her side.

"No not insecurities – Abili –" Halfway during Quick's impatient recital Tre snatched the phone from his hand.

"Damia, I've come into contact with Professor Jinx's sample of colloidal supersilver and I am experiencing some strange after effects."

"What kind of side effects?" To answer this latest question, Tre pulled the bandage from his arm and localised the camera, so the wound was now the centre of the video.

"Several hours ago I had a machete halfway in my arm."

"It still looks pretty bad though, you should get it see—" Damia's words seemed to seep away as before her very eyes, she saw the ends of Tre's umber skin began to pinch together from within the opening of the wound. It was as if an invincible sewing needle was at work.

"'Tre..."

"What do you think?" Tre returned the camera to its original position and she could now see a hopeful face.

"I've never seen anything like that in my life. Your body is healing... the Professor said it was being used for medical purposes, but this is incredible." The crowd were now moving around a stunned Damia because she had stopped in place.

"What else are you experiencing?"

"He can control heat or something."

"I can see around corners," Tre added.

"Flaming balls!" Damia cursed. "We need to get you help, there might be health risks."

"No!" Tre jumped in, "Listen I didn't ask for any of this to happen, but whatever comes with it I am going to deal with. I haven't even told Cap yet. I appreciate all of your help, but this doesn't change anything for me."

"How could you say that?" Damia asked.

"This is a fearless man. He took down a group of armed criminals today, by himself." In the background of the video feed, Quiqhin could be seen helping himself to a glass of scotch whiskey from one of the cabinets. Uncovering Tre's mind bending symptoms was more hard hitting than any alcohol he could find.

"Are you sure you should be drinking that?" Damia said.

"In England the age limit is eighteen." Quick responded, putting no halt in his actions.

"You are not even eighteen yet!"

"Two months won't kill anybody." Two seconds later, the drink was down his throat. Damia sighed and turned her attention back to the anomaly at hand. She brushed under her chin in thought, before her next outrageous statement came.

"You'll need to wear a sling from now on."

"What?" Tre replied at once. Quiqhin pulled a face of surprise.

"You just had a machete in your arm a few hours ago. If people see you walking around fine, they'll know something is up. You do want to keep this between us right?" Damia explained. Quick dashed into the room by the side and remerged with thick bandage and a cotton sheet. He covered Tre's faux bad arm with it and fitted the sling around his neck to complete the façade.

"Perfect. You'll have to keep it on, at least until we figure out what's going on with you."

"Looks well nippy," Quick noted. Tre had no idea what the British colloquialism meant but the amusement on Quiqhin's face was sufficient enough of an indicator.

"I can already tell this is going to get uncomfortable. What is happening over there?" Tre diverted the conversation.

"There is a twenty-four hour protest going on, for the appeal against Sargent Boston's militarisation movement." She swept her sentence quickly aside to reassume her former stance however, "As soon as I can, I am going to come to Signot. I'm sorry I missed the event tonight, if this chaos was not happening here I would have come. But Tre, we need to figure out what is going on with you. You might not care what happens to yourself, but we do." Tre could not help the warm feeling that washed over him. He could see no lie, from the line of beauty marks from Damia's neck, to her eye. Then the hand of Quiqhin Isles found its way to his shoulder.

"Thank you for saving everyone's life, back there, mate. You're braver than you are crazy," Quick said. Just as those words left his mouth, the sound of a metallic swoop roared from the phone. Damia was amongst the hundreds of heads now faced upward in awe. The camera then dropped, showing a view of above. Damia seemed to have forgotten to disengage the live feed. Though the boys in Signot could not see what the Heavens Conquest protesters were looking at, the enigma building whispers gave them some clue. Afterward, a sonically altered voice could be heard. The very voltaic nature of this voice sent hallows to the very marrow, but the message it had told Tre two things. It stood for peace but expected cooperation in return.

"Citizens of Heavens Conquest: we are not losing the city and all that you stand for, we represent something much bigger. Sergeant Boston and his regime may be growing, but for them to complete this move they will need my consent... I do not give my consent. I am the watcher of the people. Everyone needs to go home right now because no more innocent people will be put in harm's way. Tonight, I will confront the army personally and request that this whole process be dropped. If they don't, then they are in for a long night. I never opened my arms to oppressors and that does not change today. For Heavens Conquest!" This declaration sent a surge of cheers all across the city streets and the haunting chant of 'N.O.M.A.!' soon formed from the applause. From all of the rough movement the feed was capturing, the camera would occasionally jog in different directions. In two precious seconds, Tre glimpsed the fable. A crimson angel pressed into the sky like an idol; against the sable night, he hovered like a totem of hope. The prayers from Heaven's Conquest would be answered from above.

CHAPTER 8

Emily Di Pinto

Coming to terms with the reality that he had power beyond that of a normal human being was nothing short of life changing, however, having the support of others made the surreal surreption that much more bearable. Over the next month, the research group consisting of Tre Moon, Quiqhin Isles and Damia Ascot began spending more time together. Half the reason was the looming expectation of progress their research project brought; the other half was the urge to uncover the mystery of Tre's condition. That very urge served to bring them together, again and again, beyond their standard obligations and under the unlikeliest of circumstances. Where Tre had no visitors prior, Damia and Quick would now frequent his apartment. Internet cafes, university libraries and any other student inhabitable space were other spots they made commonplace. The trio became so familiar in fact, that at suggestion one day, they began calling themselves 'AIM'; an anagram for their collective last names. After the inception of the group title, Quick, ironically, was first to give reminders that the group name was, by no means, in order of importance. The Quarters of Isles naturally became the base for their most pressing meetings, especially ones regarding Tre's powers. It boasted privacy, space, resources and most importantly, room service. It took less than three meetings for the combined scientific minds to culminate scientific and medical apparatus in the room that would be known as AIM's home of operations. As Tre's contact hours with AIM's members increased, so did his touch on who they were as people. Quiqhin Isles did indeed live up to his nickname. He was a brash individual, but Tre learnt that he was also the first to contribute ideas and pick up the team's morale when it dropped. His first aid training had been useful to treat his injuries at the carnival incident and his speciality in biological engineering proved helpful only to further their research project. But for the cause of helping them understand Tre's powers, Quick would be the first to admit he had reached an anomaly. Not that it stopped his endless suggestions, of which 'fire powers' was the least wild. Both Quiqhin and Tre learnt the hard way that Damia's easy going guise was one misspoken opinion away from peeling away in hot appeal. Damia Ascot was like an onion, seeded in the rare grounds of parti pris; therefore, she gave a palaver of reasons for her grounds of belief. If you peeled one layer she was a political activist, if you peeled another layer she was an avid environmentalist, if you peeled another she was a speculative futurist and with another, an untiring supporter of vigilantism. It was tiring just to think of how she juggled all her interests with her physics major, but her knowledge in that exact major had been their only breakthrough toward learning of Tre's bizarre abilities. When they ran base tests and recorded Tre while performing his powers, it was through her expansive knowledge in her discipline that they gathered several ground breaking facts of what exactly was happening. She figured out that his optical gifts were not limited to physics bending sight. A series of eye tests revealed that he had magnified sight (allowing him to see and focus on distances past normal human capability), retroflective sight (allowing him to see at low light levels, where one would normally not be able to) as well as concave sight (which had no beneficial effects and only left him with a painful glare for a few minutes.) Her information did not line up with the heat energy he could summon to his hands or his ability to stutter out of sight, so past his optical gifts, the AIM team were positively stumped. It was Damia's scientific hunch that some data showing energy being manipulated around Tre's body was the answer to all their questions.

It was a mid-February afternoon and Tre Moon's love for scientific collectors' items brought him to his local miscellaneous shop. It was largely shabby and rundown, but it procured new merchandise at such a fast rate, that one could find the item of their dreams if they came at the right time. Tre did not have a particular item in mind when he went through the stained, glass doors. What he was truly trying to buy, was some alone time. Amidst his constant preoccupation with AIM's dual investigation, he had not found a single moment to himself. On another note, it felt somewhat refreshing to spend time alone instead of spending to impress someone else. Tre ventured the various aisles like he usually did, only to notice that the store was looking particularly bare bones on this day. Usually, hordes of items would clump the shelves, but they were so empty he could see the greasy surfaces that held them. Moreover, he noticed a particularly rugged stall that looked like it had been destroyed and reassembled along with merchandise so chipped and dented, it was arguably more useless than his perfectly healed arm being hoisted in a sling.

"Looking for anything special?" called a voice from the front of the store. Tre assumed the owner was in the back as the counter was empty when he entered, however the light voice did not belong to a man.

"Nah, just looking." Tre poked his head out to see who the voice had come from. Even as his convex vision dipped to the left and right of the corner, he could not find anyone. He returned to his shopping. In his free hand he held out the baseball bat of Signot's resident baseball team (The Signot Silvers), it was splintered in the middle. At the moment when he held the thought of how exactly the owner expected to sell an essentially useless item, a female emerged from the near end of his aisle. If Tre did not drop his jaw, he would have dropped the item he was holding. The girl's skin was coloured peach but sun kissed like the coastal beach. Her Latin-American features could not be missed and her individuality could be defined as a conglomerate of amulets. Her face was square; her jaw bones were cut like glass, giving her jawline the perfection of a polygon. Along her cheeks she had many deep pores that were perhaps born from a past war with acne; however, they were bilaterally columned with such accuracy that they actually added personality to her canvas. Her hair was golden brown and was locked into a single plait, but this did not stop her cute baby hairs from breaking free. Lastly, her eyes were deep set and her pupils were flushed with the unnatural colour of coral pink. Thanks to Caprice, Tre was no stranger to the extensive measures of female cosmetics; nonetheless he found it a strange colour choice for contact lenses. Tre assumed his six foot frame and he had about four inches on her, still there was not an inch of fear when she spoke her next words.

"I hope you're going to be paying for that today." She was eyeing the baseball bat with her coral stare.

"I would not bet on anyone buying this to be honest." Tre dangled the splintering half of the bat from his large hand.

"You're right. Definitely not you, with that arm." The girl then began chuckling to herself as she stepped toward the direction of the counter.

"Er, are you running the shop?" Tre was still somewhat at loss.

"Someone has got to run it."

"When did the old dude leave?"

"He left about two weeks ago. Are you from Signot?" The girl made a suspicious half turn.

"Hell yeah, I live just down the road. I just haven't been here recently."

"I see."

"What I'm wondering, is if you know why store owners change so much?" he asked. The girl pranced slowly to the desk as she spoke.

"Why? I mean sure, it's not the biggest shop and it's in a patchy part of the borough. But it also helps out a lot of people." As she finished her sentence, she lifted herself to a seat on the raised counter. Her voice had a grapey tune to it, which added to her innocent air. Unfortunately, in Signot, innocence went hand in hand with ignorance and to walk in ignorance was the first step toward being a victim of a crime.

"Yeah it helps out the good folk." Tre joined her near the counter before he continued, "Listen I'm just going to give you a heads up. Miscellaneous stores are often targeted by criminal's cos they see it as a quick way to make a buck. So, watch out and call the cops if you get the chance." "*Not that they will even come on time.*" Tre thought aloud.

"Oh, criminals. I've had a few already," she said with cheer. The tone of the girl's voice and her words did not connect whatsoever.

"Really?"

"Yeah, as you can probably tell they kinda trashed that stall over there but they didn't leave with anything."

"You called the cops on them before they could steal?" Tre guessed.

"Didn't have to. Must be something about this face that made them change their mind." Her coral eyes made their way upwards in positive wonderment. Tre's jaw was still agape, but it was purely because he had never met someone like her in his life. Even though she had been faced with the toils of the inner city reality, she managed to wipe away all of the pessimism with one humorous remark. With so many reasons to be in fear, she found just as many to be at peace. Who was this girl?

"Who are you?" Tre could not help himself asking.

"My name's Emily, Di Pinto. You?"

"Tre Moon."

"How old are you, Tre Moon?"

"Seventeen why?"

"You're young but your expression is hard like you're ancient." She chuckled again.

"I find there's not much to smile about," he murmured.

"I bet you don't come out to the coast much?"

"You live in the Hetashi district?" Tre propped himself beside her on the counter. Emily pulled up her roll neck jumper a little.

"Yeah, pretty much. It's somewhere everyone should go. We get a lot of sun, a lot of tourists too. It can be pretty windy at this time of year but I think it makes the waves in the water even prettier. Just as pretty as the ones in your hair." Emily observed with a smile that made her jawline even more profound.

"Have you lived in Signot all your life?"

"Yup, all 3007 years." Her words were bizarre enough to make Tre frown uncomfortably. He expected her to declare a joke or at least give her true age but she held her smile, which only added to her offbeat ambience. Tre looked at the shoddy interior of the store then back at the glowing owner.

"What?"

"It's good to see someone smiling in the city for a change," Tre said earnestly. Emily took some time before she replied; when she did she spoke upwards again.

"I used to be conflicted. I think when there is a part of you that you are hiding, that you are denying, then you cannot truly be happy. To be yourself is happiness. I mean I haven't got much going for me and this job will just about keep me afloat, but

I'm okay with that. I think it's nice to be free of responsibility. Just being here, in this miscellaneous shop and meeting people like you, means a lot to me."

"Did you drop out of school or something?" Tre asked. Emily chuckled.

"Oh, there's nothing the education system can teach someone like me. There are other people who could make better use of it."

"Hm." Tre hummed. There was nothing exactly breath-taking about Emily Di Pinto's aspirations, however her contentment with life was a breath of fresh air. She seemed to be happy just, existing. She had the innocent temperament of a creature of the wild, and her whole attitude made Tre consider that perhaps simplicity was truly a descendant of divinity. Something he could never achieve. A turbulent and blood stained past, a now passive psychological disorder and the recent complication of superhuman abilities assured that Tre's life would be the furthest thing from it. Emily noticed his mood darkening and so caught the shadow before it could fully form.

"I think there's another side to you, Tre."

"What makes you think that?" He panicked slightly. The image of his burning house flashed in his mind.

"Well I know actually."

"Yeah?" Tre put his hands atop his knees in order to stop them from revealing his nerves.

"There's a saying my family have. 'No one is truly evil or good because they came from love to get there'."

"You are something else," Tre said with relief.

"Meaning?"

"It's a saying and it means you're a cool person. Very chill. Do you smoke or something?" Tre put out light heartedly. Emily found Tre's comment so hilarious that she could not prevent herself from howling in laughter. As she doubled over, her roll neck pulled backward some and he could see flesh like scars on the left side of her neck.

"Delightful you are just!" she proclaimed loudly, "there is nothing on this land strong enough for me." She adjusted her roll neck upward once more.

"I'll take that as a yes. Anyway, I got to go; my friend is probably waiting for me, so she can start dinner." Tre motioned to leave but he found himself caught mid-stride.

"Having second thoughts about the bat?" Emily jested. Tre weighed how his next sentence could be misconstrued, but he boldly spoke them anyway.

"Take my number. I live down the road, if any more criminals come, just call me."

"Oh." Emily placed a sleeve to her face.

"Wait, this is – I'm not hitting on you. I'm serious, if there's any trouble, call me. I can help."

"I'm flattered but you are a bit on the young side." Tre could now hear girlish fritters from behind the sleeve.

"No for real," he maintained with his usual hardness. Guilt kept him from succumbing to the embarrassment of the misinterpreted rejection. If he found out Emily had been hurt, it would be another casualty he felt he was responsible for. Especially since he now had the means to prevent it. Emily caught on to the fact that his figure had now broadened. She pulled a scrap of paper from the receipt machine and passed it to him along with a ballpoint pen.

"How sweet. If it helps you sleep at night, I'll take it."

"I wrote my address too. If anything whatsoever happens, call me and I'll come as soon as I can." He passed her the note of his details before becoming caught by a gust of urgency.

"Maybe you should let your arm heal before you start thinking about saving anybody."

"Just call me if there's trouble, okay?" At that, Tre dashed down the road in hopes of making his dinner arrangement with Caprice. Alone now, Emily Di Pinto looked over the note he had left her.

"Tre Moon," she recited to herself.

Tre ducked under the doorway into his student apartment and briskly shut the door behind him. The afternoon was settling into night and the winter winds did not let up. As the velvet of evening blended into the sky, Tre could not help but hope that Emily Di Pinto was shutting shop soon.

"Yo, Cap!" Tre removed his trench coat and hung it on the clothes rack at the entrance.

"I'm in the kitchen," a low voice called back. Their apartment plan was so tight that it took Tre only five strides to reach the kitchen.

"Is Damia and Quick here?" Tre asked.

"Nhnn," came Caprices' coy reply. She was over the kitchen counter rubbing seasoning into what was going to become her signature fried chicken. The sleeves of her grey knitted jumper were rolled beyond her elbows; however, this was not the only tight aspect of her. She was taking the process of seasoning rather laboriously and her brown and alabaster curls were covering the majority of her face. If this was the latest hairstyle trend, then Tre would be naming this one the 'frowsy palm tree.'

"Good thing you got started with the food, I'm sorry I was late. I know how you get when you're hungry." He took a seat on the single chair by the door. Opposite him was the small fridge Caprice and himself had brought when they first moved in. He chose to look over the lecture timetables and the profanities Left had written in colourful fridge letters as he waited for Caprice's oddly, delayed reply.

"It's cool," were the only words she managed to find.

"Are you okay?" Tre's relaxed posture faltered in place of a concerned one.

"I'm good, sit down. Dinner will be ready soon," she said sheepishly. With his convex vision, Tre could see her mowing the chicken between her fingers with such pressure, that blood was seeping from it. His convex sight was able to curve under her frowsy hair mask also, but all it revealed was her staring into the seasoning dish, blankly.

"Uh Cap, I think you forgot to wash the chicken... are you sure you're okay?" Tre rose and took the dish from her hands and still after, they did not move. Emotions had her stuck between the motions.

"Cap!?" With his free hand, Tre wiped her hair to the side and the blank feeling that was failure, froze him in place also. The area of Caprices' left eye was bruised and her eyelid had swollen so much that you could only see one of her hazel globes.

"No-no-no." The guilt that he had felt years ago when he realised he was holding the lighter that set alight his home, remerged. A guilt so heavy that it made whimpers from his strong voice. Tears began to stream from Caprice's open eye; it made her scared to see her best friend in such a state. They shared a few moments where his nose touched her nose, his hand held her face and her hands held his forearm; it was their pillar of healing. Finally, Tre spoke.

"Who did this to you?" Tre mouthed, the pain in his heart was too much for him to carry his voice. This question was met with a hesitant look to the floor.

"Tell me who did this!" Tre blasted with such suddenness that Caprice broke into instant cooperation.

"Lancis. It was Lancis." After her confession, she wilted to the floor in a defeated sob. Tre was overcome by the same flames that took his family away from him. Her words made him lose his mind for a second, but a second was all it took for him to slip and give control to the other identity.

"Tre, where are you going?" Caprice wailed after him.

"*For a walk,*" replied an eerie voice that was not of his own.

CHAPTER 9

<u>Traphouse Circuit 1-9</u>

<u>**Camera 1 – (Traphouse entrance) 21:46pm**</u>

"Yo, what time is it?"

"Nowhere near the end of our shift, I'll tell you that much."

"That's not what I f*%#ing asked man. Anyway, I'm finishing up early today, I clock in at the nightclub by the beach soon."

"So, another bodyguard is taking the night shift?"

"Yeah."

"How comes Lancis asked you to bouncer at the club and not me?"

"Two reasons probably."

"Go on, smart ass."

"Firstly, cos nobody in this place pays to get in when I'm guarding the door."

"I'd do the same sh*t man. He's the one paying my bills at the end of the day."

"And two. I call him Chef, not Lancis. It's a respect thing, homie."

"You're a damn suck up, have I ever told you that?"

"That's why you gonna be down here in this damn trap while I'll be letting in all the sexy women. Have you seen the kind of babes down at the coast?"

"I wonder how you'll feel if I told your baby momma about what you're up to tonight?"

"Tell her? I hope she's damn well there to see it herself. Ungrateful gold digger."

"Hahaha!"

KNOCK! KNOCK! KNOCK!

"Hey kiss ass, get the door."

"I am. Someone has gotta do the work here. Chef gonna dismiss yo' ass soon, mark my words."

"Yeah, in your f*#%ing dreams. I was appointed to this trap by Maximov himself."

"Really?"

"Yeah I used to bodyguard for the Bolivians main base."

"So, you've met Maximov huh? What's he like, is he as big and bad as they say he is?"

"You know what; he's actually a chill guy. But when I say do not, I mean do not, mess with his money... Who the f*%# are you—"

SMACK!

With one light swarmed punch, the bodyguard who answered the door was knocked backwards with such force, he was forced from his feet. The second guard looked back and forth, perhaps expecting some sort of monster to emerge from the doorway, but to his astonishment a hooded figure wearing a cap came instead. Both guards had a considerable amount of height on the hooded boy and were at least double his width and it was this continued underestimation that lay wake to the next lumbering attack. The second bodyguard swung at the hooded assailant with everything he had, but the boy proved too swift. A wave of light followed every movement and when he swung back, the wave of light that came with his strike, gave him strength deceiving for his size.

BRACK!

Another punch landed and yet another bodyguard was floored.

"Argh!" The first guard had found a way to his feet and had begun charging at the hooded boy. In a moment that would not have been believed possible unless a camera had caught thef footage, the boy grabbed the incoming bull by the collar and threw him over his head as if he was a rag doll. Three hundred pounds went flying into the wall behind and three second later the boy had his breath back.

Camera 2 – (Hallway 1) 22:02pm

The hooded boy proceeded from the fight scene and through a curved passage until he reached a single wooden door. He did not immediately proceed. Instead he put his hand outward and began observing the unfamiliar wavering effect emanating from his motions. It gifted him swiftness and lent him strength; the recompense, he suspected, of sacrificing his ordinary life. The boy pulled down his fleeced hoody, revealing a navy cap holding a tide of black waves. The beak cast a sinister shadow on the face below; a face intrigued by the power in the palm of his hands. The uninvited assailant did not look enraged or desperate; instead he looked calm and calculating. He pressed his ear to the door to hear what was happening in the next room. After he was content or perhaps discontent with the results, he descended to a heeled kneel. He then began muttering words to himself.

"Pay. They all have to pay. Like we did."

Camera 3 – (Pole Room) 22:07pm

The pole room was alive. Twenty-five individuals made up the frolics that consisted of flashing, kaleidoscope lighting, an exciting urban soundtrack which incited the group of enticing strippers to heighten the hormones of the male on watchers, to the point, they would change the climate. Showers upon showers of dollar bills would rain from the sky just to raise the chance of a personal lap dance. The room was full of egos and countless zeros. When the intruder finally came through the door, hardly any of the components of the room slowed. Not the music, not the money throwing, not least the sensual dances from the stars of the show. One of the occupants apprehended him however.

"Can I help you, soldier?" The Traphouse dealer approached the hooded assailant with such arrogance; one would think the piles of money on the floor somehow put a wall of safety between them.

"I'm here for Lancis Green," the hooded boy said with no fear in his voice.

"You are 'here' for him? Just who the f*%# let you in anyway? You can't just talk with him my g; there are motions you have to go through."

"Who said I was here to talk?" Silverlight eyes traced the alarm in the face of the approacher.

"Who the f*#% is this clown?" The dealer alerted the rest of the room as he backed up slowly, "why the hell is your face blue? Are you one of them crackheads—" The rest of his words were lost in the force of the assailants' knee and blisters of his broken teeth joined the hundreds of dollars on the floor.

"Yo who's this guy?"

"What the f*#%!"

"Damn!"

"Soldier, get the strap!"

SMASH!

As one of the dealers took off for the door on the left, the assailant covered twice the distance in just as much time. The end result was a body collision that immediately knocked the dealer unconscious. Everyone watched as the wave of light settled from his previous location, to his current one. Before their very eyes, they were witnessing something spooky.

"Get him!" That one order caused the ten remaining males to swarm at the hooded assailant, each to different effects. Some dealers used brute strength at the expense of being overpowered. Attacks to the assailant's blindside were punished, as he seemingly had eyes at the back of his head. Even when they had him cornered, he would stutter out of sight only to reappear behind them. The more time went, the more they realised that their attempts were futile. With a few minutes more, it was now bodies raining to the floor. By the time the barrage had finished the assailant was the only person standing; the strippers had either ran way squealing or had cowered to the floor themselves.

Camera 4 – (The Gun Room) 22:19pm

A dealer is leant against the door. He is breathing nervously with one hand to the door handle and a pump action shotgun in the other.

Camera 3 – (Pole Room) 22:20pm

Assailant begins moving north of the room toward the nearest door. Suddenly the door furthest springs open and he is caught off guard.

"Don't you move or I'll shoot your damn head off!" The dealer hiding in the gun room, begins pacing toward the assailant who was caught off guard.

"That's right don't you f'#*ing move soldier! In fact, don't even turn around. Put your damn hands up!" the dealer shouted and he gave satisfied nods as the intruder progressively did what he said.

"Who the f@#k are you?" the dealer called.

"I–" The assailant began his sentence at a half turn, but his words were excised by the roaring demands of his perpetrator.

"I SAID DON'T TURN AROUND!" A clucking sound signalled that the shotgun was loaded and ready to fire. The dazzling lights of the pole room seemed to have taken its effect on the wielder of the gun, as he was now seeing three separate figures of the hooded assailant. The camera also captured the three figures and the footage did not lie.

"What the?" The illusion took some of the intent from his grip, however, when the figures started turning around one by one, starting with the furthest right, he fired the weapon. Most of the bullets passed through the figure and found a home in the wall behind. It was a hologram. Before the dealer could initiate another pump, the middle figure gave him a taste of reality. A punishing boot to the chest that sent him flying like a Frisbee.

Camera 4 – (The Gun Room) 22:26pm

Dealer flies through door of the gun room.

Camera 5 – (The Stash Room) 22:26pm

Dealer is still airborne. Breaks through the door of stash room and crashes into the solid wall. The shotgun lands beside him. The hooded assailant follows soon after. He makes his way toward the edge of the room, making sure to step on the dealer's outstretched hand as he does so. The intruder first unseats the rug, and then pulls the trapdoor upward revealing a ditch of money. The assailant palms the money and after his hand glows white hot, the money is set alight. Before the assailant leaves he makes sure to set the rug alight as well. He closes the door and leaves the injured dealer to his fate.

Camera 4 – (The Gun Room) 22:30pm

Hooded Assailant closes what is left of the door to the stash room and leaves the injured dealer to his fate.

Camera 3 – (The Pole Room) 22:31pm

The hooded intruder re-enter's room just as one of the strippers tries to make escape with a bag of dollar bills. She looks horrified as she bumps into him.

"P-p-p-please don't kill me. Please!" The assailant gives her a reaction bluer than his complexion. He simply walks past her, over the bodies of the sprawled dealers and toward the door he originally set upon.

Camera 6 – (Hallway 2) 22:32pm

Hooded assailant enters the extended hallway.

Camera 7 – (Greenhouse) 22:32pm

Two herbal farmers are waiting at the corner, leading to the room. They both have knives in hand.

Camera 6 – (Hallway 2) 22:32pm

The intruder proceeds down the hallway and roughly two metres from the ambush he stops instinctively. The assailant projects a hologram of himself directly in front of the corner. The farmer nearest the corner lunges out into the hallway, stabbing furiously. As his knife clashes with the wall, he realises that nothing is there. The hooded assailant takes advantage of the confusion and socks the first farmer with a running right hand. The second farmer grabs the intruder from behind and pulls him into the greenhouse room.

Camera 7 - (Greenhouse Room) 22:35pm

A struggle begins where the farmer is trying to plunge the knife into the assailant's chest with all his might. The couple trample over rows of budding marijuana plants, all the while, the struggle does not budge. During the test of strength, a hologram splits from the assailant, to no avail. Just as intruder's blue face began to pale, a blinding glare of light flashes between them, forcing the farmer to loosen his grip in pain. With the waver of light back in his movement now, the assailant easily puts the farmer to ground. Afterward, he drags the farmer through the groves of plants to the corner of the room which the camera does not cover. A series of hellish howls are accompanied by sickly crunching sounds.

"Where is Lancis?! Where is HE?!" Flickers of blood periodically splatter into the cameras view. By the time the hooded assailant leaves the Greenhouse, the marijuana plants are painted scarlet.

Camera 8 - (Hallway 2) 22:47pm

Hooded assailant re-enters the hallway. His fleece hoody is stained red. He proceeds to the end of the passage.

Camera 5 - (The Stash Room) 22:47pm

The entire room is now ablaze.

Camera 4 – (The Gun Room) 22:47pm

Black smoke is beginning to fill the room.

Camera 3 – (Pole Room) 22:47pm

The dealers who are conscious are coughing heavily trying to pull their unconscious friends from the fumes billowing from the splintered gun room door.

Camera 8 – (Cookery) 22:49pm

Night vision mode activated

The entire room is pitch black. Three cooks and a cowering Lancis Green can be seen waiting for the assailant to arrive. The bloodied assailant begins to descend the steps to the Cookery.

"I see all of you," the assailant announced. One of the cooks flips a light switch, however, the fuse of the entire area blows. All areas of the Traphouse are thrown into darkness beside the light of flames from camera three, four and five. The duel in the darkness begins. With perfect precision, the assailant begins fending and defending against the aggressive cooks. The wavers of light in his movement are absent. The only flashes of action that the occupants can see are the blind gunshots that Lancis fires in the sequence. The flashes reveal the crazed face of the assailant who looks like he is enjoying the whole ordeal. After realising the pistol is out of ammunition, Lancis gives an exasperated roar. He missed most of his shots and the ones he did not, sunk into two of his three cooks. The assailant finishes pounding the third. It was just him and Lancis now. Lancis held his breath in hope that the intruder would not be able to locate him in the darkness.

"Do you know what else hides under furniture? Cockroaches," the assailant called. Lancis could hear footsteps steadily growing louder and so he made a last resort escape. Lancis passed the intruder, but he caught a fistful of Lancis' polo shirt with impeccable timing. Once again there was a struggle; one that put Lancis an inch from death. The hooded assailant had his hands around the woman beater's neck and had him curved backward over the counter. Lancis' ear began to singe on the electrical stoves that were heating the drug products. A sadistic smile followed. With his ear being pressed further into the scorching stove by the Traphouse's grim reaper, Lancis resorted to drastic defence. With all his might, he uprooted the cooking pot and threw it into the assailant's face.

"AAARRRRGHHHHH!!s!!!" There was no sound quite like someone's wail of agony as their face scorched alive. The intruder crashed to the floor for the first time since his hostile takeover. Sensing that this was his time for escape, Lancis sprinted toward the light of the cookery's staircase.

Camera 6 (Hallway 2) 23:11pm

Flickers of light from the greenhouse sporadically light up the hallway. Lancis Green rushes desperately down the passage. Wails of pain can still be heard from the direction of the cookery. When Lancis opens the door to the pole room he is met with a gust of black smoke. He immediately closes the door, coughing hoarsely. He then turns around and makes his way through the first door in the passage.

Camera 1 – (Traphouse Entrance) 23:24pm

The guards have evacuated. The entrance is empty and the door is wide open.

Camera 2 – (Hallway 1) 23:24pm

The hallway is empty. The door to the pole room widens every now and then.

Camera 3 – (Pole Room) 23:24pm

The pole room is ablaze.

Camera 4 – (The Gun Room) 23:24pm

The gun room is ablaze.

Camera 5 – (The Stash Room) 23:24pm

The stash room is ablaze. Through the lapses in black smoke a burning corpse can be made out.

Camera 9 – (The Board Room) 23:24pm

The light from the candescent Heron Institute building can be seen through the window. The room has a low, eerie glow. The board room was a few levels higher in the building and was disguised as a corporate building while the illegal activity ensued at its depths. Lancis attempts to climb to the geometric windows at the high reaches of the large room. Despite his attempts to stack chairs, his efforts amount to nothing. Dry whimpers could be heard from his direction. Lancis keeps checking the entrance to the board room, as if he was expecting the devil at his door. He worked himself to such a state that he took a seat at the roundtable by himself. He assumes a praying position. When a silhouette appears at the entrance of the room, he keeps his eyes closed. Once again, the sounds of footsteps grow louder and louder until he could hear battered breaths beside him.

"Just do it." Lancis squeezed his eyes tighter.

"How dare you pray. My Dad used to tell me no matter how much you pray, it won't undo the bad thing you have just done. Maybe you should listen to him. He was a wise man. A good man." The voice was ghast and low, however, there was an undertone of familiarity about it. Nonetheless, Lancis dared not open his eyes.

"You aint gonna get away with this. When my boss finds out you did this, you're dead and so is everyone you know! DEAD!" Lancis shouted into the floor spitefully.

"Even Caprice?" the voice asked.

"Wait, Tre?" Lancis muttered under his breath.

"This is not Tre. Look at me," the voice told him. Fear did not let Lancis face the hooded assailant, however.

"I SAID LOOK AT ME!" the ghastly voice commanded him. Lancis opened his eyes and when the face came closer into the light of the room, he gripped the arm of his chair several times. Due to the scalding hot water, a plane of baldness was seared into the boy's silky hair. The face of the boy was an unnatural blue colour, but worse yet, scattered across it was red strips of muscle fibre where his skin had burned from his face. The most unsightly of it all was the large portion of his right eye which seemed to be scalded from his skull. It was now a pus-filled globule that retained the precession of old. Scarier still, was that the boy's eye, right before Lancis' own, was slowly reforming; loose muscle strands were overlapping each other in the distinct formation only human physiology could allow and the cones of his cornea were blooming back into the place, with the complimentary colour of dark brown pigmenting soon after. The process was akin to watching the reimagining of a reanimated corpse, a reification that made him reconsider his very reality. Under the indigo of the spoiled mask, he could not get over the fact that it was undoubtedly the face of Tre Moon.

"Tre? Tre Moon? You did this you—" Lancis tried to lash out under the presumption that he could overpower Tre, but the events leading up to that very moment was indication that he was facing a force he did not know.

"I'm not Tre," the imposter exclaimed with annoyance, "I'm his brother, Blue." Once again the scarred assailant had a hand to Lancis' throat.

"There is no forgiveness, for people like me and you. We made our choices and we have to live with it. We mean nothing to the people we hurt. This is who we are now. I've been looking for forgiveness all of my life, it doesn't exist. The pain only stopped when I embraced this," the boy named Blue told the choking drug dealer. As he spoke, a glow on his hand began. The distinct sound of a steam iron could be heard from Lancis' neck. The slow and deliberate snuffle of life filled Blue's face with a satisfaction that could not be manufactured. He enjoyed seeing pain. A few moments later, moments from Lancis' complete suffocation, Blue's hand faltered. As did his sadistic glee. The assailant backed up a little as Lancis' gasped for his life.

"I-I- My brother is begging. He's begging me not to kill you. He sounds distraught." Blue was blinking rapidly as if every blink formed a cognitive barrier to stop Tre regaining complete control. Finally, the scarred assailant seemed to gain some autonomy over himself.

"I'm not going to kill you, because I love my brother. But you are not going to make it out of here alive anyway. You'll burn with this place. I hope you feel every single flame because you deserve it, rotten woman beater." With two sandy crunches, Blue crushed Lancis' hands in his own.

"ARRGGGHHHHHHHHHHHHHHHH!" Lancis screamed, holding his now malformed hands up to his face. His fingers were bent in every unnatural position and they now resembled an unoperated string puppet.

"If you can't live with the pain, you should have never chosen this way," Blue said darkly. A light-led knee followed and with another crack, Lancis' jaw was broken. Looking dissatisfied that he could not finish his deed, and with the waver of light behind his movements once again, Blue scaled the board room's huge walls with one jump and swooped through the geometric window, leaving Lancis to die in the burning Traphouse.

CHAPTER 10

<u>N.O.M.A.</u>

The voice that called itself Blue had long withdrawn and it was Tre who was left feeling the true shades of that colour. That same night, Tre returned to his apartment in a cold sweat. No matter how much he tried, he could not forget the lives that were taken that night. Despite this, it would still be him who would be responsible for the violent acts. Logic tangled with guilt and Tre wrestled the stained outerwear from his body before sealing them in a plastic bag under his bed. The weight of blood-soaked clothes was light compared to his self-reproach. In their place he threw on a fresh sweat suit and a grey hoody to cover his grossly recovering face. Afterward, he put his left arm in the sling Blue had thrown back into the room before leaving, however, he knew full well that neither feigned injury, nor supernatural healing factor could mend his broken self-image. A shaky hand rummaged the drawers of his dresser for anything of use – three loose bars of Xanax were found and swallowed consecutively. As the hazy effects settled in, he knew he would be safe from the voice in his head for at least the next few hours. After dressing, Tre spent three minutes in the dark kneeling. He had let everyone down; Edith Hill, Caprice, himself and most importantly, his parents. Just when he thought the days of being plagued by the voice were over, history repeated itself. There was nothing but uncertainty in his future. He did not know what atrocious act his hand would be forced to commit next and to Tre, that was not the kind of life anyone should live. Tainted by the infamous. Smite with strife. Tre raised from his kneel. The darkness forgave him for his sins, it always did. But with the journey of his life marked with such bloodshed, he decided it was finally time to meet the light.

The deaths that night in the city of Signot could paint darkness for a thousand more dusks, but dawn had other plans. The shade of hopeful orange sprouted from the skyline; once the city saw the light of day, one more life could be saved. As for Tre, who was atop a nearby rooftop, contemplating the prospect of a sixty foot fall; it would be the easiest decision he would make that night. Besides, he thought, a drop to his death would be but a drop in the ocean among Signot's murder rates. His absence would bring end to his absinthe. He felt the rooftop winds luring him closer and closer to the edge and he wondered how it would feel to be as free as the wind itself. He found it ironic how his incredible new powers helped him scale the tall Claxon Borough skyscraper but it was his shortcomings that made him want to jump it. He took another step forward. The toes of his right foot were the first part of his body to feel solid ground leave. Tre could see the suburbia below, small and indistinct. When he activated his magnified sight, he could see the details of the sidewalk that would be his resting place. His left foot followed next, but he did not immediately jump because he recalled the words his father had once told him when he first asked why there were so much people being murdered in Signot.

"Tre there are a lot of people dying in this city and I want you to understand this. Don't throw away your life; don't give anyone the reason to throw away your life. To not live is to be a coward. I want you to live your life like every day counts. Do you hear me, son? Like every-single-day counts. Your daddy and mummy could be one of those people who lost their life today, but we are still here. We get to spend it with you and we are grateful for that."

"Coward?" Tre mumbled to himself. His father might have called what he was doing cowardice, but his father had never been a slave to his own mind. No one could understand, except the voice of course. Tre and itself were several years removed from their relationship of old and Tre did not want it any other way. When his other identity had burned their home to the ground, their bridge went with it. The very thought that he used to consider the voice as one of his family made Tre angry with himself for giving home to such evil in the first place. He began to step from the roof and in all in one moment his greatest fears and desires came to mind. Disappointing his parents – reuniting with them. Cutting his crimes short – coming short of his potential. Leaving in peace – leaving Caprice. His final thoughts were that perhaps his father was right; maybe he was a coward. Suicide was something the sober him had considered many a time, but only an action the drug induced version of himself could follow through with. In that respect, he was going to rightfully die the way he had lived most of his life; in fear and alone.

"Why?" Tre's final moments of solitude were thwarted. Behind him came a steely voiced masked by an even more metallic equalizer. He was certain that he had heard the voice before and so when Tre faced his interrupter, he beheld the vigilante known as N.O.M.A., in the flesh. The drugs had sedated his emotions so much; surprise was not his initial reaction. Instead, a bout of honesty came.

"Too many reasons. You don't have to worry about killing me; I was going to do it myself," Tre tipped the vigilante.

"I'm not here to stop you. You look old enough to make your own decisions." N.O.M.A. walked forward and there was poundage about his steps. There was nothing brittle about his suit or his countenance.

"I want to know why a person like you would do something as risky as shutting down one of Maximov's drug spots, by yourself." The Heavens Conquest native was now closer than Tre could have ever imagined and there were just some components that a live video feed did not do justice. N.O.M.A.'s suit was the genuine article. It was arguably made of steel or tungsten and this stemmed from the robust design. From foot to shoulder, the wearer was enveloped in complex, armoured plates the colour of blood red, these were sleek and clearly combat-ready. From the shoulder blades, finger tips and along the side profile, ran streaks of grey that had a sandstone finish. The plates of armour compressed and decompressed seamlessly, giving N.O.M.A. a degree of flexibility, and this was the biggest indication that the suit was a product of extraordinary, mechanical expertise. At the crane he wore a half-helmet that was perched upward like the beak of a proud eagle. Underneath, was fitted a pointed, fibreglass visor, stained for anonymity and under that, was the most exposed part of the whole suit – a black mask covering the lower half of his face.

"How do you know where I was earlier?" Tre pulled his hood down some.

"I keep camera-intelligence circuits in Indiana, especially in crime areas. I had one in that coastal drughouse, until you burned it down that is."

"Are you here to take me in? Because if you are you're gonna' have to kill me first," Tre promised the armoured apprehender.

"F*@k it, jump if you want. I wanted to thank you if anything. It's not every day you see someone brave in Signot," said N.O.M.A.

"Thank me? For what?! I murdered people tonight!" Tre cried out.

"I know. I saw."

"You have no problem that I killed those men?"

"No one said lives won't be lost in war. Who wins that war is what matters."

"No one deserves to die!"

"From the footage it doesn't seem that you stand so strongly behind those words." Even though his name was destined to be blackballed, he would not let this whitewash what he saw in the vigilante N.O.M.A. – false heroism.

"You think that the life of an individual does not matter, what kind of protector are you?" Tre winced a little, through his frown. The skin on his brow tore a little; it had not fully recovered from the scalds he had suffered just hours before.

"I am a watcher. I watch over Indiana," said N.O.M.A.

"What is the difference?! Lives still do not matter to you!" Tre found himself frustrated at the thought that someone as capable as the person in front of him could overlook someone in need, someone like his parents.

"They do matter!" N.O.M.A. flared, as did the volume in his voice changer. "Don't you ever doubt what I f*@#ing stand for. I used to think like you, think that maybe I can do everything, but when you spread yourself to thin you'll lose everyone. Everyone. I need to stand for the greater good. I go where I am needed, usually to stop things from becoming worse. I do not have the firepower to deal with all of the bad things in this city, but I have the resources to keep track of it, until the day I do strike." The sleek, crimson armour flexed powerfully as he spoke and even the systematic voice changer could not filter out pure emotion.

"Why stop things becoming worse when you could make things better?"

"Who do you think has been getting all the new Signot politicians to resign so quickly? I can keep the slippery bastards from ruining the city more, but the drug and crime... I can't change that. It's been like this for a long time. Maximov and his Bulgarian Conglomerate run the city and they are more powerful than you think. Busting one of his drug houses is not going to make a difference. I guarantee that another will take its place by evening." It had been three hours since he was at Lancis' Traphouse and it was the second time he had heard the name Maximov, a name he had not heard once in his life before his visit. This fact meant three things at least:

1. The drug plague that he had known his city to suffer all these years was conducted by one of the most powerful men in the United States.

2. It was almost certain once the conglomerate found out who he was, they would be after him. He needed to make sure he remained anonymous, for the sake of the people around him. Thankfully, this task was second nature to someone who hid their face for a living.

3. Now that he was one of the few people who knew the name Maximov; he was now also one of the few people who could put an end of the drug tirade, once and for all.

"Why aren't you here in Signot if the Bulgarian Conglomerate is such a big problem?" asked Tre.

"You don't listen, do you? If I were to spread myself thin, then no good is accomplished. I serve where I can and put eyes where I can't."

"The Bulgarian Conglomerate is the biggest problem, soldier. They have been murdering and oppressing the city for years. If we find Maximov... you could change things forever."

"The biggest and most dangerous private army in the world is trying to mobilise in the city of Heavens Conquest as we speak. I think I'm definitely where I need to be right now." N.O.M.A. folded his armoured arms. The sun of the new day sprinkled over the rooftop and gave a new light to the conversation. The rays seemed to sit on the plates of the blood red suit, revealing a more complex colour scheme; an infusion of materials that had a distilled but cemented appearance. It was as if the red steel was being chased by the black of wurtzite boron nitride. Similarly, if the red of N.O.M.A.'s valour was being chased by the black of his unknown, but apparent, personal story, then the man and the suit were one and the same. As the rising light reached Tre Moon, he reckoned N.O.M.A. had the chance to see the truest version of himself too. Scarred and trying to conceal it. N.O.M.A. had a first-hand account of seeing Tre's healing factor at work and the dawn allowed Tre's new eyes to gather equally as important information about his apprehender. Where average human sight would fail, Tre's retroflective eyesight thrived. N.O.M.A's stained visor was a window to the man under the suit. His sight revealed only the area from the eyebrows to the nose, as a black open facemask hid the rest. The man under the suit had a thin nose, both of his eyebrows had a single slit and his eyes were oriental in shape. The most surprising fact that his supernatural sight revealed, was that the alter ego of the notorious vigilante was in fact a young man. Closer to his own age, if Tre did not know any better. If the figurative locked horns of their previous logochamy did not already, this revelation made Tre even more sceptical of the man under the suit.

"Why did you decide to become N.O.M.A.?" Tre posed. The crimson angel tilted his head slightly as if to answer, but then inverted the way he was facing, as if to take a different angle on his words completely.

"If I did not become N.O.M.A.," He began, "I would be half the person I should be. I am N.O.M.A. because people should not have to go through the things I have been through. I represent my people and where I come from." The vigilante guided Tre's attention to the rhombus -shaped insignia on his chest and at the forehead of his helmet. The symbol was quite simple in design and did not strike Tre as any he had seen before.

"And where is it that??"

"*Not Indiana*," came his short reply. Tre turned away because he considered the conversation over, but as he turned to the edge of the rooftop, jumping from it did not have the same appeal it had just minutes before. In fact, now, it was the last thing he wanted to do. His teenage years made him obsess over how not to leave any more marks in the world. Never did he consider what kind of mark that could be. Tre examined the burns on his right hand. Burns suffered in valiant fashion. When he realised what his other identity had done to his home, his first reaction was not to restrain himself but to help his parents. To save them. N.O.M.A. watched Tre's attentions evaporate into the moment.

"You should get a mask – next time you decide to do something on your own." N.O.M.A. inverted his facing position once again.

"If you knew who I really was, you'd know I'm already wearing one." Tre lifted his head and removed his hood. Aside from a single blood-shot eye, the healing factor had reinstated the architecture of his face. His strong bone structure had been carved out once again. His true, dark, smooth skin once again ruled his face. Even his long eyelashes had remerged from the cinders of the once destroyed follicles. Where the first fire had taken away his ability to feel life, this second instance had imbued him with it once again. He could make out impressed eyes inside the helmet.

"I saw the footage. You can do things I've never seen before in my life! And I don't know what has happened in your life before tonight, but I do know why you haven't jumped."

"Yeah?" doubted Tre.

"*Yeah.*"

"I don't care what you think you know."

"You are looking for retribution. Deep down you want to prove it to yourself or to the world. Either that or you were protecting someone you love. Those are the only two reasons someone would do something as crazy as you did tonight. Especially taking the lives of the criminals. There's a difference between doing what is necessary and savagery." If understanding was truly in conjunction with experience, then he and N.O.M.A. had indeed tread similar paths in life. Tre wondered now more than ever, who the Crimson Angel really was. Until faced with it, he never realised how much a suit and voice changer could conceal for a person.

"You're right. I want retribution and recognition for who I truly am. All my life I've been in the shadow of... somebody else. I'm misunderstood. Sometimes I even question who I am... I know who I am, but if no one can see that, what am I really?" Tre compared the differences in his two hands as he spoke, as these were relative to the imbroglio of his life.

"Who said you will be in the shadow of that person for your entire life? If you took your own life you lose. As long as you are still alive, you can still win the war."

"This is not something I can win or change. The battle was lost a long time ago."

"You," N.O.M.A. emphasised, "*are a dark guy, you know that?*" The straightforward comment caught Tre off guard and he was forced to take a breath of mirth. He saw N.O.M.A.'s eyes fold in only the way a smile could. After the brief moment of agreeability, the vigilante pressed a finger to the side of his helmet, triggering his visor into patterns of telemetric coding.

"What you do with your life is your choice. But it'd be a damn shame if the Bulgarian Conglomerate never even knew that they once had a big problem on their hands." A steady hum signalled a series of mechanical algorithms to be processed inside the crimson suit and soon enough, the suit itself sprung into sentiency. The various flaps and plates folded and rearranged into different formations across the entire surface area, eventually the plates that had previously covered the length of his arms had now been modified into steel gliders the length of his wingspan. The speed and efficiency this modification was carried out gave Tre the impression that armour he had seen previously was merely a template. It was more than simply a suit.

"What does N.O.M.A. stand for?" Tre said, assuming it would specify what kind of technology the vigilante was branding. Suddenly from where the insignia in

N.O.M.A.'s chest was placed, a circular piece of the armour displaced. It removed itself from his suit and formed a crimson ball, complete with a camera lens and, surprisingly enough, its own artificial intelligence.

"Node-Operating-Management-System online. Mr B, should I continue to run a full scan on this individual?"

"Not at all. He's about to jump anyway," said N.O.M.A. With a beckon, the circular node reattached itself to the suit.

"It used to stand for No-One-Matters-Anymore." A burst of propulsion sent N.O.M.A. tens of feet into the air and moments later he was voyaging the skies in the direction of Heavens Conquest. The odds of their encounter were next to none, however, in retrospect, N.O.M.A. seemed to have dominion over even the smallest of numbers. Tre was completely beside himself. The dawn had completed its transition and the hopeful horizon had now found its place in the sky. It took Tre three minutes of staring down at Signot, tens of feet below, to realise what it meant to be standing where he was. As his father would say, the world was at his feet.

CHAPTER 11

<u>Wrong My Rights</u>

It had been two days since the incident at the coastal Traphouse and one day since Tre had attempted to take his own life, and despite both low points, Tre Moon was alive at Claxon Borough's subway station. Head bowed as if in grace. Both hands together as if grateful. Nail in knuckle as if grated. Eyes closed in laze. Thoughts racing like the many trains that passed the platform, and just like the trains, the thoughts went both ways.

"Tre...Tre...Tre! I know you can hear me. Don't ignore me; you know that's a bad idea."

"I'm not scared of you."

"You should be. Since you stopped taking the drugs I've felt stronger. I could take over right now if I wanted."

"Why don't you then? And ruin my life some more."

"Because then you'd hate me more."

"Trust me, I cannot hate you anymore than I do now."

"You say such hurtful things, Brother."

"A drop in the ocean compared to what you've done."

"No matter what we've been through I've never left your side. If you should hate anyone it should be the people who have tried to pull us apart since we lost our parents."

"I'm not having this conversation with you again."

"Of course. The only time you seem to want to talk things over is when someone's life is on the line!"

"Those dudes didn't deserve to die, no one does. If the world could see what you truly are, my life could have been better."

"Hahaha! Really? That is what you think? If I was gone you would have no one. No one!"

"I don't have to justify myself to you."

"Let's not deceive ourselves here. Your science friends only like you cos of these new powers we have."

"Think that. The Hill family love me."

"Not like a real family. Love is not making us stay in a damn mental home for a year right after we got free from Juvy'."

"Yeah, they wanted to see if you would show up again and hurt people and I don't blame them."

"Prison must have been better than that home. All those drugs and psychiatric sessions they put us through, just to try and split us apart. I hate that woman."

"That's the difference between us. Edith sees me, but she sees right through you. You're a monster."

"Well she treated us both like monsters. So, she was noble enough to put us in a mental home but not brave enough to let us stay with her. We are nothing to that woman but a case study."

"If I didn't go to the home the judge would have sent me straight back to detention. It was my only way out."

"We were never really out. Control of our lives just went from the law to her."

"Maybe for you. Caprice visiting everyday got me through it."

"Brother, you must really be out of your mind if you think that witch wants us near her precious daughter."

"We're best friends."

"You know, Caprice probably does care about us. It's a shame she might not be around for much longer because you can't even protect her."

"I hate you..."

If hate could build gates then Tre had fenced himself in the past. Every bad thing that happened in his life, he was sure the voice had steered them both into. Crippling Caprice's boyfriend was just the most recent. Since that day, Tre felt like he was in quicksand. He could not escape the feeling that he was capable of the same acts the other identity (that called itself Blue) committed that night, and that scared him. To even consider losing Caprice would cost him a piece of himself. Tre let the hood of his beige trench coat sit over his head a little more than usual, then, he ran his fingers over the burn on his right hand that was hanging from his arm cast. The healing factor had managed to reverse a severe stab wound and even reformed his scalded face, but it had not changed his scarred hand whatsoever. His body may have fooled itself that the burn was healed, but Tre knew that would never be the case.

"You can hate me all you want. That's not going to stop me from being your brother and as your brother I need to pick up your slack. You were not man enough to kill Lancis' goons, so I did."

"How comes you didn't kill Lancis then."

"Because.. of you. You were upset."

"Since when did you have a conscience?"

"I felt... bad... If I knew the medics would get him before the fire, I would have finished it off."

"Why do you think it's okay to kill people, that's not how we were raised!"

"Because that's who I am now."

"No, that's who you're choosing to be. A murderer."

"Maybe, but at least I can protect Caprice."

"Don't bring her into this."

"Someone hurt her and you want them to walk free?"

"He's in jail. She's safe now."

"Safe? So, people don't get released from jail? Are we going to pretend he was not direct partners with Signot's drug empire? You are a coward and this will come back to haunt us sooner or later. Poor Caprice."

"She doesn't even know you exist!"

"She will..."

"What is that supposed to mean? Don't ignore me! Don't ignore me!"

"Caprice is getting off the train. We'll talk later."

Right on cue, Caprice stepped from the stream of people heading toward the staircase exit. Tre stood to greet her and it took one sweep of her alabaster and brown curls to brush aside his wrung feeling inside. Once Caprice stopped in front of him she smiled weakly. There was a tepid, combined vibe between the two; they were both wrapped in their own issues.

"How's your arm?" asked Caprice.

"Better. How's your eye?" replied Tre.

"Do you think it has gone down?" Caprice lifted her thick eyeglasses and angled her face.

"Yeah," Tre assured her. In this instance Caprice's infatuation with cosmetics had effectively covered up her bruise. The way her makeup neutralised the colour of the black eye, a neutral onlooker could not be more in the dark of what she had endured. Despite all the wonders she could achieve cosmetically, what she could not draw on was her usual glow.

"Thanks for meeting me here, Tre," Caprice told the floor.

"You know how dangerous the city is, can't have you walking places by yourself."

"Especially after he let Lancis get away with hurting you,"

"Should we get going then?" Caprice offered as she tightened the scarf around her neck. Tre knew it was no coincidence that the scarf was bulky enough to hide most of her face. After all, he was no stranger to the feeling.

It was a stark and quiet journey. There was an art in the silence and though it was disturbed by the occasional siren or gunshot, this was their life in Signot. Tre and Caprice understood each other enough to know that the strange silence was revealing but needed. No matter how much he wanted to, Tre had always refrained from confiding in Caprice about the true depths of his Dissociative Identity Disorder, in fear he might lose her. His strange powers just added to this reluctancy. He did not know what to think of it himself. It was beyond explanation and beyond comprehension. Beyond anything Caprice should be dealing with. The pair made their way through the Claxon Borough streets and through the pop-up store marketplace until they reached the suburbs toward the East End. Home. When they turned onto Cherry Lane an ominous shiver ran through Tre, from his shoulders to his feet. This put a harden in his next step.

"It's been a while?" Caprice guessed.

"I haven't been here since we moved out to college." If it were up to himself, he would never walk the street again, "Nothing has changed."

"You have changed Tre-Tre," she half-smiled.

They proceeded and Cherry Lane was just as he remembered it. Antique, compartmented houses stood one after the other. Birch trees sprouted from the lawns of the larger abodes and driveways were fitted with family vehicles of various makes. The street was narrow, reaching straight giving it the illusion of endlessness, much like Tre's memories of it. He received his first telescope on this street, rode his first bike, even made his first friend. He lost these very same things on the street too. Signot was generous and ungracious, but life had set Tre up for failure to begin with. When Caprice clutched Tre's hand tightly he knew they were passing his old home. There was nothing left of the Moon residence, just a mossy cemented base. Tre's new eyes could see almost anywhere, but all it took was for him to close them to see his house of old on fire again. Tre pulled on Caprice's hand to signal that they should proceed as normal. At last, they reached a door not much further from the old Moon residence and then rung the bell. Before the door opened, Caprice made sure to let go of Tre's hand. No more than two seconds passed and the door had swung wide open.

"Tre, I wasn't expecting you too. Come in both of you please!" exclaimed Edith Hill.

The Hill home bore symmetry to the home Tre remembered, only the interior differed. The house maintained the traditional Cherry Lane design: large, rectangle rooms, grand staircases and a convex shaped kitchen complex. Edith ushered them to the dining table of which a television on the wall was overlooking. The tablecloth was tinted apricot, as was Edith Hill's knotted apron. A clicquot bottle was centred between an inch perfect table set up and the backdrop was a get up of buttercup patterned chiffon curtains.

"It gives me great pleasure to be given consent by the Council of Signot to expand my company, Isle's Oils, to the United States of America. A lot of people have asked me: why Indiana, or why Signot? Well the reason I first came to the states was for my son's college education. The Heron Research funded science programme was an opportunity of a lifetime for him. So naturally I supported him and brought myself to this city too. It was different from London, and very different from Dubai where I first started my industry, but if you spend long

enough in one place you start to see the beauty. I chose to bring this project here because I see potential in this city; such beautiful views and iconic buildings like the Liami Sphere in Hive. The diverse population. There's something here indeed. When we build these oil factories in the Hetashi Borough, Signot will become the wealthiest city in the whole of America. My factories will single handedly fix Indiana's economy and be able to fund the city in ways that have never been possible before. On this day, as you accept me, Isaac Isles − I give back to you, the people."

"Have a seat you two." Edith nudged the two juniors out of their trance by shutting off the television, "They have been playing that speech all day. The way the states love him I wouldn't be surprised if he ran for president next. That man Isaac Isles."

"Isaac Isles huh?" It had occurred to Tre that he had now seen Quick's father for the first time.

"Yeah. Love his British accent. How have you two not seen it, it's been all over the radio and internet all day?"

"Been busy," Tre said.

"Yeah same," Caprice added.

"If I didn't know better I'd think you kids lived in your own world. Tre please take off your hood in the house, it is bad manners."

"Sorry Miss Hill." Tre complied. He almost made a move to remove it with his sling arm, but he was able to play off the recovery. Caprice, who was sat across the table from him, seemed to take an interest in his newly unhooded face.

"I don't know why you like to hide so much, you've grown handsome. Right Mum?"

"Maybe," Edith teased as she moved two dishes to the table. In the large pot was a lobster soup and in the smaller bowls: cream linguini with garlic, sautéed spinach.

'You wouldn't be saying that if you saw his face a day ago, haha!' Tre chose to ignore the voice.

"If you're lucky you might take after your mom, Cap." Tre returned the double edged compliment.

"Enough you two. Help yourself to some food." Edith Hill had dressed as casual as Tre could remember in recent times: her curls were tied back with a primp headband, she had a suitably cream blouse and rings on her fingers for every day of the working week she had competed with. Though Professor Hill had achieved this relaxed look, like Caprice, her temperament refused to be dressed. Her tendency for imperatives went untouched.

"When Isaac Isles brings his oil industry to Signot, I think a lot of things are going to change. For the better," Edith began twirling strands of linguini around her spoon, "all of those dreadful pop-up stores are going to disappear. Also, I heard the standard salary is going to rise. There's no better time than now to look for a side job if you guys want to make some extra income to help with your study fees."

"I'm dropping out of college," Caprice said abruptly. Edith Hill's investigative scowl knit itself back onto her face. Tre's good hand, which was inches away from delivering a forkful of delicious linguini into his mouth, was forced to level.

"Not going to offer us an explanation?" Edith Hill did not realise that her cream blouse was now blotched in linguini sauce as a result of leaning forward so much. Tre used his long reach to gently remove it from her path.

"I've been invited to an interview for a photography internship in New York. If I get it, I'll move over there and start later this year," Caprice added.

"With who?" Tre asked. In his eyes, this could get no worse.

"Which company?" Edith asked.

"YOTT in Manhattan."

"Who?"

"Young & Oliver Trent Times. Does it matter? You should be happy for me, not trying to put me down!" The food was destined to become cold, because the family dinner had evolved into a family dispute.

"No one is – hey!" Edith Hill snapped her fingers when she saw Caprice's attention becoming lost in an eye roll, "no one is putting you down. It's just very sudden, Caprice. How comes you didn't tell anyone?"

"Because I can make my own decisions."

"So, you are just going to throw away your tuition? What is Tre going to do for the next two years with his rent?"

How he would handle the rent was the last thing Tre was worried about. The very thought of Caprice moving state increased his heart rate. Worse yet, why did she not tell him any of this? He did not voice this, however, and like he so often did, Tre became a watchful gargoyle.

"Not my problem. I'm doing it, I'm moving out of this city and making something of myself." Caprice's cavalier might as well have been literal because Tre was cut up inside.

"Are you okay, darling?" Edith Hill now looked concerned.

"No, I'm not okay! All these criminals and murderers running around... I'm sick of it! I'm sick of being scared, not knowing when I might lose someone I love!" Caprice was general in her sentences, but Tre easily read between the lines.

"He was part of the drug business. He is lucky to still be alive," Tre stated bluntly. His reality check only spurred her escalating emotions.

"Who?" Edith said searchingly, but her question became lost in the intensity between the two juniors.

"I thought you of all people, you would know that people are more than their past." There was a tone of disappointment in Caprice's voice.

'*Ouch,*' echoed Blue mockingly. Tre did not hold back; he matched her tone when he retorted back.

"I thought you of all people would have some self-respect." Today he would let the spores of jealousy he had held back since meeting Lancis, see the light of day.

"Is that what you think of me, Tre, is that what you really think?" A quaver of hurt was now in her voice.

"I really do, you are better than... him."

"You don't know him—"

"You just let him walk in your life and—"

"You don't know us!"

"—treat you like some skeezer!" The pair stopped shouting over each other when Caprice pushed her plate from in front of her. Lobster soup stained the apricot tablecloth.

"He's the only person who has been there for me – supported my goals."

"That's where you're wrong, Cap." Tre placed his cutlery together now. His sentence was general, but Caprice read between the lines.

"I love him. Him!" Caprice slammed on the table and rose to her feet upon reiteration.

"Sure. But he doesn't love you or he wouldn't have put his hands on you," Tre whispered slowly. He wanted her to feel every moment of his spite. Caprice glanced at her mother who put a hand to her mouth. She gathered her possessions erratically and made for the door. Before she left, she turned back toward Tre. She swung her handbag over one shoulder and brushed the chip off the other.

"Your parents would be ashamed if they knew you were a drug addict," she said her final words of ivy before leaving.

"Caprice! Who hit you? Tell me immediately, don't you walk away from me—" Edith chased Caprice into the doorway passage but her orders were met with a stupendous slam of the door. Disobedience was the order of the day. Two arrows to the heart were exchanged and with the reactions that followed, both had landed direct hits. Tre's powers could heal wounds, but they could not amend burnt bridges. He did not have a second of rue, firstly, because of the commentary within his head and secondly, because Edith Hill had now reappeared. She stopped at the doorway in such a way that it hid half of her face, she chose to excavate him with her visible eye.

"You lied to me. You lied to yourself." Edith's voice was swollen now. Tre did nothing, including make eye contact with her.

"I don't even know what to say about any of this to be honest," she continued, "drugs Tre? Don't you care about yourself?" Tre's chose to hold his silence still, which was two letters easier than his true answer.

"We'll talk about this at our next session. Also, this came through the post." Edith offered Tre a letter and when he reached to take it, Edith grabbed his forearm with her free hand.

"Your life is yours, Tre. It's yours." Her hazel eyes had sunk in hurt.

Tre left the Hill home feeling powerless and ashamed. He could not change his past ways, he could not take back what he said. This was his life now. Just when he thought he reached the lowest point of his day; his expectations were one envelope seal away from rebate.

Tre swore as he took in its contents:

Dear those concerned,

It has come to our attention that Project CSS001 (colloidal supersilver) has gone missing from the premises of High Claxon University. We have launched a private investigation into what occurred and we have been given authorisation by the Indiana Police Department and Federal Bureau of Investigation, to bring the following suspects in for official questioning on Monday 15th April 2013:

Tre *Isiah* Moon
Damia *Alexandra* Ascot
Quiqhin *Moulbar* Isles
Professor Noel *Colin* Jinx

The CSS001 project is a multibillion dollar project funded by many investors and if you are found in possession or liable for the absence of said project, you could face prosecution from all involved parties. You may not bring a lawyer or solicitor to this questioning.

Attendance is mandatory.

HERON RESEARCH, TOWER HEADQUARTERS
INVESTIGATIONS DIVISION
LINNING WALK, HIVE BOROUGH
SIG C40, INDIANA
UNITED STATES

CHAPTER 12

<u>The Effigy</u>

With the claws of the law sunk back into his shoulder, it was no surprise that Tre once again felt like the minority stakeholder of his life. As he reached the Heron Research enterprises, any hopes that he would walk free from the questioning, began to unsolder. The irony was that the AIM members had spent the weekend ironing out the creases. Each member had added their own theory of what would unfold but they resolved to condone their position of unknowing. At Tre's suggestion they would enter the questioning at different times and from different destinations so much as to deter dangerous pre-decisions and designate enough time to develop their individual, invincible depositions. Quick claimed to have experience dealing with police accusations on many occasions and so pressed to Damia and Tre, the significance of pleading ignorance. If they had no ears, they would avoid hearing. If they had no eyes, they would not see trial. With no trace of the colloidal supersilver it would be near impossible to be incriminated and for him, it was a closed case. Damia's stance was completely adjacent and was based on everything but complacence. She pressed the importance of the project. She expected court procedures to be present and she brought forward a reasonable prospect. That it could be the chance for Tre to finally find out what happened to him on the evening he gained his powers.

After being directed to the elevator at the lobby entrance, Tre was escorted to the department of investigations by a tall guard who had mastered the 'nobody's home' expression better than even himself. In most cases, an elevator ride was an awkward experience, but today, for Tre, it proved informative. Once his corner cutting eyes discovered a wire inside the guard's blazer he made a note to be careful what he would say from there on. Once they had reached a floor level high enough to make a statician ecstatic, the guard led him down a glass passage with views that would give a vulture vertigo. It was this same single passage that connected the two Heron Research towers, giving it the infamous 'H' shape. He always wanted to visit the Heron Research building, but never under such circumstances. Along the walk Tre could see all the sights of Signot. To his left was the Hetashi Borough, accompanied by the flashing lights and swarming rides of the Belly Carnival. To his right was the majestic building, the Liami Sphere, in the prestigious Hive district, and because the diminution of peripheral was a thing of the past, he did not even need to pirouette to capture the propensity of Signot's national park. The escort reached its last few feet and Tre was introduced into one of many executive rooms in short corridor; a room branded 'Office of Aaron Heron CEO'. When he entered his expectations were flipped on itself. Yes, the room was executive in size, but it was religious in design. It seemed the crucifix was a crucial aspect of Mr Heron's latter days at the company, as there were countless wooden crosses planted across the room, and even between the many framed portraits of himself in his infamous glass-like suit. Old Testament pages were pinned to the noticeboard on the back wall. Atop his stationery desk were an assortment of silver daggers and silver pliers and these were amongst the brightest objects in the room because obvious obstruction had been made where the windows would be. Instead, several standing candelabras burrowed the space in a lowly glow, reminiscent of a castle hallows.

Tre was so caught up in the mysterious office that he did notice the occupants. Professor Noel, Damia, a guard Tre presumed brought her, and a busty, plump woman who was sporting a mink coat dyed with an assortment of synthetic colours. Along with themselves, this woman looked like she had no business in an office, let alone one that closely resembled a prayer room. Her ponytail was gelled backwards, but she was leant back further in her chair. The exactness in her makeup detail was only bested by the crass of her dress. A pentagon crossed string shirt lay across her chest. On her legs were designer denim jeans that were filled to the seam and varicose, yeti pumps graced her feet. Tre was convinced the lady could very well have fit in at Signot's annual fashion show at the Liami Sphere, but the settled aroma of malt and citrus warned that she had been in the room for some time and was therefore expecting them all.

"Who is this lady?" Damia said when he took a seat beside her. She plucked the words right from his thoughts.

"I'd watch what you say." Tre faced her deliberately and scratched his ear in the slow shape of an ear piece. As always, Damia was quick to pick up on things and batted her eyes in faux wonderment to why the conversation should end so prematurely.

"Tre, do you know anything about what happened? Anything at all?" Professor Noel fired desperately.

"Everything you say before the questioning will be used against you," a guard warned, "discussion about the article can be held once Signorina Baelel commences questioning." Professor Jinx was effectively silenced by these words, but Tre's guilt grew louder than ever. A confession could free everybody and clarify everything, but he knew that confession would only be the beginning of a whole new line of problems.

Any air of confusion was wafted away when the lady withdrew a fancy fan and began airing herself, letting everybody in the room know that she was the person whom went by the name Signorina Baelel. The charity in her look also let them know she possessed the authority in the meet.

"Where iz the final suzpect'"? Signorina Baelel asked.

"We have an agent tracking him. He is three blocks away Signorina," one of the guards informed her with the utmost courtesy.

"I grow *impaetient*. I wish to start the questioning now," she said.

"But Signorina–"

"I said, I wish to start the questioning now!" Baelel snapped her fan together at these words, "Three ladro iz better *thaen* one. *Staert* the recording." The guards did not reply, they just pressed the inside of their blazers where Tre had warned Damia the wire would be. Once the proceedings began, Noel Jinx ruptured into a weekends' worth of overbearing defence.

"Listen, there has been a terrible mistake. There is no possible way that the colloidal supersilver could have escaped containment. When Aaron and myself first had the initial components validated, we tested it in all conditions. High temperatures, pressure – you name it! There is no way for the containment to have been opened either. The only mechanism capable of that is in Heron Towers! Baelel, do you think that trialling me and my students will bring you any closer to what truly happened? It is an anomaly." Signorina took a moment to reflect on his words.

"That is Signorina Baelel to you," Baelel emphasised with a strong Italian accent. "*Aeron* and our partners put a backing of one point four billion dollars collectively and you are telling me that it just disappeared? I'm sorry but I cannot use that as an answer at the board meeting."

"Ungrateful. As always," Professor Jinx arrowed in, "you couldn't give a flying monkey about the scientific community. All you care about is the money still. I hoped when we lost Aaron at least that would change."

"Do these children even know who *Aeron* Heron iz? If they did they would have never let this happen to his most prized project!" Baelel shot back as if they were not even there.

"Aaron Heron founded Heron Research in 1982, before I was born. He is America's most recognised scientist for his companies work in bioengineering, genetics and charity. Heron's distribution into independent regulation services is the reason my father even had a job in this city," Tre spoke up and his tone was so firm that it commanded the immediate attention from everyone inside the room. Signorina Baelel gave a sarcastic, slow clap to gift wrap her next fact.

"Well young boy, I am Signorina Vallila Baelel and I waz *Aeron's* mistrezz throughout hiz marriage. He iz not here now and neither iz hiz wife. I am the successor of thiz company now. If you love Heron as much az you claim, you will tell me what happened to the sample that night. It meant a lot to him," Baelel said with a smoky smile.

"I don't know." Tre lied. Damia folded her thin lips inward.

"He iz a liar. He was one of the last people to leave the premisez that evening." Baelel unsheathed her fan to air herself once more. She was clearly not used to things not going her way. Tre thought it ironic that Signorina Baelel would accuse another of being a liar when the story of her acquisition of Heron Institute was more questionable than what the acronym N.O.M.A. stood for.

"Why did Mr Heron go missing?" Tre shuffled the subject of conversation.

"Mr Heron suffered from PMLE – a sun condition," Damia added when she saw Tre's mouth move in confusion. "Not many people know that, that was the true reason he built the suit; it reflected all forms of light and he could lead a normal life. They say his condition drove him mad and he ran with his wife."

"That is utter nonsenze. *Aeron'* would never run from what he built because of a sun condition. That waz a small inconvenience for him. He ran coz he waz a coward. He could not face our love." Baelel began to fan herself furiously. Tre could not help but inspect the celebrated preservations of Heron's inheritance. He found it extremely strange why the man he looked up to during his childhood would have daggers, pliers and harmful objects of that nature. The ability to magnify his sight allowed Tre to read the Old Testament pages that were pinned behind Signorina Baelel. They foreswore treachery and tragedy; lost treasures from a man in trepidation. His eyes could also qualify as forensic tools because upon magnifying his sight further, he could see that the many pages had creases only disposed material could have. He could also see faint stains of blood across each one. Visible enough to know blood had seen parchment, but faint enough to know someone had tried to cover it up.

"The truth is, we don't know what happened," Professor Jinx admitted with some trouble, "he willingly gave up his suit; it is being protected by Sargent Boston's private military and though you may have convinced yourself otherwise, you were nothing but a habit to him, Vallila." These words prompted Signorina Baelel to gasp with offence and chuck what little water she had left, in Professor Jinx' direction, until the bodyguards came to settle her.

"I'm fine!" Baelel stressed to the surrounding guards, all the while she pressed her ponytail back into formation as if her moment of madness had unpocketed it completely.

"Where iz the last suzpect?" Right on cue, Quiqhin Isles was made to enter the room. He was dressed in a rosé red tracksuit and held a blasé blue profile.

"Hurry up, I've got somewhere to be," Quick announced.

"How many contact hours have your students had with the CSS project?"

"Maybe fourteen or so, I don't know."

"Did you alter the substance at any point without moderation."

"That is a stupid question, an absolutely stupid question. You know that that containment vase cannot be opened outside of this HQ."

"Do you take full responsibility for the missing CSS project as it was contractually and administratively under your care?"

"This is f*cking wrong and you know it is!"

After a line of questioning that, surprisingly, forced Quick, Damia and Tre to be spectators; they saw Professor Jinx crawl closer and closer to the brink of helplessness. With each question it became more obvious that the questioning was a legal procedure to incriminate their professor and hold him liable for every aspect of blame: financial, public and otherwise. With every question, Tre was forced to hold his words and see someone else, totally innocent, face the consequences of the blind truth. A feeling he knew all too well since the day of his parents' death. This breached the limit Tre was willing to go to preserve his secrets and just as he was about to speak up, Quiqhin nudged him roughly under the table. A stern shake of the head followed.

"Given the answers that you have provided Heron Institute is holding you, Noel Jinx, liable of one point four billion dollars of lost investment and two trillion dollars of projected profits lost. We will repossess everything you own to settle this debt and if the debt is still outstanding, you will be forced to serve community service in your state prison until your contractors are satisfied." The guard had finally reached the end of a long paper he had been reading from. Damia's line of birth marks were reduced to half when her hand found her mouth. Quiqhin's head shaking become more furious and Tre's guilt had formed a life of its own, in the form of Blue's remorseless laughter in his head.

"I have a feeling that repossessing everything you own won't settle that debt," Baelel smiled.

"Baelel. I have a wife and kids..." The students had never seen their professor plead before; the prospect of losing your life's work, moreover, your life's worth, could do that.

"I'm sure they can just drop the habit of having a father, no Noel?" Heron's mistress was toying with an innocent man's career and future and it burned every single one of them inside, Damia was first to vocalise it however.

"You are a heartless b@#ch, in case no one in this building is honest enough to tell you," she sneered.

"And you all are liarz. I am not going to stop until it is returned; I will get your whole university shut down if I have to!" Signorina Baelel's arms sprouted like an angry peacock and the flames of the candelabras flickered some. Tre did not know how accurate this statement would prove to be, but he was under no circumstances ready to find out. No more people would suffer for his secret.

"I can tell you what happened to the supersilver, just let everyone else go," Tre wagered calmly. The supersilver incident was not his fault and if he knew a way to reverse it for the purpose of that very moment, he would give up his powers. On the other hand, he harboured the feeling that he did not get to truly experience what they had to offer, especially after witnessing what Blue had done at Lancis' Traphouse. Nonetheless, if anyone's future had to be sacrificed, whose was better than his? Up until this point, he had been living half a life anyway.

"I knew there waz something to be said under that cool act. The quiet onez alwayz have a story." Baelel fleeted her hand outward in signal that the others were dismissed.

"Tre?" Professor Jinx croaked in disbelief. Damia had taken a pink complexion from the applied effort of not speaking up.

"It's okay, Tre. You don't have to tell her, I will." Quick stood up. "It was me who disposed of the supersilver." The confession only served to knot the owner of Heron more than ever.

"What do you mean dispozed?!" Signorina Baelel hawked in a high pitched voice.

"I broke the containment and it evaporated in thin air. It is never coming back." Quick was fearless. He took pleasure in delivering this story to the equally spiteful owner and apart from becoming the latest victim of her flammable retaliations (she hurled the empty glass at him), he smiled throughout it all. He knew that most of her threats would fall flat against the width of his financial situation. Money was not all that mattered, but it was an effective mattress for when legal threats were laid. Signorina Baelel was too couture to allow anything but her outfit do the screaming, so she brought her voice extremely low for her final words. She turned hostile to everybody in the room, including the guards.

"You chumpz make yourself useful for once and call Sargent Boston! Tell him to put the suit on lockdown until we can find a way to harness it." She thrashed back toward the suspects when she had finished.

"Jinx. This iz the last of you. These ribaldo are still under your care and you will pay for this loss, even if it is reduced." She kept her undertone when she turned toward Damia and Tre, "You two can forget about ever working for Heron Institute. EVER! Once I list you as conspirators no scientific council will take you on," she warned them, with cutting words, but it did not take Damia long to slash back.

"I doubt it. Heron Research has less clout since you have taken head. Plus, I don't even want to be part of this company; I heard it is in partnership with Isaac Isles oil industry. You clearly do not care about the environment." Damia was faster than she was feisty, because she was the first to exit Aaron Heron's office.

"You," she pointed a rattling finger at Quick, "forget about a career in... anything! You do not even know what you have caused. Get out, get out now!"

In one day, the second strangest incident that had occurred in Tre's life had been exorcised, but not in the manner he wanted it to. The repercussions of Quick's false confession were evident after one discussion. Tre, Quick and Professor Noel joined Damia outside the office door and if remorse was measured in floors then the AIM members were still several levels short.

"I don't know why you would do this, Quick. I gave everything to you kids... She is still going to hold me financially responsible, I hope you know that." Professor Jinx bowed his bald head for a few moments, before uttering words that were beside his usually utilitarian self.

"I will never forgive you for this. Don't even bother coming to university tomorrow, Quiqhin, you are expelled." The Professor watched Damia and Tre with something close to hate and then he followed the path toward his now destroyed life. Tre remembered how the professor would always preach that every action had a reaction. Today was no different.

"Why? These powers are not worth what just happened in there." Tre squared himself in front of his brash friend.

"I didn't do it for your damn powers, bro," Quick laughed off Tre's words.

"Why then!?"

"You've already had your future taken away from you before, this time you deserve the chance to have one." Quick gave Tre a sincere hand to the shoulder and decided it was time to leave himself. Quiqhin Isles was always trying to make time for his ventures; it seemed he would have a lot more of it now. Afterward, it was just Damia and Tre alone. The pair made way for the elevator as well. Having received the most mercy from Signorina's Baelel's wrath, it was justified that they had the most to say.

"Tre we gotta find out what has happened to you. It might be the only way to get the supersilver back," said Damia finally. The elevator blinked and invited them inward.

"I know. I'm just scared if I can't." Tre pushed the button labelled 'G'.

"We," Damia reminded him.

"Thanks." With the hovering feeling that his friendship with Caprice might be gone, and her physical presence soon to follow, it was comforting to have companionship elsewhere.

"Quick is such an idiot," she chuckled.

"I know," Tre felt a smirk invade his face, "the worst part is, I don't think he cares."

"I do. Without him are we eligible to continue our group project? Is the project still on if the professor leaves? Argh, so many questions. I'm just going to go back to Heavens Conquest tonight and scream into my pillow."

"Wait."

"What?"

"Heavens Conquest."

"Yeah? What about?"

"Baelel said that Herons suit was in the military base. Before she kicked us out she said that she will get the base to lock it down until they can extract supersilver from it."

"Sorry. Usually I'd be following but today has been hectic to say the least. Just tell me what it is you are thinking, please."

"If I can get the suit from the base, maybe we can extract it. If my powers can help us extract the supersilver it is made of, we can undo this whole mess."

"Tre that is ridiculous. Suicidal too." The elevator blinked once again and invited them onto the ground floor, "You may be on to something, but if you think can successfully get in and out of America's—"

"Strongest private military. Yeah, I know, heard it before." Tre clenched his jaw. He was adamant that this was the only solution. If the suit held the answers to harnessing the supersilver, then not only could he restore order to Quiqhin and Professor Jinx' lives, but he could perhaps learn of what happened to himself and maybe even his idol.

"It's too risky, I like the idea but it's too risky." Damia stumped herself to a stop when they reached the Claxon roads again.

"If there's anyone that can do this, it is me. If there is any time to do this, it is now. If there is anything that deserves to be stopped, it is what has just happened," Tre contended so much that his sling arm almost sprung into animation. Three solid points and two ankle rolls later, he had won her over.

"Okay!" She pushed him.

"I was going to go anyway; it would just be easier with your help. I need to know everything I can about the base. In detail too." He eyed her and watched as her expression changed from hesitation to the reliability he was so used to.

"Tomorrow meet me at High Claxon station at 3pm and I mean 3pm on the dot. I'll be driving."

"Don't even sweat it. They won't pull you over in Signot, the police here have their hands full to be bothering young ladies."

"Tre, I'll see you tomorrow, there's a lot I need to think about. Remember Claxon station at three." With that, Damia made her way toward the nearby subway that Heron Towers had conveniently arranged to be built. He had convinced Damia that infiltrating Boston's Base was a good idea, but the truth was that he had not convinced himself. His only option was to convince himself, to convince himself.

"Blue... Blue! I'm talking to you!"

"*Brother?*" echoed an excited voice.

"'I need your help."

"*I never thought I'd see the day you asked.*"

"It's here."

"What do you want? I was busy."

"I want you to teach me how you used the powers at Lancis' Traphouse. I want to know how you did everything."

CHAPTER 13

<u>Boston's Base</u>

"Brother, I know you have felt the energy too.
"The energy is with us most of the time.
It feels... right. Like we are made of, light.
I know you have felt it too. Since the supersilver bonded with us.
Its shows us, through our eyes, what it is capable of. Showing us things that shouldn't be possible.
Cutting corners.
But, while you have been trying to run away from it, I have accepted it.
How do you expect to move like me when you are still stuck in the past?
How do you expect to use it for power when you are scared of your own?
You will never be able to make more versions of yourself if you can't control it.
It is a sensitive power.
I love power.
Toying with someone's senses. Distorting how someone see's you... that's power.
No one would ever cross us if they knew what we were capable of.
I've been reflecting recently.
The energy has been teaching me new things every day.
So, I'm sorry if I haven't had time to play.
I've just been here in the dark, just absorbing.
I hope you can catch up before it is too late."

"Tre!?" came a forceful voice. When he broke out of his trance, he took in where he was again. Inside a Ford Explorer. On a hill in the city of Heaven's Conquest, readying himself to invade Sargent Boston's private military base.

"Uh yeah, I'm listening." Tre tried to focus on the task at hand, but he could not stop thinking about Blue's words. They kept repeating in his head like an insidious poem and more strangely, he had not heard a single word from him since. Even calls of his name went unheard and were rendered into empty echoes collected at the pits of his mind. If that was not enough of a distraction, Damia's serpentine shaped plan meant that Tre was overloaded with information, inside and out.

"You're listening?" Damia intoned. She now turned in his direction even more and raised one eyebrow to complete the gesture of dubiety. Today she strayed from the simplistic style of work dress and opted for layers. A lightweight, khaki parka was worn over a thick, grey, velour hoody.

"Yeah. Can you just repeat it, it was kinda' long." Tre tried to carefully herd the matter on, but Damia was two steps from her comfort zone to allow this. Given she was assisting an illegal infiltration into one of America's most prohibited territories, of which her friend was risking his livelihood.

"Repeat it, huh?"

"Yeah, if you don't mind."

"I didn't even begin!" she blasted so forcefully that the one long vein along her wide forehead made its ungraceful reappearance, "If we are doing this then I need your full attention, all of it! I don't care what is going on in your life right now, you asked for my help and I said yes. I didn't have to, but I want to. So, listen, Tre!"

"Sorry," Tre agreed quietly. Damia was in the right. He could see that the very thought of the mission had put her in a place of worry. The bags under her eyes told him that she had lost hours of sleep mulling over a plan. Today she had even adopted Tre's own signature look and subsequently, most of her brown head of hair was hidden inside a hood. Her star line of beauty spots were cut short by the hoody's neck and if this was anything to go by, they were entering the path of the unknown. If her paleness was anything to go by, Damia had never done anything like this before. If Tre's heart was anything to go by, he was about to make his biggest mistake and if the evening sky was anything to go by, this would be the Moon's brightest moment.

"Okay," she said when she saw Tre had buffered his full attention.

"First thing is first. You get in and out as soon as possible; do not spend more time in there than you need to. You are not N.O.M.A.; you can't take them on alone." Some part of Tre wanted to dispute this sentence; he could hide his pride, but the ego acknowledged no equal.

"I don't know exactly where Heron's suit is being preserved but we'd be frikkin' fools to think it's not deep in that place, heavily guarded. Be aware of security systems and do what you have to do to get it." Tre remained stone faced through this statement and Damia continued her checklist.

"That base is jacked up, but I think once you breach the main border you'll have passed the worst of it." She began sifting her view to the rear window to see the gigantic base clearly. Tre had no such troubles. Line of sight was his prisoner. It bent and transfigured without as much as a blink. It curved until perpendicular and bounced from window mirror to rear view mirror, until a clear view of Boston's Base behind him was delivered. The base truly was elephantine. Though it was a considerable distance from Heaven's Conquests hub, it had miles of clearway and equally spaced border gates that started from the outskirts of the city's motorway. The main body of the base was rectangular in design and boasted fifteen square miles between its longest sides. High, carbonfibre walls were ribboned in electrified barbwire. Carbon rifle wielding service fighters patrolled in single file, with the sole purpose to fight and fire. Freighter planes, tanks and cargo trucks were held at the banks of the base. Enough fire power to put out the fire of a freedom fighter. Huge watch towers had been implemented at every corner like a turnbuckle in a sports ring. These towers were not built to buckle either; they were the first point of recon for the base. Brick after brick had been laid and bullied into place with cemented paste. This was the foundation of the forty foot obelisks that had floodlights for shoulders and mounted rifles for a nose. If the phrase 'man builds in the image of himself' was anything to go by, then Sergeant Boston believed he was untouchable.

"You're right. The base is heavily protected. They have men on operation at every point too." The exactness of his optical control meant that Tre made these observations within a matter of seconds and due to this, Damia became the latest object of focus.

"It's amazing what, and how you can see. But I'm worried. Your eyes won't help you protect yourself." Tre's started a bout of quiet and so it took Damia one read of his stone like face before moving on.

"I thought about your question yesterday. Why I was helping you... it's because I know how it feels to do things alone. To have no support."

"Yeah?" Tre said in his obtund way.

"Yep. My folk are old fashioned. I'm from Dallas, way out in the country. Ever since I was young they never really supported my interest in science. Especially molecular physics. When I was offered a place on Signot's Brightest programme, I tell ya', that was one of the best days of my life. To know that my life goal meant something, somewhere in the world. I was around them for so long, sometimes I felt like I was wasting my high school years – chasing some dream. I love them and I miss them every day, but I had to move to Indiana for me. People like you and Quick remind me that I made the right choice to follow this path." Her head leant on her shoulder as she recalled her story and warmness swarmed over her previously pale face.

"You live by yourself?" Now that he gave it thought, Damia did not strike him as someone who was Indiana to the core and he liked this about her. A written but hidden past, something he wished applied to his life.

"I always have, in a way."

"Living by yourself in this state must be expensive, you aint a drug dealer are you?" Tre joked, in hopes of sifting some truth from her answer.

"I get by." Her return was considerably heavier, "I'm also helping you because I think you can help other people." The thought of her sentence made him frown. After all he had been through in his life, he reckoned it was himself who needed saving.

"I'm only fixing what happened. That's all. The suit could help get Quick and Professor Jinx what they lost."

"What if they can't get back what they lost? Maybe all of this happened for a reason."

"Look. I'm not a hero, okay," Tre protested strongly. Damia respectfully did not follow up.

"Good luck in there. I hope you find Heron's suit. I hope you find what you need too." Damia reached across the passenger seat and grabbed Tre into a deep hug. The type of hug you give when you do not know whether you will see someone again. The type of hug he would have given his parents to cherish, if he knew that fateful day would be their last night.

"Thank you for everything Damia," came Tre's tame reply. She could see that loss had hardened him, but she could also see something different in his eyes. Tre's eyes were like a talisman, people looked to it for meaning; today Damia saw closeness.

"Don't say it like that. You're going to go in there and when you come out, you will have exactly what you need." A face that believed in him was enough to inspire Tre to face what he believed in. He climbed out of the Ford Explorer. With only: dark jeans, his old Reebok sneakers, a long beaked cap, a black hoody and a tan backpack on him, he was ready. Living in failure scared him much more than dying in peace. It was now one teenage boy against an entire regime.

In the city of Heaven's Conquest there was considerably less pollution, so the sunset took on the shades of bourbon and while Indiana was readying itself for rest, Boston's Base grew more alive. Patrols per hour increased and more infantry were dispatched to every crevice of the bases' outer bank. Floodlights swung dangerously across the perimeter and the only thing that did not change was the weapons being full of ammunition. The private base had many eyes on watch, but it took one blink for a crouched figure to blink out of visible sight. A few minutes later, a small debacle broke out at one of the base's ammunition shacks.

"What do you mean you lost your access card?" repeated one of the loaders.

"I swear to God, I put it right there when I checked in for my shift, right there!"

"Coney, you are a f*cking moron you know that. You have probably just misplaced it again."

"No, that's why I keep it tagged to me now."

"If it's tagged to you why the hell would you leave it lying around on the crates?"

"I had blood on me from the shift I did in the city. I changed my jacket."

"You wouldn't have no damn blood on you if you just shot the loudest protester, then they would all fall into line."

"Well I didn't, okay?"

"Not even a pigeon can get into the base without an alarm being raised. So unless you are telling me that a ghost took your access card, then you prob' left it in the supplies room or something."

Like a ghost was at a work, a floating access key card pressed itself against one of the base's discreet, supply room doors. After the shutter had opened, Tre Moon stuttered back into sight. With dedicated concentration to the feat, Tre had disappeared out of sight for a record long two minutes. Long enough for him to breach the entrance (In what would otherwise be plain view), pilfer the access card of a careless member (one he spotted from a mile away) and enter the base's interior. Tre noted that the crowded room was labelled the supply room and so he placed the access card atop a crate of bullets and proceeded inward. At every corner he would turn, he had to avoid some form of personnel and each instance became closer than the last. He was not confident enough in his use of the stutter ability, to activate it at will. So, his near misses ranged from physically hiding out of sight to activating the ability so late that the onlooker stood in utter confusion until they convinced themselves that they had just experienced a form of pseudo hallucination. Like Damia had predicted, it soon became apparent that aimless wandering would not lead him to the suit. The military facility was extensive enough that he could explore it for an entire night and still not find what he was looking for. This was not time he had. The next member of personnel Tre passed had the specification 'Communications Operator' on their badge and he decided to tail him in the shadows.

After ten minutes of dedicated stalking across a series of passageways that Tre would never be able to navigate from memory alone, the member of staff reached a room suitably named 'Operation Room'. The man opened the door and held it open with an arm, but he did not enter. Tre had now bested his personal record of being invisible through the stutter and carefully slipped between the ajar door and under the stubby arms of the employee. The man had sweat patches at the site of his armpits and so Tre had to quickly become a master of breath control as well. He tried to fold as much of his six foot frame as he could, but the top of his waved hair brushed the underside of the employee's forearm as he passed. Thankfully for him, the man perceived this as an itch and pulled his sleeves down to do so. Tre let some air go in relief. The room was blitzed with an electric red glow due to the infrared light bars that were installed in the ceiling. The room was extremely short but stretched for many metres length ways. A spiderweb of communication screens were fitted to the wall. Each served a different purpose, whether it was live footage from around the base, satellite sourcing, department information charts or streaming an MMA pay per view event, each screen was active.

"Hey Kai, I'm gonna head home now. Already stayed an hour past my shift," announced the sleazy communications member.

"Cool, see you tomorrow," replied a young voice. Tre poked his head around the desk he was behind and there was only one person seated. More importantly, he looked as young as he sounded. There and then, Tre knew interrogating this boy would be his best chance of finding the suit.

"Why do you always stay late, I'm starting to think that you don't have a life." A frowsier smell came when the man laughed. Tre ducked back behind the table.

"That must mean something coming from someone who smells like they don't." The young man's head zipped left when the screen showing the mixed martial arts started roaring because of a knockout.

"Wow, you are a douche like your dad."

"Always a pleasure, Henry, close the f*@#ing door on your way out!" The young man leaned backwards gloatingly until his colleague had sealed his exit with a middle finger. When the door closed, the room fell redder still. The young man instantly followed a peculiar programme. He assured that the door was indeed locked and afterward he tapped a key on his computer's board, automatically transferring all twenty screens into a live video feed from the streets of Heaven's Conquest. His head was angled toward the corner that held wading protesters and with two fists over his mouth, he watched the action unfold with such concentration that his knee rattled underneath his desk every time a strike landed. Tre silently moved in when he convinced himself that no better opportunity would present itself. Like a satellite in the steady trajectory of station keeping, Tre slowly circled behind the lone member of the communications team, and then he extended his long limbs outward in the motion to put him in a submission. Tre's breathing became denser as the defining moment drew closer. The rattling of the desk increased more and more, until it was synonymous with Tre's beating heart. At the moment before Tre exited from his shutter, one of the screens at eye level blinked off, and in the reflection, Tre could see two dangerous, thin eyes zero in on him. Before Tre could even see, let alone believe, what happened, the communications member rotated, thrust his wheeled chair into Tre's groin and connected a menacing back hand into Tre's reappearing face. This backhand contained so much force that Tre was sent rolling to the far sides of the room as a result. His hat was unseated from his head, but the boy was on the attack before he could outstretch another hand. Tre blocked the first punch with his large palm and a crackling sound was the least of his worries because a kick was closely tailgating. When the kick found his ribs he shrieked in pain, as it felt like a regmaglypt had been left in his side. Surprisingly, the young man backed off and knelt arrogantly.

"I'm going to let you get up and defend yourself." The sides of the boy's face now cradled a thin-lipped smile. His hair was black, somewhat long and styled backwards. His eyebrows were sharp and had two fashionable slashes at the ends each one. His face was flat and visibly rosy even through the infrared of the room. His jaw was strong and protruded from his face ever so slightly and his eyes were leaf shaped and filled with delight.

"C'mon asshole." The boy planted more seeds of provocation as he weeded closer to the grounded Tre. Tre noted that the name on his personnel badge read 'Kai Boston'.

"Kai," Tre began with a grimace of pain. Upon hearing his name called, Kai Boston could not help but appreciate the modesty of his opponent.

"Not fighting back is the smart choice. But I'm gonna have to take you in; you've broken into a private military base."

"I need to know where they are keeping Aaron Heron's suit."

"Why?" Kai Boston suddenly became overly interested. His gung-ho stance dropped some.

"It can help people," Tre said, still holding his ribs.

"You know what you have to do to get it." Kai's stance lowered again. Tre reluctantly got to his feet; his healing factor had been fast at work during the respite and despite the fact that pain still resided, he had reached fighting shape.

"You picked the wrong guy, soldier." When Tre squared up with the military hard-man, Kai smiled a welcoming smile. The rematch began. Both boys battled through bruises but Tre's sprawling, brawling style could not measure up to Kai's clinical display of the martial arts. Tre's punches rarely landed because of Kai's agility. His movement was not guided by the light that Blue had used and it was hard to keep up with wave after wave of his opponent's sine wave technique. He would fall further hapless when Kai employed the coy style of hapkido. It had been five minutes into their second duel and Tre could not see how he would pass his greatest test yet, moreover, he could not see literally, because his eye had blackened from repeated damage.

"Hyaa!" grunted Kai as he leapt into the air, on the spot. The next moments seemed to get lost in the flow of time. The leap was nothing short of fantastic, as the young man was several feet in the air. With verticality at his whim, he had enough time to complete the following maneuver: he tucked himself into a ball, put a diagonal spin on his roll and finally, extended a leg outward. The tax of this incredible airtime would be the force that the leg came down with.

SMOCK!

Kai Boston's heel slammed Tre square in the face and it left him bewildered as the polarity of his vision changed completely.

"Ahh. What?" Tre gushed to himself as he staggered backward. The red room had disappeared from his view. Now, all he could see was blackness and sporadic swarms of colour. Had he lost his sense of sight? His head was thrumming notes that suggested something was amiss. He looked in the direction of Kai and saw something that completely changed his perception of what he was experiencing.

"You must not want that suit badly enough." Through his eyes, a swarm of red rushed to Kai's head. Tre had seen similar images before. He looked at the ceiling and realised, that somehow, his eyes were interpreting infrared, thermally.

"No way." Tre observed his own hands, his palm was yellow, but his fingers were all but blue canals extending from it.

"Enough of this." Kai's next attack came at the same speed; however, the heat signature of his body allowed Tre to telegram exactly what he was going to do. A frustrating sequence played out for Kai Boston, where Tre dodged every attack he had to offer and eventually the tact in his attacks went out of the window. After Tre was satisfied with toying with the arrogant teenager, he slammed him to the floor and pressed him into submission.

"I'm not here to play with you, where is the suit?!" Tre exclaimed while fighting off Kai's struggles to regain control. Tre's upper body strength proved too much for the downed martial artist however.

"I told you to wear a mask next time," Kai's crimson face managed through Tre's grip. These words were enough to single handedly snowball all of the previous tension and animosity into something much bigger: realisation.

"You, you are—" stammered Tre, who was in positive shock.

"The suit is held in the basement. In a secure suite. You need to hurry though; the base will know that something is up soon. Just look at this room." The thermal rendering of Kai's hand waved around to what, Tre suspected, was a thrashed control room.

"I have so many questions," Tre started, with the thought that Damia probably had twice as many, "why did you try and stop me? And why aren't you stopping me now?"

"Because I wanted to see if you were ready," said Kai simply. Tre finally grabbed his hat from the floor without interruption and pulled it onto his head. The burn on his hand was the coldest region of all his vision. Tre took heed of Kai's words and proceeded on his quest for the suit. Never did he think that the man he was fighting just moments ago would prove to be his greatest aid. Perhaps fires could build bridges.

"Tre Moon," Tre introduced himself huskily.

"You think I didn't already know that. N.O.M.A. – Night-Operations-Military-Apostate."

"Doesn't your father own this military?" Tre said.

"Blood is nothing to me." All it took was one command for the multiple screens to blink off. "When I 'wake up' I'll sound the alarm. That way they won't suspect I helped you. Be out of the base before they come because, trust me, they will come." Tre nodded. Even through his defective, infrared vision, Kai Boston had a heart of crimson.

Just how there was a thin line between rivalry and trust, there were also many sides to a hero.

The further Tre descended the levels of the base, the closer the walls became. With his descent came fewer and fewer distractions in the form of active patrols. At the lower ground level, the walls were closer than ever. On this level he was the only person in what was otherwise, a single absent hallway. When Tre approached the door at the corridors end he knew he had reached his end goal.

'DO NOT ENTER!'

'HAZARDOUS!'

'HIGH RISK!'

These signs were plastered over its head, accompanied with the traditional colours of warning: yellow and red. Not one of these signs could wilt his will, not after coming so far. Tre twisted the doorknob, but it would not budge. After several tries, he barged the door with such force it seemed to barge back. Out of all the outrageous ways he imagined failure could come, it did not once cross his mind that a highly secured, steel door would be his greatest obstacle. He sighed flatly. Ten dull minutes passed where he was forced to stand before something that could not be easily moved or negotiated with. Now he knew how people felt when they tried to embrace him over the years. Ten tenuous seconds and a bruised shoulder later, he remembered one invaluable lesson. The principle in physics that was universal – every form of matter was in a state and states could be changed. Nothing was truly indestructible. Not Professor Jinx's pureness. Not his own innocence. Not even Caprice's friendship. He removed his coat for the next attempt. He put a steady grasp on the doorknob again, but instead of force, he felt. When spiking light layered his arm, he knew that his mysterious powers were under his whim. His hand became increasingly heated and soon enough the door handle and the lock itself has completely dehisced in place.

"Simple enough." Tre opened what was left of the door. There was nothing stopping him from proceeding, but he stopped anyway. Behind the secured door were three equally sectioned rooms, which made up one, larger one. These rooms had no doors, windows on the walls, weapons, or any other visible features separating the last from the next. Hypothetically, Heron's suit was hoisted on the wall on the furthest side free for anyone to walk and take.

"This is a damn trap." Tre's thought could exist without judgement today, because Blue was still silent. He magnified his sight to find the smallest of inconveniences, but he did not pick up on anything. Another cautious instance played out where he removed both of his shoes and chucked them at differing distances across the room to see what would happen, but they both landed and settled like thrown objects would. Tre knew that if he was trying to throw an object as far as he could trust then he would be there for his entire life. He had to make the walk now or never. Even a decree from the President of the Unites States assuring his wellbeing could not make him feel less apprehensive about what lay ahead, and so he took his first step.

CRACK!

The howl of several sonic booms consumed the first room and cocooned Tre in place. The wind came from plates that had unfolded in the walls and by the extreme reverberation, Tre was held prisoner by the process of acoustic levitation. There were immense forces being applied to his body, so immense in fact, that his anatomy was sent into anarchy: his ear drums were tapping out from the sheer volume. He could feel his bones rattling against the surrounding tissue and he was being held in place, against his will. Over the roars of sound, he was sure he could hear a faint alarm blazing from outside the room. Heron's suit looked fainter than ever through the murkiness of the colliding waves. He struggled to move and to breathe because the power of sound knocked both momentum and oxygen from the stream. Just when Tre thought he would find no salvation from his asphyxiation, calm struck. Gently, Tre returned to the ground and an ever so smooth stream of air was available for him to breathe. When he looked around the sonic shockwaves were still blasting from the folds of the first room, however there was a thin layer between his skin and where the shockwaves would have made contact. This thin layer drowned out the noise around him and gave him peace in the chaos surrounding him. Tre did not question, he merely proceeded to the second room. Once again, his first step was met with instant reaction. In the walls of the second room, seven square folds disappeared and, in its place, seven turrets emerged from within. Without warning, each turret fired a beam of laser directly at him. Tre felt the unknowingly hot singe of the laser for a millisecond before it cooled to a warm ambience that spread to this layer around his body. Unbelievably, the point the lasers contacted his body was only the beginning of a new path, as they were redirected outward. All without leaving a single scratch on the teenager. He noticed that when he moved at certain angles the laser would refract at different angles also. Overcome with the natural urge to do so, Tre opened his hand outward and focused. Suddenly the point of the laser's redirection changed once again and he watched with his own eyes as the beams slowly crawled across his body like obedient serpents and formed at the destination of his palm. Tre admired the ball of laser; he felt the consistency in his hand and even tracked the harmless trail from the ball, across his body, the point of contact and back to the turret where it came from. It truly was a thing of xenology. Tre squeezed his fist tightly and watched as the lasers fought to free themselves from his hand. They slipped from the gaps between his fingers and shot outward, destroying the turrets that originated them in a series of destructive ricochets. Feeling both assured and astounded, he entered the third room. Like before, it took one step to change the landscape. Steel shutters were sealed around the third room, preventing him from turning back. A flap in the ceiling opened and while he expected something momentous to come next, nothing did. Tre slowly approached Heron's suit and took a minute to realise that he was face to face with his idol's greatest invention. The suit was like silk to the touch and it would have been completely invisible to the eyes was it not for the translucent polymers of what it was made from. Before Tre could hoist it from its hold, his vision flickered like it had done earlier when he fought Kai Boston. All around him he could see luminescent waves bouncing across the room. A vast influx was coming from the flap in the ceiling and most importantly, he could see these waves were slowing down and lengthening when they touched himself and Heron's suit. As he looked at his hand he would not believe his eyes if they were not showing him otherwise. He could see clean through his hand. The anatomical layers, skin and muscle, that made his hand were now translucent. Underneath he could see his bone structure in bright luminescence. If he was not versed in particle physics he might have thought that he had been reduced to a skeleton by the lasers, but his actual summary was logical and explainable. The room was a death trap. The room was being filled with gamma radiation and somehow, the suit and himself, for that matter, were capable of taking enough energy from the gamma waves to transform them into X-rays. How he could see waves that were not within a human's range of sight, or better yet, how he was still alive from radiation was a question for later. With his skeletal looking hand, Tre took the suit from the wall.

"So, he's definitely in there?"

"Yep. After Henry clocked out of communications that's when he attacked me."

"How'd this person just sneak up on you like that?"

"Dunno, just happened."

"Maybe if you spent less time being a communications operator and became a fighting soldier, that wouldn't have happened to you."

"You'd like that wouldn't you?"

"Like it? As my son, I expect it." After these words, Kai dismissed himself from the conversation, leaving just Sergeant Boston in front of the base's main entrance. Sergeant Boston was a tall, Caucasian, brawny man with a squared head and an even more square speaking pattern. He did not have Kai's oriental eyes but instead wide, blood-shot ones. His face was carpeted with a prickly, trench qualified stubble. He had bladed scars over his chest and forearm but his current attire of a pink, flossy dressing gown showed that this evening, the last thing he was prepared for was a battle.

"Oi you!" the Sergeant barked at a passing guard.

"Y-yes sir," the youngster in infantry uniform responded immediately.

"Make sure that every single exit from this base is locked and secured, with at least two men surrounding it. And check with the technicians that the lights in the base are lined up, to direct this sneaky f*cker right to this exit," Sergeant Boston specified as he put a pricked finger into a palm for every figurative exclamation mark that his sentence would have contained.

"Sir, you asked me to do those things just twenty minutes ago. They are all secured," confirmed the soldier at question.

"Did I ask if I asked you to do it before?" The Sergeant hovered over the soldier now.

"Err, could you repeat that please—"

"GO AND RUN THE CHECK AGAIN BEFORE I KICK YOUR GODDAMN!" the Sergeant exploded. He attempted to boot the soldier as he scuttled to his duty, but another man stepped into his attentions. In one smooth motion he also pulled out a packet of cigars.

"Have a smoke, Serge, you are going to scare our new recruits away again." The man had grey, slicked back hair and a grey moustache. His uniform was rather presidential compared to the standard infantry uniform. His epaulette had enough badges on it to justify the senior air about him and his name badge revealed that he was one of Boston's army's Lieutenants; 'Lieutenant, Major Rashkin'.

"What I say goes, those little bastards are gonna learn the hard way. Around here if you aint serving you aint earning." Sergeant Boston took a pull of the robusto cigar, in which all fairness to the Lieutenant, did seem to mellow the fireball that seemed to dictate all of the sergeant's actions.

"Also, sir. I know family matters are none of my business—"

"You got that damn right," Sergeant Boston muscled in.

"But maybe you should give Kai some credit. Since he joined the Communications department our intelligence division has grown the most," Lieutenant Rashkin finished. The sergeant faced his Lieutenant head on, giving him an unobstructed seat for his next words.

"I built this entire regime. Me. And I don't care what anyone tells me about statistics, figures, money. I don't give a f*ck. That boy is a disappointment." After two pulls, Sergeant Boston discarded a perfectly good cigar.

"Sergeant! That's him! That's the intruder!" From one of the watchtowers, a voice amplified by a megaphone alerted the base. In one impressive instance that was a culmination of training, practice, protocol and fear of the Sergeant's reprimand, the base seemed to spring into motion. A dozen armoured trucks pulled up behind the Sergeant and the Lieutenant. Soldiers holding a range of weapons hopped out and assumed shooting stances. Extra infantry rolled at the notice of a moment and even a pair of attack helicopters secured the skies. All four floodlights swung to the main entrance of Boston's Base, revealing a tall, dark skinned teenager with only a backpack and a hat. As soon as the target was identified by the floodlights a flock of red dots followed soon after and tagged the target on the places that would disable him from escape, namely, the legs, heart and face.

"It's just a kid? I can't believe this."

"How on earth did this runt get into the base at peak hours?"

"He hasn't even got a weapon?"

"Biggest mistake of this kid's life. Might as well give his life to the Sergeant now."

The Sergeant looked amused for the most part. He flapped a hand in the air, which was apparently a signal for the snipers because the red dots fell on command. Amongst the tens upon tens of bodies, Tre could make out the figure of Kai Boston in the crowd. Unlike when they met in the communications room, he now looked tense.

"Rash are you seeing this?" Sergeant Boston gave a smoky laugh.

"I can indeed, sir," the Lieutenant replied promptly.

"A worm."

"I think it would be unethical to shoot down a boy, even if he is trespassing."

"Well we'll shoot him if he runs, but you're right." The Sergeant saw reason for the first time that night, "Besides at this army, we eat worms." Boston's eyes lit up with malice.

"Are you going to run, boy?" the Lieutenant asked.

"No," Tre replied as he shielded his face. The combined strength of the floodlight made it incredibly bright. Also, as usual, he did not want anybody to see his face.

"You coloured folk can run fast that's for sure. But nobody is gonna outrun a fifty calibre round, and that's a guarantee," mocked Sergeant Boston, to the amusement of his followers. From the skies to the ground, Sergeant Boston had every angle covered. No improvised plan he could think of lead him to any other fate than death or imprisonment. Tre cursed under his breath.

"Before we take you in there's one thing you need to know about Indiana. You don't f*#k with the big dogs. You don't f*#k with the Bulgarians, you don't f*#k with Heron Institute and we may be a bit outta town, but you do not f*#k with Boston's Base either." Boston had caught his mouse in the cheese trap. On Tre's side however, these words may have had more weight about them, if he could ignore the feeling that he was becoming progressively lighter.

"He's a quiet one," the Lieutenant pointed out.

"I don't blame him," the Sergeant said. "Any last words, before we take you in?"

"Yeah," Tre said.

"Well? We aint got all day. I've got two women I need to get back to." Boston filled in the origins of his pink gown. The unmistakable look of dislike was now visible on Kai's face.

"Your base aint sh!t." In a spectacular moment that could never face decadence and that would be forever present in the memories of those present, an unworldly sight unfolded. A true parallax. The very spotlight that Tre was beamed under seemed to instigate a strange phenomenon around him, wisps of light came and for a moment, he glowed brighter than any star that night. Another moment later, Tre had burst from his very position into the air and through the sky at untraceable speeds. A line of heads was forced to watch as the boy disappeared into the night sky. Their only remembrance was a line of light that stretched for miles in the direction of Signot.

"Spectacular." The Lieutenant could not help but comment until he saw Sergeant Boston's face become pinker than the ridiculous dressing gown he wore.

"Everybody back to position, let's go now!" Lieutenant Rashkin dismissed himself. Kai could not comprehend what he had just seen, but apart from seeing his father humiliated in front of his entire cavalry he knew he had witnessed something special. The beginning of the legend of Tre Moon.

CHAPTER 14

<u>The Electromagnetic Spectrum</u>

Heron's suit being stolen from Boston's Base was the biggest scandal in many years for the state of Indiana. The news was big enough to reinvigorate the conspiracy theories of past, as to why he went missing in the first place. It was also big enough to further obfuscate Tre Moon's mysterious case from 2008. Breaching the private army's perimeter was unheard of, let alone surviving the high security room that was designed to bring death to any intruder. Sergeant Boston and his regime, without question, had only grown since their inception but upon losing Heron's legendary suit they experienced their first public exorcism. Signorina Baelel spoke out against them and consequently, ended their prosperous relationship with Heron Institute. In a state that held Aaron Heron as a beloved hero, Boston's army suffered a broken public image. Protests that had previously infested Heaven's Conquest died out. For a regime that promised to fix so many of the state's problems, they now found themselves in an irreparable state. Sergeant Boston's hope of becoming the nation's symbol of safety was crushed and it took the work of one highly pondered individual, to turn a once feared army, into an unreliable non-factor on the outskirts of Heaven. The breacher remained unnamed and Sergeant Boston himself could not be reached for comment. Tre Moon delivered Heron's suit to the Quarters of Isles that very same night for study. Against all doubts, he made it out alive. Against all odds, he even gained an ally. After conquering Boston's Base in the face of danger and failed salvation, Tre had gained a new strength. The hope of better days. He remembered Damia's notion that the powers were given to him for a reason, and the more he reflected on this, the more he committed himself to the idea. What was the likelihood that a rare sample of altered silver could affix itself to him and change his very biology... the same chance that he would be born to share a mind with another being that would ultimately murder his parents? From the waters rose a whole plateau of understanding and from that, the island of loneliness he had inhabited since young did not seem so small anymore. From incarceration between four walls to the ability to soar to the heights of free fall.

From dependence on drugs to others depending on him. From having years' worth of turmoil to being able to heal wounds within a matter of seconds. Lessons had transformed into blessings and if anything was a testament that hope could exist even in the most arid of circumstances, he was the living, breathing proof. No matter how deep the hole was, there was light to be salvaged. He would not give up on Caprice. He would not give up on the city of Signot. Blue appeared to have given up on him.

While Heaven's Conquest was under heavy investigation for the suspect of the missing suit, its sister city, Signot, was undergoing changes of its own. The fire of protest that dewed in Heaven's Conquest had now reignited in the beach borough of Hetashi. The rallies opposed industrialization of the beach borough after Isaac Isles had announced to expand his oil industry by the coast. On any given day you would see the streets alive with cries to save water supplies and marine life. To add to that, many of the miscellaneous shops mapped across the region made the less than generous acquaintance of gentrification. New investors invaded, pollinating every field of business and forced existing owners either to match or be made unfit to lead in the new and fast, economic climate. Tre saw this shift in the city's infrastructure when he passed his local miscellaneous shop on the way to an impromptu AIM meeting. Outside the convenience store were roughly a dozen cardboard boxes, in the size of the moving variety, and hoops of rope he assumed were brought to hold them together. Retro, was his first thought upon seeing the ropes. The word, retro, being a near fitting word for Emily, was his second. Tre stepped between the boxes and into the small store and as he looked around, it looked more bare than usual.

"Hello?" Tre called when he saw nobody at the store's counter, moreover, his corner-curling optics once again failed to find anybody between the three aisles the store contained. It was not too long before Emily Di Pinto burst in from the door leading to the backroom. She was completely drenched to the point it looked like she had been attending to a particularly unruly water leakage.

"You okay?" amusement managed to bubble its way to his surface.

"Yeah, why wouldn't I be?" Emily said through heavy breaths.

"You are soaking wet," Tre pointed out despite the fact that he felt it was quite obvious.

"Ah, yes, yes." Emily removed her ribbed jumper that was dripping the most and then gave a toothy smile as if this had solved the problem. Apart from the fact that a thin white t-shirt was stuck to her torso and that her attention seemed to be stuck with whatever she was previously doing, something did not stick.

"You buying something?" Emily asked as she wrung the water from her jumper to the shop floor; either disregarding or unaware of the hazard a wet floor may cause.

"What were you doing in there?" Tre noticed that a puddle of water was slowly crawling its way from the backroom to the shop floor. Typically, his bending vision would have allowed him to see under the small crack between the door and floor, but the aqueous body threw his sights into multifarious directions, too many that a clear image could not be formed.

"Having a bath as you would say." A hearty laugh punctuated her words and Tre was immediately stripped of his suspicion. Emily Di Pinto was absent of any of the normal emotions his schemas had scripted; he did not see humiliation, lies nor tameness. Despite the fact she was proudly doused, the truth was cut and dried. Emily Di Pinto was indeed a free spirit.

"I saw the boxes outside. I was gonna ask if you needed help, but clearly you have bigger problems," Tre said.

"Problems? There's been none, otherwise I would have called, remember?" Her coral pink eyes lined him up. Tre huffed.

"So, I heard about them shutting all of the miscellaneous shops down."

"That's what they're saying."

"How long you got to move?"

"A month, probably less."

"I'm sorry. It's not right that they are kicking everyone out."

"I'm not sorry. I'm happy."

"Why?"

"Life itself is a living thing like us. Opportunities are like breaths; they must always begin and end. I enjoyed being here. It was different for me, but a new breath of life awaits."

"Are you sure you're from Indiana?" Was the first response that came to Tre. How her ocean of optimism ran concurrent to her faltering situation was beyond him.

"Yes, young boy." Like she had done on their previous encounter, Emily broke from their conversation and progressed behind to the counter, dripping water carelessly as she stepped. "Did you manage to get that camera you were looking for?"

"Camera?"

"I was fiddling around in the back and I found the old owner's stash. There was a note to reserve a camera for Tre Moon."

"Someone got it first," Tre replied meekly. When he remembered Caprice's declaration of love for Lancis, his chest tightened some.

"Ah," the lax store owner made out through a mouth of vinegar greens. She had pulled out the container and the surrounding area was not just wet, but now smelt highly alkaline.

"Do you want to try some?" She offered when she caught him eyeing the dish.

"I am not even going to ask what it is." Tre chose not to vocalise his true aversion.

"You could do by trying something new once in a while. A smile would be a good start." Emily hurled a side of her wet curls behind her back because it still fell at a length to interfere with her meal. Like before, Tre saw the mysterious slashes on the sides of her neck, but he had a clearer view this time. The scars came thrice and were lined one atop another. They were also red, blotchy and raw in appearance, giving Tre the distinct impression that she had endured and survived a horrific accident of some sort.

"If you don't mind me asking... what happened to your neck?" Tre hesitated.

"Oh, those," Emily shuffled nervously and pruned her hair back in front of her shoulder, "I was born with them." Given the breezy coolness she had exuded prior, Emily Di Pinto's reaction was indeed out of the norm. The change from open-minded conversation to closed body language was telling, and Tre could not shake the small moment of symmetry he had seen. If one was to substitute her hair for his hood, both equated to trying to hide something deeper than the surface.

"Emily, I gotta go for a check-up." He excused himself with a slight raise of his faux, casted arm.

"It's still not better?" Emily said.

"It's had some complications," Tre started, "I'll see you around." Before he left Emily and himself shared a look of farewell, of which Tre held his trademark stony expression until she finally gave in.

"If there's any trouble I will call." She forfeited quite quickly because he did not appear to be caving in anytime soon, "Now either help me mop this floor or leave here."

"Good luck." Tre sealed his exit. When the tall teenager finally left the premises, Emily placed four tender fingers to one side of her neck. After the first, she placed a hand to the other side of her neck, revealing another stripe of identical scars. Shortly after, she skipped toward the backroom door and called through it.

"It's okay, the customer is gone now. Hello? Hello?" She swung the door wide open only to find an empty backroom: a mop and bucket, a fire extinguisher, a sink and locker cabinet. Emily closed her amaranth coloured eyes. Miraculously, the entire backroom was completely dry and even the swarming puddle of water that had been emerging from under the door, was now nowhere to be seen. Emily returned to the main store, pulled on her drenched jumper (which was now the wettest aspect of the store), pulled herself atop the counter and lay backwards across it. Horizontally, her straight jawline stood like two towers and her damp hair, that was now sprawled across the counter, lay like many tentacles. Her scars could be seen freely. And so, Emily Di Pinto would lay carelessly supine, replaying the moments before Tre's interruption in her mind.

"I think we have finally figured out your powers, Tre. We've been studying this suit and it is nothing like we have ever seen." Damia could not help but rise to a jittery stand as she greeted Tre's arrival at the AIM meeting room. Tre was not sure whether it was a product of Quiqhin's financial reach, or the extensive testing that they had to carry out, but the discreet room was now decked out with almost twice the number of computers and scanning equipment. The most notable upgrade was the tall glass cylinder that was constructed in the middle of the room, which held Aaron Heron's sun suit.

"This place looks... different." Tre did not know if he was more impressed with Damia's statement, the upgrade to the room, or the alacrity of the upgrade's implementation.

"I know you like it. I like it." Quick swaggered over and gave Tre an Indiana style handshake.

"Where you been? You okay, man?" Tre asked.

"Do I look okay?" Quick smiled. Everything about the Londoner suggested that he had been on holiday; from his Arabian tan to his jersey grey shorts. He had black, designer shades and a cap on too. He also donned a new forearm tattoo that depicted a formula one racing track eventually turn into the head of a serpent. The tattoo was immaculately done (money could do that) but the drastic change, like the AIM room itself, alerted Tre that he was trying to prove a point.

"No. You look like you are going through a mid-life crisis," Tre said. Damia had to scupper a laugh into her hand.

"I've been vacationing in Miami, man. Brought my boys over from home and lived life. I'm actually glad I was kicked out of uni cos the best thing has happened to me because of it."

"What?" said Tre and Damia in unison.

"My father has let me head 'Isles Oils' in Signot." Quick removed his shades to emphasise the glory of his statement and the moment could have gone according to the script in his head if he did not receive a whooping blow to the arm by the third AIM member.

"OUCH! What was that for you weirdo?"

"You are the head of Isaac Oils in Signot now and you are still behind it? If the move to the coast happens, do you know how much sea life will suffer?" Damia's passion bested even Quick's naturally loud tone.

"Don't start again with these environmental protests, leave that in Heaven's Conquest."

"What about the sea life!?"

"I don't care about the sea life. I'm probably having lobster for dinner today luv – OUCH!" His mockery was met with another bruise to the arm. Damia was frail in size but she definitely packed a punch.

"If you let the move happen I will never forgive you, Quiqhin." Damia now traded physicality for iniquity.

"I go Mosque every week that is forgiveness enough." Quick's comebacks proved impervious to both.

"What were you saying, Damia, you figured out my powers?" Tre made a timely cut into the incoming argument; because if the meeting had become further side-tracked his anticipation might have eaten him alive.

"Oh yeah," Damia took a breath, before mouthing to Quick - 'We are talking after.'

"Before Quick came back I was running industrial CT and thermography scans on the suit and it contains some of the colloidal supersilver that Professor Jinx had. The same sample that caused your powers. It's pretty much made of the stuff. Jinx was right, supersilver is unstable it needs to bind to something in order to normalise. I've tried all kinds of tests and the supersilver won't un-bond. It is embedded into the suit. I fear that it may be irreversibly bonded to you too. I don't know how it could bond to a human but hey... we don't have all the answers. Not yet anyway."

"I guess only Heron would know," Tre said, "and he is—"

"Missing," Damia pieced together, "this suit was designed for his photodermatitis. It reflects light completely. This was our first clue to what your powers may be."

"You have the power to alter the way light waves reflect off of your body," Quick stated, "think about it, mate, it makes sense. How else could you see around a corner unless the light was curving?"

"You can see more in the dark because your eyes are reflecting the waves in enough directions for you to see more things." Damia pushed on.

"Also, that little fire trick with your hand. We solved that too," Quick said.

"I solved," Damia corrected him.

"She solved," Quick fixed his words, "when enough light is collected it creates more energy of course. And more energy causes heat. If you had the right kind of concentration of light you could even change that heat into a laser beam because they are, theoretically, made of rays of light."

"Because the suit can change the way light waves move, they can also change the speed at which it reaches the eyes of others. In other words, making yourself appear closer or further than you really are. Also, when you told me about what happened at Boston's Base I could not figure out how you could possibly disappear that fast. It annoyed me, so I did some research. It turns out that there is a process called photosailing. Satellites in space use this to increase the speed they move in the vacuum, by using the energy of reflected light particles for momentum. It only increases the speed of the satellite slightly, but in theory if one was to increase the efficiency of photons reflected... you could increase speed or power," Damia concluded. The rate that these revelations came at Tre made the foundation of his understanding of science and even life, crumble before him. Fantastical theories laced with logic. From the grounds that his AIM colleagues had already established, Tre applied his extended understanding of particle physics, to explain some of the other abilities he had experienced more recently.

"I don't think it is restricted to just light," Tre continued the thinkers' café and Damia and Quick reached for their figurative tea.

"How so?" Damia inquired.

"You can do more things? Why couldn't I get these powers," Quick joked.

"Certain things that happened inside Boston's Base have led me to believe that these reflective powers, allow me to also control the other frequencies on the electromagnetic spectrum. I was able to see infrared waves. I was also able to slow down gamma waves to the frequency of x-ray waves, and I say this because I saw my skeleton through my hand." When Tre had finished his speculation, both Damia and Quick looked positively stunned.

"I've never heard you speak so intelligently Tre. Or even that much to be honest," Damia admitted.

"Does that mean you won't be able to tan because you do know that means you reflect UV light?" Quick pondered.

"I don't tan," Tre said shortly, ending what was a short lived demonstration of his acquired acumen.

"What do we do with the suit now then?" Tre watched the translucent suit through the cylinder.

"Sell it," Quick said.

"Keep it." Damia gave Tre a telling look, "We need someone to protect it, until we can figure a way to un-bond that supersilver."

"I don't think there is anywhere better than this secret room," Tre pointed out, to which Quick flicked his shades back down in flatter.

"We need someone to protect us... no more hoods." Damia gently lifted Tre's hood from his head. The waves in his hair were stronger than ever and the absences of bags under his eyes were a product of the estranged battle with Dissociative Identity Disorder having recently being won.

"Quick let's give him a minute." Damia lead the way out.

"If the suit doesn't fit, there's a tailor on the lower ground floor," Quick whispered to Tre as he passed.

Tre went to the room's latrine to begin the routine. The suit was light to the hand just like he remembered, but unlike at Boston's Base, he had all the time in the world to process the otherworldly effects that occurred when he touched it. Upon contact with his skin, the translucent material of the suit would ripple like waves in the water. This strange seismic effect only multiplied when he put it on and he watched as polymorphic effects took hold. The translucence in the suit faded out and was replaced with reflective shards that layered its surface, lining his arms, chest, legs and neck. These shards were purely visual, however, they shifted between each other like concentrated particles in a telescope. Tre noticed that the reflective qualities in the suit were an extension of his impulses. He played with the suit's translucent grading some until he decided that the metamorphic mirror effect agreed with his metaperception the most. On the suits mask, he noticed that a chandelier of shards was made where his eyes would be and the shards would shrivel or enlarge depending on how he magnified or focused his sight. The shards on the suit would also bend inward to help his eyes curve the light, aiding for near three-hundred-and-sixty degree vision. The suit was a physical extension of his powers and with it on; he felt the connection to the electromagnetic spectrum. The suit was his translator. Each wavelength on the spectrum had its own language and the fact that Tre, as a human, was only accustomed to visible light, had made his interactions with the other wavelengths mystifying. Radio, Microwave, Infrared, Violet, Ultraviolet, X-ray and Gamma. They all were all present in some capacity. They all could be utilised.

With Heron's altered sun suit on, he walked to over to the large mirror by the sink. However, what he saw follow him into the mirror took his breath away. Not in the magnificent way like what he had just learnt, but in a cold, looming fashion. His own reflection in the mirror was exactly the same but instead of the mesmeric, mirroring suit that he had created; his reflection was fitted with a blackened suit. The reflections in the black shards could just about be seen through the dark, distorted effects it made. The reflection's eyes were the only aspect that resembled the mirror suit he was currently wearing. Tre looked around sharply because he could not believe what he was seeing was possible. The reflection mimicked every move he did, slow, fast and otherwise. Seconds after convincing himself that what he was seeing was another episode of his amateur understanding of the spectrum, he was proven wrong. The reflection committed blasphemy upon the laws of nature and stopped in place. With his reflection now out of sync, his heart began to sink. His eyes told him something was amiss, his mind told him his eyes were playing tricks, fear told his mind to fix his vision, but the reflection had a message of its own:

'tius eht rof sknaht'

Were the words scraped into the centre of the mirror with one long pointed finger. Afterward, Tre's reflection gave a faceless stare and walked out of view. His reflection was nowhere to be seen and Tre was left to study a perfectly empty mirror. No matter how many times he re-entered the view or took off his own suit, his reflection would not return. Since the day his parents were murdered he had prayed to become just a trace, but now that the prayer was partially fulfilled, he felt like half of himself. He grabbed a handful of his face to make sure he was not a ghost, but this was hardly consolation. He could not help but feel like he was a victim of interjection and so the blues of independence settled in. Tre Moon: the man with no reflection.

CHAPTER 15

<u>The Man With No Reflection</u>

"How are you doing, Tre?"

"I've been worse."

"Are you still taking drugs?"

"I don't do that anymore."

"Right... I only ask because over the past five years, not once have you scheduled a session outside of the one per month obligation."

"I know."

"Is there anything on your mind? Caprice?"

"To be honest, no. Haven't seen her for two weeks. She hasn't been at the apartment."

"I know. She's not been here at home either."

"Where is she?! Has she left the city already?"

"Still here, said she needs 'space', so she's been staying with my sister who I don't talk to. Probably to get to me."

"You should appreciate all the family you have, Miss Hill."

"You're right, Tre. So right, but in this situation, it is a bit more complicated than that."

"All of the family I have left cut me out of their life because they think I was responsible for my parents' murders. I can't explain or prove otherwise. That is complication."

"Hm. Something is bothering you?"

"I want to know everything about my disorder."

The monthly instalment of de ja vu was due and it might have settled into a routine session if the setting was not so oppugning to the norm. Tre and Edith Hill had taken their usual seats in her towering office as counsel and counsellor, but it was clear that he had come to seek rather than to share. In his acute state, his hands were clutched together and even his hood was removed; today, nothing would go over his head.

"I've told you many times about it," Professor Hill said.

"Tell me again... please." The unexplainable gravity of nerves clutched Tre's hands even tighter.

"DID is present in all races but is more common in American children. Usually it is caused by trauma occurring at less than nine years of age. Dissociative patients who are not appropriately treated or who attempt to treat themselves tend to get worse and it then becomes one of the most difficult psychiatric conditions to treat." Edith listed each point from memory.

"More..."

"The average number of alternate personalities a person with DID has is between eight and thirteen. The other identities can periodically control the person's behaviour and have their own unique way of viewing and understanding the world. If DID is left untreated it can lead to further abuse – Tre. Why are you making me say this?"

"What else?"

"Why are you making me say this?!" Edith repeated, at a louder volume this time.

"I can't say," Tre said. The serene surroundings could not let Tre release his darkest fears despite having shared years of intimate, psychological discussions in the very same room. The truth was his life had changed so expeditiously over the past months that not even the principles of the counselling room could cater to what he was going through. For him to open up about his current onus would be the equivalent of bringing the rendition of her volcano-painted canvas to life. The origami sculptures above their heads were rendered simple if they were compared to the folds and knots that Edith observed in Tre.

"I don't know what you are going through, but drugs are not the answer and ignoring it is not the answer. You must fight and own the life that you have been given. The life that we have fought so hard to get back for you." For once her pen was pendent and the only thing that was written, was faith in her face. Tre looked up warmly at his saviour.

"Let me tell you something, kiddo." Edith Hill crossed one leg over the other before continuing, "I remember way back when I was around your age, I was studying and working to become a Professor. One of the most stressful and expensive routes you can take is being a Professor, but I did it. They told me because I was from the drug era of Signot I was not going to make it. Then they said because I had dyscalculia I wouldn't make it far. After that, they told me that because I didn't have money I would never be able to afford the route anyway. When I had Caprice, I was apparently a done deal. Then her father left me to raise her by myself, I could never be a Professor at this point. That's what they said. I am a product of everything that I have been through and we all have our own challenges, but if you know who you want to become... you can always rise above the things holding you back.

When the incident in two thousand and three happened. People saw a juvenile. They saw a crazed, murderous kid who deserved to be locked away for the rest of his life, but I saw me. Someone with something to prove. You still do. You are you, Tre, you always have been. It may sound impossible but once you truly separate your life from the other identity that is when you will truly realise this. Don't lose yourself to the thought that it was your fault."

Edith spoke pained words as if she longed to borrow Tre her perspective for one session. Her desperate frown did not leave her face when Tre replied.

"Edith, if I told you I don't think I was suffering from Dissociative Identity Disorder, what would you say?"

"I'd ask you to read the diagnosis again," she said.

"And if I told you that what I am going through is something that psychology, or even science cannot currently explain?"

"Then I would ask this pioneer to happily create this new field of thought," came the second spate of selective sarcasm.

"What would you say if I told you that avenging my parents is the only thing I can think about lately?" The Tre Moon Edith knew was always sedated and laidback in manner, but the Tre she saw before herself was composed of conviction and vindication, an indication that his afflictions of old had mounted tenfold.

"Tre, what you are doing is called projecting. It is perfectly normal for suppressed emotions to surface sometimes but that is why I'm here to talk if you need."

"I hate him; I hate him so much..." Tre's words were so enveloped in despise, Edith Hill could not recognise who was speaking.

"Tre? Are you still there." Edith became quite tense in her chair.

"It's me. You don't have to worry about that,"

"Yes, I do," Edith retorted in a motherly tone, "no matter what happens around you, every day that you are given to walk this earth, you need to be able to look in the mirror and be proud of the person that stares back at you. The day you can't look yourself in the mirror is when you know you've become something you weren't before," Edith said. According to her standards he was now a completely different person and this explained the hate that had found refuge in his heart since the day he lost his reflection. For him, a reflection was now a thing of the past, a bare reminder of who he used to be. It was now an eerie message that he had ascended the boundaries of rationality but also escaped the reach of conclusions such as the diagnosis of Dissociative Identity Disorder. His reflection in the mirror was now a fitting figure of speech for how empty he felt inside. Since the loss of his reflection, he now knew there was no such thing as perfection, and this is where he found acceptance in vengeance. Because with every mirror he found bare, spelt that his parent's killer was out there.

"What is Blue like?" Tre asked.

"Who is Blue?"

"The other voice. You have spoken to him a lot right, to keep notes?" Tre pressed at a dangerous pace. Edith shuffled her set of notes hesitantly.

"Blue huh? He is very hateful, extremely hateful and he has no remorse for others. That is why he did what he did to your parents. He hates everyone who has tried to keep him where he belongs, including me of course. He believes he is entitled to do whatever he wants because he has never been taught what was right. Naturally, this other personality has never received affection or acknowledgment a day in his life and that is why he is a murderous sociopath. There's certain chemistry in psychology that is destined to lead to disaster. Despite everything I had just said, he has convinced himself that he loves you, Tre. To him, you're brothers—"

"Hey Mum, I—" Mid-explanation, the door to the office swung wide open and it was none other than Caprice who stood before them. The sight of his best friend made Tre drop his intensive session of research altogether. Professor Hill's eyes flickered between her daughter and Tre because both seemed to have become embroiled in the silent act of unsettlement.

"Can you two watch the office while I make a call outside?" Miss Hill's workplace discourse was so convincing a neutral onlooker would presume the call absolutely had to be made. When Edith Hill wedged herself from the room, the tension was thick.

"Hey," Caprice started.

"Yo."

"Can I?" Caprice motioned to the bean bag next to him.

"Sure."

She brought the ends of her windbreaker together and pinned them down with her folded arms; afterward, she half-heartedly made her way to the bean bag seat next to him. Caprice over-estimated the firmness of the bloated bag, because she shot downward when she sat, sending her frilly, alabaster curls flying about. The silliness of the moment was enough to muster a brief, shrill scream and bubble both parties to the point they could not deny their adlubescence.

"I've missed you Tre-Tre." She sighed, her expression told him that she had been holding the feeling since their last meet. More importantly, to him, her face was healed from the black eye she had suffered at the hands of Lancis, who was still locked away.

"Where have—"

"Say it back!"

"—you been?"

"Say it." Tre had to weave his question between her demands of reciprocated affection, but he had no doubts that this was the Caprice he had missed so dearly as of recent.

"I've been away. I needed to have some space."

"That makes two of us," Tre said.

"Your arm is still in that sling huh?" She ran a hand over the wrapped cast.

"It should be better soon," he played along, "I'm sorry about what happened the other night."

"Me too, but I meant it." Her hazel eyes watched the surface of his stolid face when she broke the mood. Thankfully for his pride, the only thing that broke was their eye contact.

"I didn't." Tre looked to the floor because only that was the only place that could hold any expectations he had left.

"I'm still going New York." Unlike Tre, Caprice kept a level in her face.

"I don't get it. Why Cap?"

"Because I need a new scene. A new life."

"Your life is here though. What about your family and Lancis, he's still here."

"I don't give a damn about him... he left me," she shot back, and her curls flared like leucitic pythons. The fact Lancis' name made her central features (namely her high definition eyebrows and rounded lips) burrowed into a lour, was quite surprising given her confession of love last time out.

"Oh." Tre did not know whether this new information made him feel better about her decision or not. "Listen, I'm not telling you what to do but I need you to stay in Signot, until I say it's safe."

"You need me to stay in Signot? My future job is in New York! Do you know how selfish you sound?" The okna starkmark sunroof brimmed with brightness and the cyclonic range of colours in the room was brought to life. The red of rage being one of them. Caprice was now far removed from the initial joy she had upon seeing him.

"It's for your own good." Unlike their last clash, Tre was able to keep his rebut to a minimum, "There is a possibility that you might be in danger soon."

"This is Signot, everyone is in danger. Heck, I was approached by the Bolivian drug members last week, asking who destroyed their drug house."

"Did they hurt you?"

"No. But I'm sure they will hurt the person who did it."

"Do you remember who you—"

"Why might I be in danger, Tre?" Caprice said over him. There was a long pause where Tre considered the route of honesty; a noble road but also an endless one. If he told her of the origin of his powers and what he had been through since, the questions would not end. More importantly, he would compromise her beyond the boundaries of a turbulent friendship. The Bolivian drug conglomerate and Boston's army were both eager to learn of his identity and if this happened, Caprice was a target by affiliation. The second road was determined to be much shorter and this was because it was the one he took most often. A brooding silence.

"You know, when Mum told me that she was going to convince the judge to let you get your help in here, I was so happy. I made every single one of these origami's that are hanging from the ceiling, just to make the room look nice for when you came home. I didn't know if you were going to come home, but I did it anyway. In future, I advise you to show someone how you feel before there's a chance you could lose them." Caprice had a canary complexion and left him with weary words to reflect on. Still masking her body with her oversized windbreaker, she made to leave.

"Another point of advice would be to tell a girl that you want her to stay instead of making up bad excuses like they might be in danger." Caprice watched her childhood friend in anticipation of a reaction, but his face did not even move a fraction. Even after some seconds of expecting perhaps a confession, it was evident that Tre had more prevalent thoughts. Though he was faced away from her, his bending vision allowed him to see the stages she went through before leaving: hope, disappointment and acceptance.

"I got the internship. I'm leaving in two weeks." With their friendship perhaps more tattered than before, her last words ended the short lived encore.

CHAPTER 16

2102 Noom Eulb Fo Esac Suoiretsym Eht

As if fate itself had observed Tre Moon's warning of danger, a streak of blood curdling murders was reported the following week. The first report from Signot's Police Department included the massacre of numerous individuals; the supposed files of the victims bore no connection besides attending juvenile prison at some point in their lives. The second report caught a gruesome scene of Judge Valentine bludgeoned to death in his own supreme court and the third, and perhaps most baffling for the forensics, was the murder of Lancis Green in his prison cell. The imprisoned gang member endured multiple stab wounds and the key weapon of evidence was seemingly strewed from existence. The murderer had concluded his act by seeing to it that Lancis had both eyeballs skewered from his skull. This prison killing somehow met the criteria of being spiteful, unsightly and unlikely. The murder was undoubtedly committed by the hands of another, but the twenty-four hour security footage could not account for this as not a single person could be seen entering or leaving Lancis' cell on the day of his murder. In fact, the confounding similarity in the three cases was the evanescence of every piece of crucial evidence. Every testimony that was held did not report acrimony, however, they did mention seeing a figure in black shortly before. This blackened truth would come to light when a direct picture of the perpetrator was captured; it wore a black, augmented version of Heron's infamous suit and could be seen vanishing from sight. A direct match. These small details eventually contributed to the bigger picture and so investigations were quick to link the figure in the black suit directly to the attack on Boston's Base. Regional coverage deemed that Signot was under threat from a supernatural force. The creepy, brief footage of the figure of black would continue to haunt the news headlines throughout the week and thus it was given the name, Spectre.

Tre had remained homebound for the majority of that week. He was on standby for new developments of the figure in the black suit. It was also a period of discovery, because he came to terms with things he had never had to think about before, for example, feeling conflicted on different levels about the murders that had taken place. Having lived in Signot all his life, the murders were the latest in the copious tide that had swept the city for the last two decades. Then again, as of recent, the horrific fashion the killings were committed made many take stand or hide in fear. His presence at home was perhaps an admission for the latter. If one could see a level below to his feelings, they would see that Tre felt glee to a moderate degree. Lancis Green was a misogynistic, woman beater and a catalyst of Signot's growing drug trade. He was part of the twisted sample of persons that would prosper in a pessimistic prognosis; one could say it was divine justice that he would not see the fruits of his felony. When it came to Judge Valentine's death, Tre held a personal yet distanced grudge. He found it ironic that a man, who wielded the iron fist of the law, would receive the little mercy he had so rarely showed over the course of his career. Despite the rage, wrongdoings and the right to feel how he did, he knew the murders had to stop. His conflict, like it so often did, came in couples. Would he be the saviour or fade in fear of failure? He was living a true life parable of incomparable proportions, and he felt caught between being admirable and fallible. Tre felt like a free radical; destined to be part of something bigger than himself, but inherently explosive, ready to self-destruct a moment's notice.

Tre dropped the game console's controller to the floor, as he could not overcome his distracting thoughts and for the first time they were caused by himself only. The company of his other identity was now a thing of the past.

"Bro," Left exclaimed, through a mouth full of tortilla chips.

"I don't wanna play anymore, I can't think," Tre explained. He unseated himself from the gaming set up they had arranged for the evening, their room was full of snacks, soda and a low-key the soundtrack of Left's alternative rock music.

"What is there to think about, just play. We only just fired up the start menu." He tried to incite guilt through outstretched arms, but all he would receive was Tre turning up the volume of his Signot Radio application on his phone.

"You've been here all week listening to that thing, what you tryna win tickets to a show or something?" Left let his controller rest on the hill that was his belly emerging from his marl, 'Prince of Conquest' (a popular band in Indiana) T-shirt.

"Yeah, I am actually." The way Tre saw it; predicting where the killer would strike next was as useless as guiding a laser with one's hand. His opportunity to track down the figure in the suit would be on the terms that suited the masked murderer; in other words, when he chose to reappear. A part of him did not want the news to come through as he felt safer convincing himself to be unconvinced; that the whole string of incidents was pure coincidence. That the voice in his head had merely disappeared out of existence. Fear could play tricks on the mind, but his heart was steadfast. He knew it was coming, he only prayed the bloody trail of association did not close in on the people he loved.

"Kind of a wack way to spend your birthday week. At home and stuff." Left crunched into another handful of tortilla chips. The careless debris that met the floor was but a suitable depiction of Left himself; widespread and cheesy.

"I don't celebrate my birthday." Tre's jaw was clenched. It had been a while since the Spectre had been reported seen.

"You are as much fun as throwing bleach on an ant's nest." When Left received a mildly confused look from his roommate, he decided to elaborate, "Which is not very fun by the way. I mean, first it's insect cruelty and after you get over that, you have to bear in mind that the chemicals get them extremely agitated. Then they start getting everywhere, crawling in places they shouldn't."

"Glad it's agreed across species that you are annoying," Tre returned with only the slightest hint of humour; his jaw unlocked due to jocularity.

"We all can't be as lifeless as you." Left took Tre's humoured reply with the same excitement a kitten would if tossed a knitted ball for the first time. "Where's Caprice, I haven't seen her in a while?"

"She's not coming back, soldier. Moving to New York next week."

"Damn dude... she couldn't have timed that any worse."

"Shut up."

"Seriously when she was here though, she was so moody."

"She's probably not too good now either. Lancis' death is all over the news." Tre steadied himself onto a seat on Left's bottom bunk with his non-slinged arm.

"Spectre – the figure in the black suit. That's scary stuff man. I know I don't pay my TV license and I illegally download games, but I hope I'm not on his hit list."

"Me too," Tre said sincerely.

"I think I know who it is man, also you're on my bunk again without asking. You just do what you want right. That's your style huh?"

"Who do you think it is?" Tre fished out the words of relevance to him.

"It's obvious. Aaron Heron is back from wherever the hell he was and now he's terrorising the city. I mean it makes sense. Where has he been all this time? Building a killer upgrade of his suit. No pun intended." Left proposed his theory with such spirit that his weight became a burden for the wheeled chair he was upon and it buckled some.

"It's impossible." If the Spectre truly was Aaron Heron in return from hiding, not only would it void who he personally believed it to be, but his fandom in his boyhood years would become memories of mislead. The Aaron Heron he knew wanted to contribute to the world not take from it.

"Not really. We don't know where he ran to or what he has been doing while he was gone. He knows the suit inside out." This possibility strung itself between the silent contemplation that followed, until their ancient, barely audible, doorbell sounded. Afterward, a fisted rap on the door came.

"Must be the pizza." Left licked his lips, abandoning his jumbo-sized packet of half mauled tortilla chips. Tre Moon was left to orchestrate the glum, silence by himself until Left returned, and when he did it was not fresh takeaway he brought, instead it was fresh faces. Damia Ascot and Quiqhin Isles stepped into their room and it only took two more bodies to fill the slight room to full capacity.

"Surprised to see us?" Damia guessed. On the day, she had again parroted his choice of apparel; a dark pea coat covered her otherwise spring inspired underdress. Lastly, a curved beak cap hid the wideness of her forehead.

"Kinda, has anything happened?" Tre found himself primed with adrenaline, in anticipation that they came with news of the supernatural type.

"It's your birthday in a few days man. I had to remind Damia and all. ("It's not like he told anyone when it was," she muttered under her breath.) We're here to take you out." Quick showed his loyalty to mainstream fashion by wearing an oversized, leather, bomber jacket, jeans with silver zips by the knee and branded trainers so luminous Tre wondered if his own reflective abilities could replicate their effect.

"That's nice of you, but I don't really go out," came Tre's amateur mastery of what was expression of gratitude.

"Sure. But for Caprice you'll go Belly Carnival which is only the most fun place in Signot," Quick quipped. Damia, who seemed to have chosen Quick as her personal punching bag of late, socked him in the arm again.

"C'mon, there must be somewhere you would like to go?" Damia offered. Tre did not immediately reply and because of this Damia and Quick decided to make themselves comfortable in the limited space. For someone so short spoken, there were also lengthy waiting times for Tre to process the direction of his will. Left kept one eye on his on-going gaming session, one ear to the conversation around him and one hand inside the dwindling tortilla chips.

"You know what, there is." Tre finally spoke up.

"Thank goodness. I'm driving, let's move," Quick instructed almost instantly, as if the impasse had been impossible to tolerate. With that, the three AIM members got to their feet. The destination of the night would be at the discretion of Tre Moon whose birthday fell the next day – June 8th specifically.

"Sorry I'm not cool enough to come!" Left called after them, half sorry for himself, half stuffing himself.

After an hour of driving, half an hour of colloquial and fifteen minutes of educational speculation, the trio arrived at the point of Tre's instruction. Quick winced to get a clear view and Damia had to unseat her cap just to see through the extended darkness. The black of night had taken its inevitable reign of the day and only served the eerie details of the setting on that particular night. The road was poorly lit even with the assistance of the full beam headlights. On either side of the lonely road was a cluster of forest and due to the dark, the tree branches were arched in many spectral shapes. The many barks' were more worn than mossy and tried to hold on to the trunk of which it came. Further ahead a single soiled path could be seen emerging from the perimeter of the forest. The path was complete with webs, gravel, buckthorn and the faint colour of a single rose bush ingrained beyond the pitch black of the onyx.

"You've got to be having a laugh," Quick said to himself, however, fact that Tre did not see the blink of the cars reversing indicators was indication enough.

"Lead the way birthday boy," Damia said.

Even if he had not been gifted with the ability to adjust his vision to almost any condition, he would still be able to navigate his way. Just how the seasonal migration of birds would always find home, so would Tre. After some time, all three teenagers were expectedly dusty and soiled by the time they reached the bottom of the ditch-like path. Realisation came when Damia and Quick noticed they were amongst a graveyard.

"I come here every year to spend my birthday with them." Tre settled the two roses by the pair of gravestones that were noticeably close to each other; if they were any closer, they could be figuratively holding hands. Tre seated himself in front of them like he always did. A hand to the shoulder came afterward and he knew Quiqhin was honoured to be with him. Heartfelt sniffles sat right next to him and he knew that he had faith of Damia's friendship even after all of the demonising he had been through.

"We'll take as long as you need, bro." The volume in Quick's voice had considerably tapered.

"Actually, we have discussions here," Tre surprised them both, "hi Mum, hi Dad. I know it has been a while since I have brought anyone but... It turns out that I have more to live for than I thought," Tre disclosed for the first time. It was at these words that Damia and Quick knew that the mysterious Tre Moon, despite the further complications he had been through, was just a lost soul looking for acceptance.

"Mum, Dad. A lot has happened to me recently. At first, I didn't understand why, I thought I was cursed. But I understand now. Everything that you had told me back then is starting to make more sense now-"

"Tre..."

"If you could see the things that I can see... the things I do—"

"Tre!" Damia yelled over him, "I think someone has defaced the gravestone."

Tre's next words were harvested as a result of his startle. His body became transfixed and his eyes, fixed on what Damia had pointed out.

'Rehtaf Dna Rehtom Yrros Mi' was highlighted by the moonlight under the dedications to his parents. To his friends this was a case of uncalled vandalism but for Tre, this was verification of his deepest secret to this day. Because of this, they did not understand why visible fear had consumed him and not anger.

"What's the matter? We'll find who did this." Quick tried to comfort him.

"We need to get back to the city now." The uninterested undertone in Tre's voice was gone and this drastic change put worry in theirs.

"What's going on Tre? Tell us?!" Damia exclaimed, getting to her feet.

"When we get back to the city, I want both of you to get to hide somewhere safe. I need to warn the others." When he had been first plagued by the inverse writing on the day he lost his reflection, Tre smashed the mirror to cover up the trace. Perhaps in hope that it would fade, but he could not ignore the second message. Urgency birthed in him and with the momentum of the reflective Photosail, Tre was able to surge above the forest in the direction of the car. The two members of AIM dashed as fast as they could to keep up but by the time they had reached the car, they had arrived five minutes later and more muddy and tired than ever.

"We're coming with you," panted Quick, though following through with his words surely meant certain collapse.

"You can't. I won't be able to protect all of you," said Tre.

"Who else needs protecting?" asked Damia, as she winged the door of the vehicle open.

"Caprice and Left," Tre told them, "also the car is going to be too slow, I don't know if I have that much time."

"Why don't you do that Photosail thing you just did?" Quick proposed.

"It doesn't work like that. I won't be able to sail back to Signot, it's too far. I need a lot of light, a lot more." Tre's jaw clenched tighter with every passing second.

"Or, just increase the rate of reflection." Damia withdrew a backpack from under the passenger seat and threw it toward Tre.

"What?"

"Colloidal supersilver is the most reflective substance on this planet. The suit is made of it. I'm sure you'll have all the energy you need. That suit enhances your powers I'm sure of it."

Tre looked at Quick who just shrugged.

"Either that or we got wheels." At that, Tre stripped down as fast as he could and pulled the suit back on, a process he promised himself he would never do again. What was on the line that night could make even the most sanctified man drop their principles, and having being born a sinner, Tre was no different. When he pulled on the mask, it gave him an unprecedented view of his friends' awe as they saw the shards like fixations on the surface assort themselves to the shape of a human body. When they saw the mirror like plates emanating more light than the night sky was readily giving, they knew that Tre was ready to perform his spectacular feat. They backed up some and backed him with words of encouragement he would cherish during his fast-track journey back to Signot.

"Tre please be careful."

"Do your thing bro, but you owe us answers."

"I need mine first." His first words through the suit gave him instant feedback. Sound waves were but cousins to electromagnetic waves and just like them he could taper the waves to his will. For this reason, the frequency, volume, amplitude and speed of his voice could be controlled the minute it passed through the medium of the suit. He chose for the reverb in his voice to take on a mirror effect, completely divergent to his normal voice. The light reflecting from the mirrored suit grew too strong that the pair could not help but shield their eyes and when they removed their hand, all they could see was the streak of light in the sky.

By slowing down the rate of reflection from his suit, Tre Moon was able to slow the Photosail down to a speed where the fingers of light would gently deliver him back to the ground. He looked around without moving his neck. He was now in downtown Claxon and roughly four blocks from the apartment; he could only pray that Caprice was at home with Left. He dashed in the direction of his flat, but his acceleration fell flat when he passed a hoard of roped cardboard boxes.

"Dammit Emily," Tre whispered under his breath as he entered the miscellaneous store. Ironically, the one time he was not shopping, Emily Di Pinto was at the counter available for customers to consult her. When she spotted Tre she backed up in alarm, reminding him that he had to uphold ambivalence. The responsibility to get her to safety and assure her he was not the murderer, as well as keeping his personal relationship with her behind the suit.

"I'm not going to hurt you; I'm here to get you to safety," said the boy with no reflection.

"I know you're not. You just surprised me. How did you move so fast?" Emily Di Pinto upheld to her strangeness; brief fear had now convoluted into something closer to fascination. It almost felt as if her taffy coloured eyes could unwind the spatiotemporal illusion of the mirrored shards and see right through his mask.

"This is not a time for questions," Tre spelt out carefully.

"A man in a trippy suit that weirdly resembles a known public murderer, randomly visits me on my last shift in this store. If not now, when is the time?" she challenged him. Emily had less cares than they had time to anticipate the next event. Though Tre's convex sight gave him advance warning, his reflexes could not escape the sheer margin of impact.

The shell of a missile was fired into the miscellaneous store and upon impact it had incinerated everything within proximity, devastated everything outside twenty feet and ruminated outward in the Claxon streets. Tre rolled over in the wreckage of what was left of the shop. Badly concussed and somehow alive, Tre's impeccable vision had now been compromised. The shards of his suit had taken on cracks from the impact and so he was seeing hundreds of multiples of everything around him. A flummox of visual information. The site that the miscellaneous shop had occupied had now caved outward and what was left was property and products, damaged beyond repair. Smog now joined the fire, turning the scene into a health hazard. His suit, though damaged, was more than capable of deflecting the poisonous carbon monoxide particles. His worry was that Emily Di Pinto was nowhere to be seen.

"Emily!!!" Tre coughed through his words vigorously. From the smoke, a silhouette formed.

"Emily, get- out." He began feeling nauseous as more fumes formed and before his eyes a figure poured from the silhouette of smoke. It was N.O.M.A. – Kai Boston had clearly come with serious intention, but Tre could not comprehend why through his weakening mind. The armoured wings that spread several metres across withdrew inward and automatically mobilised to fill the anatomic holes in the armour, though he did not appear to have any figuratively. Even the way the red of the nearby infernos rippled against his crimson shell could not compare to the burning words he declared when he stepped over Tre.

"No more innocents die from your hands, Spectre. It's over, Moon."

CHAPTER 17

Lights Out

Lights out. Tre nodded awake and gasped a precious stream of fresh air. As he tried to resume action he noticed he was clasped to a chair. Both the secured crimson clasps and darkness was the harness. All he could remember was embers, claustrophobic fumes and the incendiary arrival of N.O.M.A. at the miscellaneous storeroom. If it was not for his retroflected sight he would not have been able to tell he was in the centre of a car park. It was deliberately empty and every source of light had been meticulously obscured, angled away or short circuited in place. Winds that the breach brought stroked his face in such a way he knew his mask had been removed. Despite this unmasking, there was only one face at his concern.

"KAI SHOW YOURSELF!!!"

"I've been here," said a dissonant voice behind him and soon, the aerodynamic suit of N.O.M.A. came into view, featuring its crimson and tungsten blend of aerodynamica.

"What have you done..." Tre uttered with a still dizzied view. In fact, he was so disorientated, his convex sight did not account for N.O.M.A. standing directly behind him before he spoke.

"I have had a tracker on you since we first met on the rooftop. I don't know how you are killing those people, but tonight you are going to tell me everything. I didn't let you get that suit to start making a personal blood sheet. I let you get it because I wanted you to mean something to Signot!" He cast Tre a look of disdain through his stained visor.

"I didn't kill those—" Tre choked on his sentence as the hands of the crimson angel plunged around his throat.

"If I was you I wouldn't lie to me. I've been watching, I watched what you have done." N.O.M.A. released Tre, giving him the breath of life for the second time that evening. He was thankful that the guise of N.O.M.A. was not as petulant as the boy beneath because his metal brace was more pestle than palm.

"Are you out of your mind?" The folds of N.O.M.A.'s grip was visible on his neck, but this did not quail his voice, "There was an innocent girl in that shop. You killed her!"

"You can't get out of this," N.O.M.A. dismissed.

"I was trying to tell the owner to get to safety. What were you thinking?!"

"I scanned the interior before I fired the missile. Only one heat signature came back. You. My intel system is one of the most powerful on this planet and you are telling me it failed to pick up someone else?"

"It's too late." Tre bowed his head. No matter how he tried, there was no easier way pain could be rearranged. A box was his favourite place to store guilt and like most baggage, it had to be opened one day. As his head bowed, he saw hundreds of absent reflections in the mirrors in his suit. On this occasion he was thankful for his loss of reflection; mirrors had the power to multiply emotions. In this case contrite.

"Your suit can change colour, how?" N.O.M.A. continued doggedly. All Tre could see was circles; N.O.M.A. circled him while bound by his misinterpretation. All the while, the trail the figure in the black suit had left, admittedly, led back to himself. Tre was used to consequential roundabouts for things he had not put into motion, but today instead of submitting to the improbable truth, he would take another road.

"Let me out. I need to stop him; I need to save her—" SMACK! The laden fist of N.O.M.A. struck Tre across the face, but even the tungsten it was made from met something sturdier - Tre Moon's will.

"He is going to murder her tonight, you have to list—" Another punch landed; an average man would have disbanded their quality of honesty, but Tre was the furthest thing from average. His entire life story had predicated this.

"I know it doesn't make sense, but it is not me!"

"Who is it then?!" N.O.M.A. fired a frustrated retort with his next punch, the force caused the suspect's chair to bundle over. N.O.M.A. followed the trail of broken chair legs until he reached him. He then kneeled over Tre ready to deliver another pulverising blow. It was a dim, grim scene.

"Someone who will take everything you love – take everything that makes you – and will never be satisfied – until you feel like him." A simple sentiment put a harden in the motion of Kai's next punch.

"If you are not going to let me go now, then I don't want to leave this car park until one of us has died for what we have done," Tre said through a bloodied mouth, "misunderstanding has already caused one person to lose their life today, but there is more to life than our past. We can still save someone. You can."

Like before, a crimson, spherical node formed from N.O.M.A.'s suit and flashed a scan over Tre's bloody face.

"Node-Operation-Management-Assistant. Mr Boston, target perspiration levels are steady. Breathing rate has maintained. Physiological signs show target is telling the truth. Facial cues could not be read because subject has a stiff expression. Advised to investigate further."

The falcon-like helmet of N.O.M.A retracted in place and in a series of mechanical gushes, it formulated as an extra layer of armour at his shoulder blades. Kai Boston's face could now be seen. From the insignia on his chest to the razor cut in his eyebrows, the crimson angel had seemed to strike a line. In this case, a line of reason. With a three fingered trace of his visor, a three dimensional electronic menu was projected. He made one gesture; the turning of one digital knob and the tone of the lighting was restored to their entire car park level.

"I couldn't see your reflection in my visor. What are you?"

"The son of a mother and father who were taken from me," Tre told him as he found his feet, "there are questions that we both have that will need to wait."

Another anomalous command from the crimson hero altered his infallible restraining cables into laffy taffy. One by one, they magnetised toward N.O.M.A.'s suit and filled in slots in the armoured plates that he would not have otherwise noticed. Once they had slipped into place, they underwent the rapidly bewildering process of hardening to tungsten. Tre reckoned perhaps the better question was – what on earth was his suit?

"You say you are not the killer, but you have the same damn suit. Who's your lookalike then?" Kai fell short of Tre's height when the tall teenager finally got to his feet.

"Someone who shouldn't exist." Tre was a long way from elaborate and so Kai decided to cut his questioning short.

"Who is this person in danger and where are they?"

"Caprice Hill and Left Miller. If they are not at the apartment down the road, then I don't know, but if you track the person in the black suit then we can get there before him."

"I've tried, smartass. The Spectre can't be tracked, I don't know if you read the news, but it can turn invisible. I can track this girl by microwaves, but it could take longer than we have."

"I'll speed them up. Just get to her as soon as possible."

"What the hell are you supposed to be, Broadband Boy?"

"Have your systems found her yet?"

"I told you radio takes a long—"

"Node-Operating-Management-Assistant. Mr Boston I have intercepted a cellular message by a 'Caprice Hill' at 43 Broadwalk, Claxon Borough. I have also tracked a gaming I.P. for 'Left Miller' at Hondown Flats, just eighty meters away. I have noted a 76.8% increase in signal transmission speed. It would be beneficial to apply this for future intel use. Do you want me to form a scouting node from the armour to investigate what technologies this human uses?"

"No!" Kai slapped the node back into his insignia like it was a persistent cough.

"Questions later. Go to Caprice you can get there faster," Tre commanded his curious contemporary.

"Aight. Where the hell are you going?" Kai asked upon seeing Tre gear for a running start.

"That building over there," Tre pointed through the breach at the pecan-shaped building, "her mother works there. Once I get her to safety, we can look for him – the Spectre."

"I hope you've healed up by then, Moon." The ledge of armour supporting the nape of his neck expanded outward and reassembled into his helmet at such efficiency that Tre was sure that his armour was a mentis metal. But that was a question for another day, because the ramifications of their current task were omnipresent.

"If I see the Spectre and take off its mask and it's you..."

"It won't," Tre half lied. In total honesty, he did not know what N.O.M.A. would find and that was the most conspicuous part of the whole affair. N.O.M.A. turned his back to Tre with clear intentions for ascension.

"After this is done, will I have to worry about something like this again?"

"I'm hanging up this suit tonight. One of my friends have died today, this is the least you can do," Tre pulled his own mask on now.

"What was her name?" There was a respectful timbre from the crimson suit now.

"Emily Di Pinto."

N.O.M.A. said no more. Like an eagle conditioned for command, he swooped through the open breach between the stories and propelled in the direction of Claxon Borough in search of Caprice Hill and Left Miller. Tre, more than anything, yearned for Caprice's safety but he also knew that N.O.M.A. was constructed, and the man beneath instructed, to deal with situations concerning life and death. He decided to shunt all of his remaining energy into his last task. Tre set his magnified sights on the Hive district high-rises and as if the shards of his suit had become accustomed; they angled light-ward all at once in preparation of a speculative jump.

CHAPTER 18

<u>Spectre</u>

The date was June 7th, a day before Tre Moon was introduced to the world for the first time. The crow summer evening in Signot could tell a story; the constellations spelt both tragedy and triumph. Such was the polaris star that defined the polarity of the Gemini. The combined will of two heroes on that night opened up the possibility for a peaceful chapter for Signot, but the hysteria in the air spelt that the city was bound to recidivation. The trail of light that streaked toward the Hive offices cast light upon the whole affair. Destiny would be sealed that night, for better or for worse.

CRASH!

Tre Moon bundled through a pane of glass on the eighth floor of the Society of Psychology building. As he rolled to a stop he was now a figure made of shards, amongst many more. He looked backward to scan his progress; a streak of light exceeding the length of a football field could be seen. It was his most daring Photosail to date, but despite his increasing handle on his reflective abilities, he did not know how fast he could get back to Caprice. For this very reason, he made haste. His progress to the tenth floor was met with an array of attention: fright, curiosity and wonder. The majority of workers meandered clear from his path, misconstruing him as the midnight black Spectre. Thus his reception was greeted with many running for their lives in the direction of their own reception. The few that would call themselves brave souls, stayed put, for the sole purpose of witnessing. Those few brave souls would live on. Ironically, the only person whose duty it was to clean was the only person who stepped forward for clarification.

"No matter what you do in this building tonight. Nothing will make you feel better," said the janitor.

"Yeah there is. Bringing a mother home to see her daughter safe," Tre responded. It only took one sentence to see his stigma disinter. Tre continued his journey and when he arrived at his desired floor, the tenth, he became deterred by the difference in details. No light could be seen from the gap between the door and the floor, moreover, the room contained a darkness not even his agile sight could navigate. Another point of interest was the creases and splinters beside the doors handle. Soon after, Tre spotted something that made him wish he was merely suffering from strabismus. When he strained his magnified sight as far as it could possibly go, he learnt that he could see microns and with this new gift, he could now see nanoscopic globules of blood on the inner side of the door handle. Tre Moon had the eyes any detective would wish for but now he also was faced with the prospect they would not.

"It can't be." The shards of his mask rearranged into worry. He gripped the splintered handle and tried to trade his assumptions for gumption, but when he pushed the door open, his heart metamorphosed to stone. Edith Hill's office was battered beyond compare. The room had been ordained in the image of the wraith; the portraits had been shredded from the wall, the positive psychology bookshelves had been scattered and Caprice's handmade origami sculptures looked like they had been clawed by a vulture. Or rather, the hands of an individual more strung than the sculptures themselves. The okna starkmark roof let only shredded light through and it centred on perhaps the most unsettling view. The lengthy figure of Edith Hill motionless. Tied to a chair. With a hood over her head.

"Miss Hill!? Miss Hill?! EDITH?!" The memory of the inferno washed into his mind and he had endured fire and rain to ensure it would not repeat itself. He was only thankful that he arrived before it was too late. He extended a searching hand toward her mask. Fear made him finger for a hold on it. Perturbation did not allow him to pull it off immediately either. His expectations were made from the extreme despair he had once known; a chilling past that could make him freeze even to that day. As he raised the small of the mask just half an inch, the face of a shard–like veil appeared beside it.

"AGH!" Tre jumped backward with such alarm that he bundled over some of the books that had been pulled from the bookshelf. It was now apparent that the state of the room was caused in struggle.

"No." No other paraphrase could encapsulate the paradox Tre was seeing. The face in black completed its entrance by allowing the rest of its body to fissure into the visible spectrum. When it rose, it stood tall at roughly six feet. Instead of hands it had claws. It wore a suit composed of black shards, the appearance of synthesised obsidian, which gave a dull, distorted reflection of that around it. The very ripples in these shards put waves in Tre's emotions and seemed to contain an ocean of matter, visible or otherwise. In actuality, it was a mirror image of Tre. Bar the oxymoron that they occupied the same physical space and the violet spectrum of colour that flushed from its eyes sporadically. The shards in Tre's own suit tried the impossible task of curving away from the Spectre as much as they could.

"You're not real. Leave this woman alone, what do you want?!" demanded Tre.

"*I have always been real to you... Brother,*" the Spectre assured him. Fallacy thundered through the room and it was all absorbed by Tre, shell shocked to the point of denial.

"N-No. You can't be— You can't do this to me again. You can't."

"*You think I'm here for you? I'm here for me!*" said the Spectre as it sunk a single claw into Edith Hill's shoulder. Her lack of reaction alerted Tre that she was unconscious.

"Blue?" Tre asked, despite being between the point of disbelief and grief.

"*This is the first time you've acknowledged me for me,*" the Spectre stated. It spoke English but there was something blasphemous about its very existence. From the way light waves seemed to avert its proximity to the emptiness in its voice. It was as if it should not have been, yet there Tre was, witnessing it with his own eyes.

"How are you here?"

"*Don't ask me stupid questions. The supersilver changed us, it changed everything... Everything is clearer now.*"

"What have you done to me, to my reflection?"

"*Don't you get it? You and I was the same person. We always have been.*"

"You are a voice."

"*I'm a person. See.*" Spectre inserted the rest of his claws into Edith Hill's shoulder and this act of reprimand was a reminder to Tre that he had to proceed with caution.

"Okay, stop, stop!" Tre pleaded, to which the claws receded. Fleshy sheaths could be seen underneath her sheen blazer. "Why are you doing this, killing more people?"

"*Why not?*" Spectre said in a way so blasé that Tre knew it was not a façade. Blue was truly a sociopath.

"Please tell you me you haven't done anything to Caprice?" Tre prayed.

"*Tre...*" Spectre had fury in his voice but thankfully for Tre, this fury made him stray toward the window and further from Edith's chair. Still, he was still considerably closer than Tre and the wrong move could cost her life. Tre chose to remain attentive to the living embodiment of his former voice.

"*You just don't understand me. You never have. That is the reason you never accepted me as a brother. You just don't think the way I do.*"

"Have you hurt her?" Tre repeated. It was a sensitive situation, but he knew the answer he did not want to hear would relinquish his sense of self-control. If Caprice was to die, he did not know what he would be capable of, especially against the very person that had twisted his sense of self to that very day.

"*You don't understand me... I would never harm Caprice, she was the only person who accepted me. That didn't try and drown me out. She said I was special.*"

"Yeah? What do you think she'll think of you once she knows that you have kidnapped her own mom?" Tre advanced toward Spectre and Edith however; it only took a flash of claws to impede Tre's progress.

"It doesn't matter what she thinks. She will never know how it feels to be silenced against your will. Do you know how many months I spent in darkness because of this woman? But I show her the darkness for a few hours and you come here on your high horse trying to make me feel guilty. You did this, you all did this." Spectre pointed the mirror back at Tre.

"Judge Valentine. Lancis..." Tre began

"The Judge locked you in that jail with me. You didn't deserve to be there for what I did. Lancis was a piece of scum that needed to be killed. I was never scared of the block boys and nothing has changed. I killed the judge for you, I killed Lancis for Caprice. Edith, this one is for me." Where there was meant to be compassion, only a void existed. There was nothing canonical about the intermittent colours that would populate the shards of Spectre's eye and Tre felt nothing but blackness at Blue's heart. Beside Edith's safety, the second most reoccurring thought Tre had was how imperfect his existence must have been, to birth something so evil.

"Blue no one else needs to die. No one deserves to die. Somehow you are given the opportunity to exist outside of my mind and the first thing you can think of to do is kill? There is so much more to life than that."

"Like what?"

"We're still young. Even though I haven't got my parents, I have people I live for. I still have Caprice. I have friends now, people who care about me. Edith is one of them," Tre said while stepping gently toward the pair.

"They are all your friends. No one cares about me. All our life it was you who was loved. The only person who truly acknowledged me was you... until that day."

"That day is gone." Tre found himself within arm's reach of Edith now.

"I know but that day I lost my brother too," Spectre revealed. Tre for the first time was calm. For his entire life he had considered Blue a demon inside of him, not once did he consider that he was another person trying to wade through their own turmoil, just like himself. Despite having being bonded to the same physical existence until recently, perhaps he and Blue were more akin than he thought. After all, Tre had also charted the barren plains of loneliness and public demonisation. Tre too had been imprisoned against his will and forced to thrive or succumb to the hardiness of prison life. Just like how his parents never knew Blue existed, Tre experienced similar treatment from his extended family when headlines of his parents' death made the news. He was granted the chance to look in the mirror for the first time in months, and this time, he truly saw himself. His struggles. His fear. His failed ambition. His regret. His loneliness. All of these things were Blue and how could he expect anything but a vengeful existence from a being that had been shown nothing of the other side. Tre made his final step and it was not toward Edith, it was toward Blue. The Spectre shifted uncomfortably at first but in the second moment he found himself within a hug by the person he held dearest.

"I'm sorry." Tre removed his mask with a hand and underneath his face was blotted with tears. Blue was transfixed by the act of compassion.

"I'm sorry I was not there for you since that day. I don't know if I can forgive you for what you done, but I'm gonna try if it means that no one else dies." Tre tried to frown through the tears, but it only made them fall faster.

"*All I wanted was for you to acknowledge me, Brother.*"

"Today the killing stops let Edith go. Be your own person now." Tre released Blue who was now suddenly quiet. After having been counselled in self-actualisation in that very room, there was something astounding that it would be him preaching those very same sentiments to another. Tre approached Edith to remove her hooded bag from her face and finally end the tortuous night.

"*I'm sorry, Brother,*" Blue said as he oversaw the unmasking.

"No..." The rest of Tre's cries were lost in his shrill heaves. Edith Hill was grey, motionless and most noticeably, the life in her hazel eyes had sunken to a place of no return. Vigorous prints could be seen around her neck; she had been choked to her death.

"*She tried to do the same thing to me for years.*" It was as if the emptiness in Spectre's voice had returned, but in truth it had never left. Tre's trembling hand managed to pull his mask back over a face scorched with utter resentment.

"*I protected you; no one ever did that for me. I did what I had to do.*"

"All those lives... today I'm going to show you how it feels." Tre bolted toward Spectre and with the force of the Photosail, he performed a crunching tackle that broke yet another window and sent them soaring over the city of Signot.

The spectators at street level that happened to look up at the right moment would have glanced the extraordinary. A comet of light, streaking across the skies, comprised of two lost souls. Both regretful and resentful. The night was destined to be both eventful and memorable for those present as they were presented with Spectre in the flesh and its symmetrical, unnamed adversary. Still airborne with a steadily declining trajectory, Blue and Tre traded life and death blows, while gliding over central, Signot was quiet at its ventral until the pair crashed right through the Liami Sphere Globe. Blue and Tre Moon rocketed through a table at some speed. The assembly of industry professionals who had attended for the movie awards were now subject to a completely unrelated show as they witnessed Tre and Blue trade power blows. Shrieks came as Blue landed a tooth displacing punch, sending Tre crashing into a particularly crowded table. Fortunately, Tre's athletic recovery made it so that the only casualty incurred was spilt merlot wine on one gentleman's fresh tuxedo.

"Are you serious right now? Do you know how much this costs Mirror Man?" The man observed the damage in the mirrors that made up Tre's suit.

"I'm sure you can get another," Tre advised the man. Following these words, the scene inside the hall began to simmer in shade. All light sources in the room: candles and artificial were suddenly extinguished and the streams of light all were consumed in the very matter of Blue's Spectral suit. Once the last ray of light had seen the obsidian, Spectre decided to send everyone in attendance to oblivion.

"*Good luck, Golden Boy.*" Spectre grabbed a nearby man from his seat by the back of his blazer. The colourful hue in his mask's eye began again and with the energy from the light he absorbed previously, he sent the man hurtling so far upward, that he smashed clean through the cleft of one of the panes above. The collision caused a chain reaction of shatters across the remaining globe. This was the beginning of Tre's troubles because not only was the unconscious man now soaring back down, but so was a torrential shower of shards. Many of the attendees screamed and scrambled in an attempt to get out of the shard's rainfall, but the spread of what was the Liami Sphere's glass design, covered the entire hall. With little time to spare, Tre took a minute to swear in panic and remember the unsettling equation that objects increase ten metres per second when falling. In the corner of his eye he saw Spectre make for a tunnelled exit. With adrenaline pumping through his system so fast, the scene seemed to play out in slow motion.

"Take cover!" Tre yelled before he leaped airwards. With what little light that was coming from the canopy, Tre was able to Photosail across the open space above and capture the falling man safely. He turned back round to perhaps see a massacre, but instead he was faced with the true majesty of his powers. When the shards reached the streak of light he left across the air, they slowed down exponentially; it was the equivalent of a mutiny in the laws of Sir Isaac Newton. Not taking any chances, Tre made a multi-directional Photosail, in essence, creating a net of this dilating paradigm. The would be victims that were screaming for their lives just moments ago were now, to Tre's dismay, applauding him as if he had just performed a nervy but titillating magic trick.

"Run dammit!" Tre called in exasperation. He then projected a waving hologram of himself at the nearest exit to emphasise the point. By the time everyone had cleared the hall below, the torpid shards had finally had enough. The sheer speed of the light rays that had enforced the slowing effect on them, forced every single one to shatter into a million pieces, and further into billion more, all until sparkling, micron sized showers of sand fell overhead. For the few craned heads that could not resist witnessing the conclusion of the glassy spectacle, Tre Moon's suit amongst the sands of glass was like witnessing diamonds dancing. Never could any circumstance replicate the way the violet spectrum refracted through the shower of shards, spectacular colours glistened back and forth only adding to the mirage of their mirrored liberator. When the light of an attendee's camera shot toward the scene, it was quickly deflected directly at them. Disorientating the camera man and soaking the picture in a blinding white flash, like he had tried to photograph the sun itself.

"No pictures!" Tre declared. Tre left the Liami Sphere in the direction that Spectre headed. Though he had single handedly calmed a calamity, the true task lay in stopping Spectre for good. Tre planned to end it tonight.

The tunnel that Tre entered continued until he exited at the Hive Common gardens. It was a boardwalk with expensive textile walkways and décor bushes. Every twenty feet a mounted statue of Indiana's most famous figures could be seen recreated in their bronzed entirety. Of the five statues that populated the boardwalk, Tre recognised three: Aaron Heron – founder of Heron Research, Nikolas Liami – architect of the now fallen Liami sphere. The third was the statue of Sergeant Boston of which Tre was the architect behind his army's downfall and the very reason why the mould was in process of being hauled down by the construction workers.

"*You know. I think our parents should have statues on this walk.*" The apparition of Blue was accompanied by the collection of every light source in the surrounding area. When the nearby guests and construction workers noticed the Spectre atop of the statue of Aaron Heron, they ran in absolute fright. Spectre gave a dim, hopeless feel to every area he visited and consequently the inspirational boardwalk now looked like a valley of idols lost and gone.

"Don't you dare talk about them," said Tre through gritted shards.

"*You can't beat me Tre and not because of these powers. Because you are the same scared little boy you were back then. You cannot protect the people you claim you'd give your life for. Our parents are gone, your saviour, Edith Hill, is gone and we both know it is a matter of time before something happens to Caprice.*" Spectre's instigation was met with a furious leap from his other, however, the light that sailed him toward Spectre was quickly soaked away by the parasitic nature of the obsidian suit. Tre fell short of his target and because of it, he took a painful tumble against the statue of his idol. By the time he hit solid ground he was at the statue's feet, as well as at the feet of Spectre who used his wraith like powers to materialise over him.

Tre tried to force a punch upward, but his arm was caught in Spectre's jagged claws. If it were possible he could even feel the absence of his healing factor while in the proximity of his other half. Tre then formed ten holograms during his struggle to free himself, but they were all drained away by the black of the suit. Furthermore, the longer that he was in contact with Spectre the more the painful sensation of aberration swept over his impeccable sight. Everything that the supersilver had provided him was being counteracted in a traumatic fashion. No more than ten seconds later, the effects of optic coma had taken over both of Tre's eyes. He could see nothing but blackness. Even in through blindness, the ghostly mask of Spectre still haunted him.

"*What you said back at the office, did you even mean it? The woman is gone, why would you let her get in between us. We are brothers.*" Blue examined the pain shown through the crippling shards in Tre's suit; remorse did not ease his grip in the same way love for his brother could not blunt his claws. Pain was all Blue knew.

"I'm not afraid to die!" said Tre through battered breaths. Through drained vitality, blindness and bloodshed, Tre was closer than he had ever been to reuniting with his parents. And despite having sought this position for decades, he wished to go no further. Not from fear, but because he owed himself the opportunity to live a future. His own future. Tre clamped his hand on Spectre's skull and he fed his hands all the light particles that were not caught in matter of the black suit. With an incensed shout, the light at his hands combusted into a flare of heat that shredded the layer of the black mask, as well as the skin and tissue that lay underneath. Tre found himself soon clutching air as Spectre assumed his ghostly form so much as to minimise the damage. The switch from physical matter allowed Tre to harness the rest of the energy Blue would have otherwise drained. In a moment of pure intuition, the mass reflection of light assimilated the heat into a siphoning, gas powered laser beam. The beam fired through Spectre's apparition and struck the statue of Aaron Heron at the helm. As Tre predicted, Spectre formed his physical form once again ready to strike him a fatal blow, however, the solid clump of bronze Tre had dissected from the statue fell directly downwards and connected cleanly with Spectre's skull. The blinded Tre flinched when he heard debris clatter around him. With no more of Spectre's passive, anti-light affecting his healing factor, nor his sight, his vision was restored somewhat. It was fitting that he could only see in black and white because that was the simplicity of his decision as he kneeled over Blue, fists clenched, ready to land a killing blow.

"*Go on... do it,*" Blue spluttered under his mask. The glow of light that formed over Tre's dominant hand informed him that he would be granted enough power to take the life of the Spectre. Literally in his grasp was the opportunity to fulfil his decade long commitment to hate. Never in his wildest dreams did Tre think he would have the opportunity to avenge his parents' death, similarly, he never thought that he would ever have to. Tre completed his third unmasking of that evening and underneath was the face of, him. Blue's face was the complexion of pale blue, a result of silver poisoning, but, of the parts of Blue's face that was not scorched to the bone or bludgeoned by the bronze, he contained Tre's features. His neat, waved hair, his clear skin, long eyelashes, broad cheekbones and even the same expression of madness that he had in his face at that very moment. Tre's held his punch still, now mesmerised by his own reflection.

"*Do it, Brother. Do me a favour. After that woman I was next on my list. I hate myself; I hate myself for what I did,*" Blue admitted in his ghastly way.

"I hate myself for what happened too," Tre told his reflection, "but you don't get the easy way out. You're going to live through every day like me, except now I can live on at least knowing that I got you. I finally got you."

"Brother, you are too noble. I should have known. Well if you are planning to keep me alive at least let me break the news to Caprice, I mean you—"

THUD! Tre knocked Blue unconscious to cease the disrespectful words that he knew would come. Tre kneeled his head. One triumph could not overshadow the fact that two people he cared about lost their lives that night.

After informing Kai Boston that he had captured the Spectre, he was told Kai, Caprice and Left were unharmed. N.O.M.A. went to find an appropriate and covert location for the supernatural murderer's confinement, but Tre had a more difficult task. Breaking the news to Caprice. Three hours past midnight brought the most trying birthday Tre had experienced in recent memory and for no reasons that were good. His eighteenth birthday brought him a cleared conscience; clear of guilt of his parent's death and also clear of the voice of Blue, both which had pushed him toward drug addiction and suicidal thoughts. He promised himself that no more people close to him would die and due to the dwindling number of these few individuals, it was a promise he chose to honour over his own life. Edith Hill and Emily Di Pinto were victims of the era of the Spectre and, just like his release from prison, just like life after the death of his own parents; he knew he had to emerge as something stronger.

Tre ducked under the shortened door frame to his university apartment. There were no lights to be seen from anywhere in the flat, but instead of danger, Tre knew it was for mourning. His bending sight found Caprice before he had to and so he entered the compact student kitchen where he found her looking through the blinds into the endless night. Caprice turned to the entrance when she heard Tre enter. Their unspoken bond told each other everything they needed to know and when she thrust herself into his chest, his usual emotional threshold was reduced tenfold. The two moon cursed friends sharing their anguish, a moment of indefinable affinity and languish.

"Tre... my mother... she is..." Her mouth quivered for words.

"Don't say anything. I'm here for you." Tre's face was buried into the sides of her alabaster curls. Today he would open up to the girl he loved behind closed doors.

"The reason why I wanted to go to New York is because I'm pregnant. I did not want to face you or Mum, so I chose to run away. Now she's gone and we hardly even talk anymore. I don't know what to do. I'm scared. I'm scared what is out there." Caprice's confession startled Tre to the very core, it even thawed his heart some, but he knew that the most important thing was that she was in his arms. That he was there for her. If Tre's loyalty could be unspun by revelations, Caprice and himself would have parted many moons ago.

"I'm here for you, I always was. You don't have to worry about what is out there; someone is protecting the city now." Tre gently held his best friend, but his expression hardened. He felt imbued with a new sense of responsibility. Just how one life had been lost under his word, he was now given another to guard. On the day of his eighteenth birthday, Tre Moon's true gift was new purpose.

CHAPTER 19

<u>Specular</u>

Just like the seasons, the cycle of crime continued, but proceeding the 8th of June, the rate of crime curbed. Gangs and petty criminals, ironically, found themselves victims of the newest movement on the Signot streets: justice. The weakened reserves of the Indiana Police Department found criminals, cherry picked and placed in front of their borough building. The fruits of Signot's police failed labour, gifted by an unknown assailant. A collection of viral footage and federal observations would soon reveal the unsung hero to be the man made of shards. Time once again proved to be the master of perception, as the absence of the Spectre's public massacre was slowly replaced by his brighter counterpart's active effort against crime. Once again, the human race would prove their capacity for change as more and more citizens left the comfort of safety to combat the judicial destitution they were so used to. Like younger siblings do, Signot imitated its older sister, Heavens Conquest, and so began political rallies to reinforce the positive changes that the man made of shards was making. The body of Indiana received the signals from Signot and invested even more money into the young city once they saw it fighting against its contagion. Drug traffic persisted in every artery that the city had, but the Bulgarian Conglomerate were forced further into the shadows than ever. There was no vernacular spectacular enough to capture the man made of shards and so the people of Signot began to call him Specular. The name was originally coined by the figures in the scientific community who figured that his powers were based upon the premise of specular reflection. The name caught on with the general public too, as most thought it was short for spectacular, despite his feats being nothing short of. Out of all the perplexing things that Specular was capable of, one thing was clear; he was an oculus into a field of physics that scientists had not even thought possible. The new field of light physics would go on to be known as 'Birma-Physics' (an extension of optical physics) and they sought the man under the shards to be the face in the breakthrough field. Endorsement deal offers would remain unanswered. Subsidy could not serve him more than secrecy because it was something Tre Moon could not afford to lose. Even more mellow messages of ethical and progressive study fell on flat ears. The answer no was not enough for the insatiable knowledge bank that was Heron Institute and so Signorina Baelel demanded Specular be captured. This was easier said than done because not once in the history of mankind had anyone tried to entrap a walking illusion. Baelel's hired arms would quickly piece together that it would be greater than just a puzzling task. Distinguishing Specular from his identical holograms would prove as successful as extinguishing flames with one's bare hands, and ultimately, so would the hopes for her plans. Signot also saw their economy flood in value with the introduction of Isaac Isles oil industry; and while only taking a record breaking two months to be fully constructed, the city was now more abundant than ever. The new and true wealth in the city was hope however. If the people of Signot could not count on anyone before, from the 8th June 2011 and onward, the poor were now rich.

The capital of Indiana, Heaven's Conquest gave up the mantle as Indiana's prized city in turn for Signot's recent rise to popular culture with the emergence of their own local hero and the Dubai oil industries. The flat city was almost grateful to be able to retire from the controversy; enjoying the blue skies of summer weather, being free of traffic-calming measures, political riots and senseless violence. Signot's sister city was so tame in fact, that it was the perfect location for covert operation. In Tre Moon and Kai Boston's case, detaining the Spectre. Past the outskirts of the city's motorway and further still, past

Boston's Base was an abandoned trial bunker. The bunker was surrounded by multiple bright signs warning of radioactive activity. It was also so far into the uninhabited borders of the state, that it was empty for the most part if you excluded the dama gazelle's, dingoes and desert shrews that had made the area their home. The steel bunker was expansive and held a single glass containment at its centre. With confirmation from Tre, they found that the bunker was indeed overridden with radioactive radiation and with second confirmation; Tre informed the party of Damia Ascot and Kai Boston that the radiation was gone, never to return.

"So, you just wished the radiation away? I don't understand your powers, I thought you reflected light?" Kai asked as he wheeled a crystal coffin along the bunker's main path. In the coffin, the irregular maya skin tone of Blue Moon could be seen.

"Not quite, he can control how any wave reflects from his body. Including those in the electromagnetic spectrum. Once you can comprehend that, then make your jokes," Damia jumped in like a defence attorney itching to highlight a fallacy. This was the latest of stinging sentences aimed at Heaven's Conquest vigilante and so Kai gave Tre a disapproving look, the equivalent to someone suggesting that the owner control their rabid pet.

"She's right. Should probably do some research later," Tre sided with her in purposeful jest. Since acquainting less than a year ago, Damia had established herself as something of a big sister for him. He found himself sharing most aspects of his life with her, of which Caprice's pregnancy was the most recent. For every instance, he would find that her advice proved useful, if not essential. Damia was truly wise and even though her selflessness could drive her to fervency, Tre knew no one else who could accept him for being both Tre Moon, student and Specular, the vigilante hero. To that day he still had not told his own best friend about his powers.

"Whatever," Kai brushed off, "this is bunker fifty-five, built to contain the radioactive tests that my father held. Without his suit, this guy aint escaping this containment. I just hope there is literally no gamma waves in here 'cause it could kill him, they pass through walls right?"

"Has working at the army left you hard of hearing, the radiation is gone?" For the countless time that day, Damia proved that she was on standby for all matters concerning her friend.

"What's your friend's problem? I don't even know her, man," Kai addressed Tre in annoyance, however, his blatant negligence of her presence only served to sour her further.

"I thought heroes fought their own battles?" she remarked.

"So," Tre intervened, "will this containment hold him?" They all came to a stop once they reached the vast, glass cylinder in the centre of the bunker. Though the cylinder was made of several layers of thick glass and was compressed together, above and beneath with reinforced steel, something told Tre that even this would not be able to secure the Spectre forever. Kai took his time before replying. Firstly, he engaged the complicated looking switchboard that was planted in front of the cylinder. Within a few seconds, shutters locked over every single window the bunker contained, effectively drowning them in near darkness. Afterward, Kai entered a complicated combination of codes at which the sole entrance to the cylinder curled open. The sergeant's son pushed the crystal coffin into the cylinder before reactivating the cyclical steel doors. Though Kai was dressed as casual as Tre had ever seen him (a retro bowler shirt, fitted chinos and a crimson backpack), just the manner that he went about the process was proof enough that he was indeed the Crimson Angel.

"He won't. Not without his suit," he said finally. Just as he finished, a crimson device literally burst from his backpack to give its added input.

"Node-Operating-Management-Assistant. Mr Boston and I have examined this being since you handed him to us on June 8th. This beings power revolves around the consumption of electromagnetic waves for energy, which it can use to magnify its own strength or tuning its physical matter to the frequencies it has absorbed. This is how the 'Spectre' appears to be able to disappear from sight and phase through physical object. Like Tre Moon, the suit enhances its powers."

"Thank you." The efficiency of Kai's ingenious apparatus allowed him to overlook the fact that his perfectly good backpack was now ruptured.

"Seems like it knows quite a bit about me," said Tre.

"Knowledge never hurt anybody," Kai replied coyly, "was this thing really inside of you for all of these years?"

"Yeah," Tre placed a scarred right hand on the surface of the cylinder when he approached it. "All of these years' people thought it was Dissociative Identity Disorder, even I did. This is something different."

"We need to find out how this supersilver material did this to you. There may be other risks we do not know about. The only way to do this is to find the creator." Kai joined him in observing the crystal coffin inside.

"There are two. Aaron Heron and Noel Jinx. Heron will be hopeless to find but Professor Jinx might just know." Kai's slanted eyes widened as Damia coupled in with practical consideration.

"Who is this Jinx?" Kai said.

"He is our university lecturer. Well he was. He has been fired; his wife and family also left him. I heard he left Signot," Damia explained.

"I'll find him," Kai said with ease and given the intelligence at his disposal, Tre believed him too.

"His life is ruined because of me, so if he chooses not to help at least let him have that choice," Tre requested.

"The Spectre is a hazard the longer we leave him here. The Professor doesn't get a choice." Kai faced Tre with assertion, but this only made the pair question the legitimacy of his brand of ethics.

"I never knew the hero our city looked up to for so long was part of the very army regime they were fighting against. I don't think you are in any position to be making the calls," Damia denounced in her dainty way.

"Who do you think has been keeping my father's army in check? They don't make any move without me knowing!" Kai exclaimed.

"For all we know, you could have set up the campaigns in the city just, so you could stop them as N.O.M.A." Damia proved herself to be an artist in instigation as with words only; she was able to airbrush indignation onto Kai Boston.

"We are all hypocrites," Tre said simply, "we fight for our cities but truly, the Bulgarians run Indiana. Gangs and criminals steal and kill to better their own home, ignoring the fact that the city is also their home. We all hurt the people we love. Every single one of us. All we can do is try. Kai is trying to help and that is all we can ask for."

"I just believe that if you stand for something, you should stand behind it whole heartedly. There's no half arsing belief. Just watch out for people who are not fully committed to what they say they are. That's all. I'm going to wait outside." Damia's brown eyes were latched onto Kai throughout her words and though there was no emphasis on whom she was referring to, her abrasion during the whole episode filled the parenthesis. When Damia left the chamber, the mood changed somewhat. Due to the many misunderstandings that Tre and Kai had faced during their few encounters, they agreed that a parley was most practical.

"Do you trust that girl with our identities?"

"I trust her and Quiqhin with my life."

"Who is Quiqhin?"

"The chief of the Isles Industries that have been built in Signot. His father is the owner."

"Small world."

"Sometimes it's better that way."

"Well, it may be too late, but you need to limit the amount of people that know about your identity."

"It is just the two."

"Right, but that is two personalities with two different views and agendas. All of these things change. I might not be your pal, but we know what we stand for. We wouldn't risk our lives otherwise. What I'm saying is, if you truly want to be a symbol of hope you are going to have to distance yourself from people you love. It's necessary."

"I've been living by that principle before I even had powers." What Kai did not know was that loneliness was not just an adjective, nor a feeling for Tre. It was a lifestyle. Like the Moon itself, Tre only found light from the stars around him. If he did not have these people he would be purposeless, just like the scarred satellite.

"Welcome to the hard life," Kai said. Once again, the floating crimson ball punctured yet another hole through his backpack before awaiting authorisation from its operator.

"Node-Operating-Management-Assistant. Mr Boston I have encrypted all combinations for this bunker's switchboard. I will stay in bunker fifty-five and link a twenty-four hour live stream to your suit. Scheduled updates on the Spectre will be given and unscheduled updates will be given should something you have not programmed me to expect, happens. I will use the time to study the Spectre when it awakens. I recommend keeping Tre Moon here also as my scanning properties have reported a one-hundred percent similarity in physical appearance. There is a strong possibility that they are one and the same."

"Thank you Noru, he's good though." Kai gestured to his node that they were leaving.

"It seems like your little robot is a supporter of the 'bring in Specular' movement to study BirmaPhysics." The bunker darkened in conjunction with their progress toward the exit.

"Just be grateful I'm not," Kai assured him. When they finally left the bunker, the entrance closed behind them automatically. The entire exterior of the bunker was shrouded, not a photon of light could be plucked from its belly. Blue Moon was once again imprisoned against his will. If the past had proved anything it was that Blue was as dogmatic as de ja vu. History could not be clearer when it repeated itself: Spectre the unexpected.

"Good citizens of Signot. I accept this key to the city today in grace. I am humbled by my journey, from the streets of Dubai, to London, and now here to this great country. But I am more humbled that you have accepted me with such open arms. I know many of you would like me to run for president, but I must gracefully decline, I am a businessman. I have no place in politics, though they say I do have the face."

Magnified laughter came from the hundred individuals who came out to the Hetashi Borough's coast to watch Isaac Isles accept the key to the city. Unlike Quiqhin Isles, Isaac was clean shaven and as a result, looked younger than his own son. He was dressed in all white; a reflection of his intentions. The scene was set almost perfectly. The horizon was a balayage of orange, pink and blue, the sea behind the beachfront spelt that Signot would see new waters due to the Arabians introduction. The beachfront hotel balconies were full to the brim with spectators and the crowd were prouder than the city had ever allowed them to be. This was a new era for the Signot, banners could be seen over the heads of the people, from "Isles for Prez" to "Specular and N.O.M.A.: Indiana's finest." – The atmosphere was magnetic and there was so much electricity in the air, that even the electromagnetic spectrum did not have the vibrations to show it.

"This is a great age for Signot. The economy is back on track, and we are seeing new health and safety, educational policies and new businesses coming here. My grandparents always told me that when someone is held back, it is only because Allah intends to launch them further. I believe the same for this city and for my son, Quiqhin Isles, who will be the CEO of the industries on this continent. I have employed over 40,000 people in this great state, but I hope I have touched many more hearts. Tomorrow the oil factories will go online for the first time." Isaac isles swung an arm behind him to show the unmissable architecture of the oil site. The site contained spires so high; one could only aspire to reach the entrepreneurial levels that the Isles enterprise had accomplished. The refinery was as far from the central areas of the borough as possible, but its sheer size put it beside both the sea and the outer rims.

"Once again I would like to thank the mayor of—"

SRRKKRINK!

In front of the of eyes every onwatcher, a snowflake shaped blade was fired directly through the chest of Isaac Isles. The combined gasps from the crowd could have made a whirlpool in the sea. Isaac Isles looked through the left side of his chest where the blade had skewered him; thrown with such precision that coincidence and misfortune was instantly dismissed. The owner of the blade had intended to take his life. Despite the horrific intermission, Isaac Isles did not fall to his knees, nor did he bleed. The moment was so confounding that the spectators did not panic, but rather tried to comprehend the supposedly tragic event without the fuse of fear. Suddenly, the figure of Isaac Isles deteriorated in place; leaving the grounded blade and a mass of confused onlookers. If those present at Hetashi Borough could borrow Tre Moon's ability to see hundreds of feet ahead, coherence would begin to form. Roughly one hundred and thirteen feet away, Isaac Isles stood without impale, but the look as if he had experienced a particularly frightening session of virtual reality. He brushed Specular's hand from his shoulder because during the whole speech he had projected the businessman's hologram to the area where he otherwise would have died.

"You're welcome. Better safe than sorry," Specular told Quiqhin's father.

"Get me out of here," Isaac Isles commanded his chauffeur at a turn, "thanks Speccy, but when you find who did it, I want..." Isaac Isles forfeited his own sentence with a nod of admiration. As he turned back around, Specular was gone and a streak of light in his place. At the scene of the attempted murder, a small quake began at the stage. The citizens backed up some, but they did not run. All anthologies and antedate pointed to an earthquake but instead a vigorous geyser burst from under the concrete stage, blasting the snowflake shaped blade upward, into the air, along with pleasant, but heavy shower of spring water.

"Specular! Specularosooo!" cried a Latin house keeper on one of the nearby balconies. As the crowd looked upward they could see a rainbow formed from the improvised rainfall, but better still, they could see a streak of fantastic white light that coloured the rainbow dull in comparison. When the citizens saw their resident hero, the consequent cheers erupted more forcefully than the geyser itself. Specular was able to snatch the blade from mid-air and also counteract the figure that had suddenly leapt from nowhere to collect it also. With the momentum of light behind him, this mid-air collision played in Tre's favour. He tackled the assassin and streaked them over to a rooftop of one of the beach front hotels. The pair blindly tussled for control as they tumbled and rolled along the floor. Finally, Tre lashed the blade downward to stop their progress and the assassin guarded her face with her elbows as he had put the edge of one of its eight points, inches from her head.

"Who are you!?" Specular exclaimed so forcefully that even the shards in his suit vibrated. Just by her physique and hair he could tell that she was female.

"Why did you try and kill Isaac Isles?" He then shook the assassin until her arms unbundled and he could see her face. Sand dune textured hair. A sunny complexion. Coral pink eyes. Latin-American features. Jawbones as sharp as the snowflake blade she threw. Painful memories impaled into his mind since the seventh of June. It was sprinkling beneath them, but in his mind raged a monsoon. Confusion, misunderstanding, joy, thankfulness. Before him, was Emily Di Pinto, alive somehow.

"Emily, I–I," Tre fluttered as he took off his mask, "how?" Though her face was one he remembered, there was a subhumanity in her appearance. Her coral cornea had a glow that even the architects of contact lenses could not contrive. The blotched gashes on her neck were now open flaps; gills if you will. The acne pores along her cheeks were now luminescent ctenoid scales, and these same scales lined other parts of her body, creating scaly renditions of breastplates, tassets, gauntlets, rebraces and sabatons. In the aquatic armour, Emily Di Pinto looked like a warrior from the sea; in the same arena of the Celtic princess Sabrina, with more spirit than Geneva.

"Tre Moon, you should have not stopped me." Emily placed her palms on the side of Tre's dark face, she then brought his close enough to hers that he could not mistake what she said next.

"I come to you as Vaniti– Submirenean ambassador for homosapiens. I wanted to stop what was coming, but now I sense even destruction of the oil building will not quell the problem. You humans would just build another."

"What are you talking about?"

"There is a war coming..."

Did you enjoy this book? We would appreciate if
you left a review of your thoughts!

You can keep up with the latest IXI COMICS news
on social media:
Instagram: @larakees

Twitter: @LaraKeesIXI

Facebook: @LaraKeesIXI

WWW.LARAKEES.COM

THE STORY OF THIS UNIVERSE CONTINUES...

VANITI AT SEA

...COMING SOON